JULES OHMAN

Body Grammar

Jules Ohman received an MFA from the University of
Montana and cofounded the nonprofit Free Verse. She
coordinates Literary Arts' Writers in the Schools program and lives in Portland, Oregon, with her wife.

Body Grammar

Body Grammar

Jules Ohman

VINTAGE BOOKS

A DIVISION OF PENGUIN RANDOM HOUSE LLC

NEW YORK

A VINTAGE BOOKS ORIGINAL, JUNE 2022

Library of Congress Cataloging-in-Publication Data
Names: Ohman, Jules, author.
Title: Body grammar / Jules Ohman.
Description: New York : Vintage Books, 2022.
Identifiers: LCCN 2021035574 (print) | LCCN 2021035575 (ebook) |
     ISBN 9780593466698 (trade paperback) | ISBN 9780593466704 (ebook)
Subjects: LCSH: Models (Persons)—Fiction. | LCGFT: Lesbian fiction. |
     Romance fiction. | Novels.
Classification: LCC PS3615.H63 B63 2022 (print) | LCC PS3615.H63 (ebook) |
     DDC 813/.6—dc23
LC record available at https://lccn.loc.gov/2021035574
LC ebook record available at https://lccn.loc.gov/2021035575

Vintage Books Trade Paperback ISBN: 978-0-593-46669-8
eBook ISBN: 978-0-593-46670-4

Book design by Nicholas Alguire

vintagebooks.com

Printed in the United States of America
10 9 8 7 6 5 4 3 2 1

In memory of Susan Watt Dunham

PART ONE

I

The women started appearing out of nowhere the year Lou turned fourteen. Scouts. Modeling scouts. Lou had grown eight inches that year, went from the shrimpiest kid in her grade to a gawky five foot eleven: more spindly legs than human girl, caving her chest in to avoid being taller than almost every other person in gym class. The women, materializing as if out of some vortex in the sidewalks, handed her cards embossed with the names of modeling agencies—all of which were coined from superlatives (*Lavish Modeling*) or Portland iconography (*Bridgetown Models*, *Rose City Agency*)—and asked her to give them a call, to come in for a meeting, to talk a little bit more. Lou never did.

Even after she turned eighteen, they didn't let up. They approached her at Target with her mom, the last week of high school, picking out twin long sheets for her freshman year at the University of Oregon. They approached the dark corner booth in the coffee shop where she'd holed up every day so far that summer, reading or drawing or just watching her friend Ivy, who was working, spray herself with steamed milk and get hit on by men in very tiny beanies. One woman approached at one of Ivy's band's shows downtown, dressed in a black blazer and black slacks and black sunglasses, pressing a card to her palm, and Lou, a little drunk, had thought for a full second that the woman was an FBI agent. After the first woman, in a mall food court when she was in middle school, Lou's mom had told her if she wanted to try it, she had to wait until she was sixteen, what her mom clearly thought of as a reasonable working age, as if modeling would be anything like Lou's summer landscaping job.

Lou knew lots of her classmates would love the chance to be a model: it seemed like a portal to being rich, to being known, being *seen*; or even, within the abyss of puberty, to just being told they were beautiful, though none of these women ever told Lou that. They all said she had an interesting face, which wasn't the same thing. True, she was tall—she was mistaken for a much younger boy all the time, despite messy brown hair curling past her shoulders, which she didn't necessarily mind. And true, she was the right size—she ate whatever she wanted and she stayed skinny and flat-chested, which she also didn't mind. But it disturbed her to think these women purposely hung out at places where they knew teenaged girls would be. Malls. Concerts. Coffee shops. Scouting beanpole girls. Somehow, no one else thought it was creepy, even her parents, who were only amused, but Lou felt like she was being stalked by the fashion industry, an entity she didn't love, didn't feel catered to by, didn't even understand was a thing until it asserted itself in her life, insisting she join it. She felt like she was being recruited to a cult that she could see through entirely, whose basic tenets she didn't believe in and never would.

One woman approached while she was mowing a client's front lawn on a Friday in early June, just a week after her high school graduation. Her boss was weeding in the back. It was a very nice and very steep neighborhood, a few miles from the house Lou had grown up in, on the edge of the hills around Skyline Boulevard. The grade made the landscaping particularly difficult; Lou was always afraid of rolling down the hill, sharp tools in hand, or the brakes on the truck going out while she was in it.

Yet Lou had been distracted all afternoon. Ivy was supposed to pick her up at any minute, and Lou was mostly watching for her dirty gold minivan, doing a crummy job on the oval of lawn by the rhododendrons. She and Ivy were going to be spending the next three nights together, which felt like a lush amount of time. They'd been friends since their freshman year but it was only this summer that Lou had let herself spend unrestricted time with her, as if before she was in some way saving up. She knew it was absurd to think time, or company, worked as if she could save any of it. But it didn't really matter if there was sound metaphysical or even physical logic to it, because anytime lately Lou tried to keep Ivy at the same careful distance she kept nearly everyone, Ivy rejected that outright.

The woman waved her hands in Lou's face to get her attention. She was walking a miniature husky. It looked like a robot toy Lou had as a kid that barked three times then flipped over backward. Lou pulled off her hearing protection and turned off the mower so she didn't take off the husky's snout.

"Can I help you?" Lou said.

The woman was dressed in a Lululemon-ish getup. Lou figured she wanted to know what the landscaping company was, even though it was emblazoned on the side of her boss's truck.

"You have a great look," the woman said, as if Lou was something she'd assembled herself. "Very striking." She handed Lou the card right as Ivy pulled up to the curb in her minivan.

The dog sniffed Lou's feet, then looked up at her with ice-blue eyes. The husky was so clean that when the mud from Lou's boots showed up on its nose, Lou wanted to wipe it off, return it to mint condition.

"Thanks," Lou said politely, and pocketed the card fast. She kept a stack of them in her room, because she thought it was funny and most of her friends thought it was funny. But she didn't want Ivy to know.

"Who was that?" Ivy asked as Lou climbed in. The van smelled of sourdough and coffee, from the free loaves and bags of espresso Ivy brought home from work, and there was a Tetris of amps and equipment in the back. They were leaving in the morning for her band Fortunato's final show, near the University of Oregon campus.

Ivy met her eyes, and for a second, Lou wanted to tell her, wanted them to be able to laugh about it like she would with any of her other friends, but she didn't want Ivy looking at her like those women looked at her. She wanted Ivy looking at her for other things. Things those women couldn't see and didn't understand about her. That no one but Ivy did.

"I don't know," Lou said.

"Well, what did she want?"

"Nothing."

Ivy didn't push it because Ivy never pushed it, content to

let everyone keep their secrets. Lou felt extra grateful for it right then, the sun bright in their eyes through the windshield, the woman and her immaculate dog already disappeared back down the sidewalk vortex: out of sight, out of mind.

The grass was still warm from the heat of the day by the time they settled at Aldenlight Park. They'd had milkshakes for dinner, then drove around in the summer air until Ivy requested they stop somewhere, try to get some photographs for her band's new album cover. Lou pulled her Nikon from her camera bag and started adjusting the aperture and shutter speed, zooming in on Ivy's impish grin. In the shadows, her face looked angular and hard, like it was cut from something solid. She had wavy dark hair just past her shoulders and dark eyes that were always lingering places, long after everyone but Lou had looked away. A straight pink scar ran down her upper lip and chin, imprinted like she'd fallen asleep on fabric. When she was a kid, she'd split her face in two on her bicycle, and Lou had never forgotten her description of it—the way she held on to most things Ivy said to her; Ivy, who seemed to think and speak in complete images. When she'd risen from the street to face her running mother, Ivy said, both halves of her teeth and jaw were raised like flags flying in opposite directions.

Ivy held her fingers out in front of the lens, and Lou took some shots of them. Her hands were long and strong, and it was easy to imagine them spreading out to reach difficult chords on the neck of a guitar. Her knuckles were thicker than Lou's, whose hands were slender and small, scarred from yardwork and a nervous habit of picking down her cuticles until they bled.

Lou reached out and held Ivy's hands still so she could focus the shot, then drew her hand back as she became aware that maybe that was a strange thing to do, leaving Ivy's fingers in midair, reaching for nothing.

"Your calluses feel like plastic," Lou said. "Like when you crush those plastic balls, in ball pits."

"I've never been in a ball pit," Ivy said.

Lou lowered her camera to stare. "How?"

"My mom never let me go in them; I don't know. Why do you look so horrified?"

"I just don't understand how that's possible."

"They're kind of gross, right? Like, how do you think they clean them?"

"That's not the point. It's like saying you've never been on a trampoline."

Ivy laughed. "I'm not a sociopath, I've been on a trampoline. In fact, I've been on a trampoline with you. At Catherine's."

"My dad lost his wedding ring in a ball pit at my sixth-birthday party. And they had to empty the whole thing."

"Did he find it?"

"Nope. And the bottom of it was disgusting. Like, human hair and a decade's worth of fruit snacks."

"What other kind of hair was an option?" Ivy said with a grin.

"Stuffed animal hair. I don't know!"

"I think you mean *fur*. What was your favorite stuffed animal? And don't lie and tell me you didn't hoard them, because I've seen the Container Store zoo in your closet. Be honest with me, were you a dolphin girl?"

"How dare you."

Ivy hooted. "You so were."

"If you're really asking," Lou said, cleaning her lens with the bottom of her shirt, which only made it dirtier, "my favorite stuffed animal was an orca named Susanna."

"I knew it."

"It's not the same!"

"You're the sweetest person I've ever met," Ivy said wistfully. "Susanna."

"A killer whale, really."

"Sweet, sweet, sweet."

Lou blushed, heat spreading down her neck and chest. No one saw her that way. She was often called standoffish, or aloof, but not sweet. Never sweet. It reflected something back at her that she didn't know how to hold in tandem with other parts of her, the parts of her that weren't soft or easy or fragile, that weren't belly-down to the world. Around Ivy, she felt like the kind of person who could admit that maybe she could be sweet and also not feel like being sweet made her susceptible, unguarded, open to anything bad coming for her.

Lou took a few pictures of Ivy. She felt hyperaware of not zooming in on her face, of keeping the shot wide-angle. She didn't linger anywhere. "Are you nervous for the show tomorrow?"

"We're not done with Susanna," Ivy said. "Nowhere near done."

"If this record goes platinum, can I have a cut of the profits so I can retire?"

"Retire from what? And I don't think anyone's retired off record sales in a long-ass time, dude. Why don't you go to law school and sue all the streaming apps and then we'll talk."

"I would really be the world's worst lawyer," Lou said.

"You'd be all, 'I don't really think there's actually an issue here, Your Honor, so why don't we get some pizza together instead, and then everyone can go on a nice long walk in the fresh air, and we'll all feel better.'"

"I'm sorry, would I be wrong?"

Ivy grabbed Lou's camera and looked through the viewfinder at her.

"Don't," Lou said, blushing.

"What if I want you on the cover?"

"It's not my band."

"Well, some of the album's about you."

Lou hadn't actually heard any of the new songs. She lunged for her camera, but Ivy held it back, laughing.

"Just a few," Ivy said. She had a perpetual slouch to her shoulders, except onstage, when her posture improved with a guitar. The shutter clicked. Once. Twice. "In case you change your mind."

"*No.*" It came out sharper than Lou meant it to. But she'd always hated having her picture taken, even before the sidewalk women started hounding her. It was definitely hypocritical, as someone who loved photographing other people, but she didn't like how she looked in photos. Unaware. She didn't like to be caught not looking.

"Whoa, I'm sorry, okay?" Ivy said, and handed back the camera. "Here."

"This light's terrible. Let's go somewhere else." The rise in her voice swelled to the very rim of needing to cry, and she didn't know why.

Lou took the driver's seat. She preferred to drive, always, and Ivy seemed to prefer her driving too, even though it was her van. They'd become friends after spending hours of ninth-grade biology trying to get their fat yellow stopwatches to land on exact numbers, killing time in the smallest of increments. But everything went fast when they were together. Even Lou's driving, which was infamously hesitant. Only up in the hills where they lived did Lou feel certain of which curves to hug, which to give room. Her handling was untroubled, the only place on earth she might find comfort in hairpin turns. There was a danger to summer that she had never liked or adjusted to, the way everything felt too open, too fast, too reckless—maybe this was the result of a static gray childhood, that illusion of safety. She preferred the overcast days that Portland was famous for, the way the sky became a physical boundary, containing her.

They pulled up alongside a chain-link fence, a plane of grass behind it, and got out in front of the red radio towers, which were several stories high. Lou had never actually been here before. The towers had always felt like a landmark of home, not a destination in their own right. But here there was light.

"What do you mean, the album's about me?" Lou said.

Ivy looked over at her, and the expression on her face suggested that Lou should know the answer to that question, that Lou was being fucking absurd in asking it to begin with.

But Lou didn't know. It wasn't clear. Or if it was, only the border of it. The insides were messy and unformed and too fragile to live in the world. She didn't want the thing to puncture and spill all over everything.

"So what you're saying is you wrote 'Ballad of a Dolphin Girl,'" Lou said, trying to turn it back into a joke. "Don't you need my permission to steal my life story?"

Ivy gave her the briefest smile. "'Ballad of Susanna,' killer whale."

Lou adjusted her camera settings while Ivy walked over to

the tall fence. At first she just gripped it, looking up. Barbed wire twisted at the top. Then she started to climb. Lou faced her while walking backward, holding up her Nikon. She knew from somewhere that this was the highest point in Portland. Her bare legs and arms were cold as the breeze picked up. She felt nervous, suddenly, without knowing why.

When Ivy climbed down and turned back, wild-eyed, running straight for Lou, there was an ember glow to her cheeks as she closed the distance between them.

Lou took her picture, and it came out blurry and perfect and strange. Like a girl turned radio wave.

2

The next morning, they picked up Catherine Ellis, who got into the back seat of the van with a backpack clinking with bottles and left her seat belt unbuckled. It was only when Lou reminded her that Catherine dug it out of the center-seat fold and secured herself, teasing Lou that she couldn't parent her the whole trip because she had plans to party, and Lou wasn't entitled to interrupt *the weekend*. Saying it as if the summer wasn't one long free weekend. They were all spending *the weekend* with Fortunato's drummer, Tuck, and Catherine's sister, Morgan, who were both about to finish their sophomore year of college. Morgan and Tuck were friends from high school and lived together off campus. Even though they had been best friends since ninth grade, Catherine rarely had Lou over, always wanting to hang out anywhere but at home, and so Lou knew very little about her sister.

Catherine was wry and talented, and seemed to get off on

giving Lou shit. They had been cocaptains of their track team in high school. Catherine had been their coach's favorite, mostly due to her perfect running posture, her lean, the cadence she never broke, and she was a state champion, committed to running for Oregon in the fall. When the girls' long-distance team won meets, it was because of Catherine. She idolized Steve Prefontaine, had a shrine to him in her bedroom, and was always quoting him in their premeet huddles. But she smoked a lot of weed and drank too much the night before meets. Their coach was always saying, *You're wasting yourself, Ellis.* Lou wasn't a naturally talented long-distance runner at all, but she and Catherine had been selected as captains because she worked hard and Catherine was a champion. Lou had none of that competitiveness, was once cited on an elementary school report card for needing to be a little less careful and a little more aggressive, which her parents had joked about for the rest of her childhood. (*Could you be a little more aggressive with that fork in those brussels sprouts, kiddo? You might be a little less careful with your merging, dearheart, so we don't miss the exit.*) Catherine had an edge to her that she never directed at Lou, even when she teased—but she was actively aiming it toward Ivy on the ride south.

"Are you and Tuck hooking up?" Catherine asked Ivy, seconds after she got in the car.

Lou actually deeply wanted to know the answer to this question, but Ivy had never offered it and Lou had never asked so directly. As far as Lou knew, Ivy didn't hook up with anyone. She was in a serious relationship with her guitars, with the kind of sound she wanted. That spring, she'd made a few offhand comments about different musicians she admired, of a variety of genders, and Lou had analyzed them for weeks afterward, trying to determine a common thread, but it was never their physical appearances. It was always their tonality, or the degree of sadness Lou felt listening to their songs.

When Ivy didn't say anything right away, Catherine added, "He's such a nerd."

Before Tuck graduated, he and Ivy always sat together at lunch and Lou had watched them from the table where she sat with her friends on the track team, trying to determine if their body language was romantic or just familiar. Tuck was a jazz drummer. They'd formed Fortunato before he left for college, and this was going to be their last show before Ivy moved to New York for school. She and Tuck spent almost every single weekend together practicing, and Lou didn't know if something had changed now that Ivy was leaving. She seemed to talk about him in a different way, like there was always something she wasn't saying.

"Tuck's a genius," Ivy said seriously. "And why do you care?"

Catherine laughed. "My sister was fucking him in high school, but she was too embarrassed to tell anyone. I caught him eating her out in our treehouse."

"Please stop," Lou said.

Ivy didn't say anything, just switched the song. Maybe she and Tuck *were* hooking up. Otherwise, why wouldn't she answer?

A Fortunato song filled the van, Tuck's kick drum pounding until Ivy's voice slipped in on the first verse. Every time she sang, Lou saw a long line of streetlamps leading around a corner.

"Do we really have to listen to you now when we're going to be listening to you all night?" Catherine said.

Lou was now very much regretting inviting Catherine. She'd invited her because it seemed way too weird to go spend the night at her sister's without telling her, no matter how much Lou wanted time alone with Ivy. Things were always different between them when other people were there, like they were tuned to different frequencies, or just Lou was, and whatever was there before got lost in other noise.

The drums got louder and Ivy matched them, banging her palm on the dashboard, concentrating. Ivy had gotten a full ride to music school in New York, but she'd been making noises lately about deferring just to collaborate with Tuck. Lou didn't want her to go to New York, but she didn't want her to stay for Tuck.

"He's so *good*, dude," Ivy said.

"Sure sounds like drums," Catherine said, over the driving beat. "Can you turn it down, Lou?"

"You don't have an ear," Ivy said.

"I've actually got two," Catherine snapped, reaching between them for the volume dial. Ivy intercepted her just as a gold pickup cut in front of Lou without signaling and she had to overcorrect, which meant Catherine and Ivy both screamed at the swerve and Lou death-gripped the wheel. She shouted at them to stop distracting her, sounding exactly like her mother.

Another Fortunato song came on, this one quieter, acoustic. Just Ivy's voice over a guitar. Lou rolled up her window so she could hear it better.

"What's the exit again?" Lou said.

"Promise I'll tell you when," Ivy said. "But it's at least an hour away."

Through the window, a red-tailed hawk lifted off a powerline and settled out of view in the wheat field beside them.

————

The proportions of the Ellis sisters' faces were only a beat apart—Catherine and Morgan had the same wide-set eyes, bleached eyebrows, and the kind of white-blond hair most people only ever had as children. From the pictures on the walls of Catherine's house, she and Morgan had been raised in matching outfits, as if they were twins or someone wanted them to be. The only physical distinction Lou might name, though she never would aloud, was that Morgan was feminine in a way that Catherine, with her beanies and team T-shirts and bluntly cut hair, wasn't and never tried to be. Morgan's hair was straightened and fell past her chest. Her nails were painted teal. She wore dark mascara and eyeliner. Stripped of any adornment, Catherine and Morgan would be nearly identical when standing still, but the second they moved or spoke or gestured, it wasn't that they no longer looked or acted related, it just became immediately clear that they didn't want to be.

Morgan and Tuck and what seemed like a dozen other people lived together in a clapboard house with a rickety back porch and a basement, which was unfinished but open enough for a show. Tuck showed Lou around when they arrived, since Catherine and Ivy had stayed there before, pointing out bathrooms and cabinets of mugs. He was lanky, well over six feet, but there was a boyishness to how he moved, like he was always on the verge of tripping into something carefully arranged. He wore glasses that he tugged up on top of his head to pull his dark brown curls away from his face, which had a down-turned nose and serious eyes. Lou liked him, in spite of herself. He was very shy, and it seemed to sit differently on a boy than it did on her. No one ever called him aloof or standoffish or, like some of the younger girls on Lou's track team who mistook her shyness for pretension, a total bitch.

Fortunato planned to practice in the basement the rest of the afternoon, so Catherine, Morgan, and Lou wandered the sprawling U of O campus underneath the cool shade of old maples. Lou had been here a few times before, for state track meets at Hayward Field, but never during the lead-up to finals week. Lou and Catherine and Ivy had only walked at their graduation ceremony the previous Saturday, but high school already felt like months ago. It was surreal to see so many students rushing around the campus paths, distraught over their upcoming tests and presentations. It made the summer feel short and urgent. Like Lou would be here with them before she knew it and everything would be different.

When the Ellis sisters walked alongside each other, they left a foot between them, despite the narrow path. They were the same size, but Morgan strode with a dancer's posture and Catherine like she was searching for something on the sidewalk. Lou trailed them as Morgan led them toward the building that housed the design department, where she was a student.

In an air-conditioned classroom full of mannequins and bolts of fabric, Morgan showed them her project for her design final, a long blue evening dress with tiny white flowers embroidered on it. The dress was elegant, but not fully sewn. There were still pins holding pieces of it together. Morgan asked Catherine whether she liked it, and Catherine glared at her like she was being cold-called in class.

"I don't know," Catherine said. "I guess it's fine?"

Of all the girls in their high school, Lou was certain that she and Catherine were the least likely pair to know the correct way to comment on a dress, let alone a dress-in-progress. One of the reasons she had been drawn to Catherine as a friend in the first place, out of the pack of their teammates freshman year, was because she was the only girl Lou had ever seen wear a suit to a school dance.

"I guess you wouldn't know," Morgan said. "You haven't worn a dress since preschool. So I don't even know why I'm asking you."

"You don't have to be such a bitch all the time. I said it was fine."

Lou inserted herself between them and ran her hand along the neckline. Apparently her main role this weekend was as buffer.

"I think it's really cool," Lou said. "It's like something Michelle Obama would wear. Or like an Oscars dress."

"You're so nice, Lou," Morgan said. She paused, and then looked at Lou with an earnestness that had surely gotten her a lot of things she wanted in the world. Sometimes being around girls like Morgan, Lou felt as if she had been given the wrong translation of something, and she didn't even know how to ask for the version that would have made sense.

"Will you try it on for me?"

"Oh," Lou said. "I don't know."

"Just so I know what it looks like on a body," Morgan said.

Lou wanted to say *No way*, but Catherine was staring at her and Morgan was smiling so sincerely that she ducked behind a white board, kicked off her shoes, and pulled down her jeans. Lou avoided looking in the standing mirrors that surrounded her as she pulled on the dress. She knew she was weird-looking, so gangly all her clothes were a little baggy—though she often wore them too big on purpose, selecting them from the men's section of Goodwill.

The dress fit, but the side zipper was hard to finagle. She stepped out to reveal herself to the Ellis sisters, feeling like she was wearing the garment inside out, or like *she* had been turned inside out.

"Oh my god, Lou," Morgan said, walking up to her, adjusting the front of the dress, which was a little big. "You look seriously amazing. You have to model for my next show. I'll pay you and everything."

Lou had no interest in being seen so publicly, in any dress. Not to mention, stumbling onstage in front of hundreds of people seemed inevitable considering how often she slipped just walking up the wooden stairs to her bedroom. And yet here she was, being scouted even by people she knew.

Folding the hem higher, adjusting some pins, Morgan explained to Lou how she was piecing the dress together, which seams she still needed to sew. She said she wanted to design a full collection by her senior year.

"But what are you going to do with a degree in this?" Catherine was asking Morgan.

"Live in New York," Morgan said. "Work in fashion. I'm so tired of that being a question. I love it, so I'm doing it, and I'll make it work." She said it like a mantra.

Catherine wove through the other projects quickly. She caught her heel on a bolt of fabric, nearly falling on the concrete floor and taking everything down with her.

"Mom and Dad are going to expect me to be a stockbroker to make up for it," she said, steadying herself.

"That's them," Morgan said. "That's not your problem."

Catherine picked up a box cutter from a neighboring table and stabbed it hard into the flat beige chest of a nearby mannequin. Lou looked in the mirror one last time, then closed her eyes against the image of herself.

———

Later that afternoon, after Morgan went back to the house to clean up for the show, Catherine and Lou walked to Hayward Field together.

"They'll never get it clean," Catherine said. "Under the grime there's like a whole other ecosystem of grime. It's disgusting."

Lou liked how the house felt, even with all the dust. It felt like a community, all the people coming and going, the coffee always brewing, meals being cooked and shared, all the different art hung or taped to the walls, the whole house a collage. Her house had been so empty lately, and her parents seemed to spend more and more time apart. She missed the feeling of being surrounded, of always being offered something, even if she didn't have to take it.

The gate was open, and runners were stretching at the far end of the field.

"Race you," Catherine said, already taking off. Lou laughed but stayed where she was standing. The sun was heavy. Catherine ran down the center of the grass until she was fifty yards away.

"It's too hot!" Lou shouted to her.

"Lame!" came Catherine's echo.

They watched the runners from the bleachers for a while. Catherine's whole body seemed more relaxed, now that they weren't around Ivy or her sister. Their energy turned lazy and silly. Catherine did an impression of their coach, scolding her. "*You're wasting yourself, Ellis!* You're wasted, Ellis! I want to get wasted, Lou."

Lou never wanted to get wasted. She just wanted to get right up to the point of being relaxed in a social group and then have it fade out like something drying in the sun. At which point, she would go to bed.

"I wish you were going to be on the team here," Catherine said.

"There is no way," Lou said. "I was a pity choice for varsity and you know it. Besides, I'm going to be too busy, like, studying for all my bio-chem tests."

Catherine laughed. "You'll last ten minutes as a science major. You are going to be a hippie art major, and I'm going to have to come rescue you out of your tree protests and shit."

When Lou came to U of O for college, she did plan to spend all her time in the woods. The main draw of Eugene was its dense rain forest, the short drive to the coast. Ecology was a more practical major than photography, which had been her first choice until enough adults in her life had told her it was a bad idea. Ivy was the one who pointed out that they had a key thing in common: preservation. One of systems, and the other of moments. But Ivy had also once told her, in an entirely different context, that the thing she hated and loved the most about Lou was that she was preservation-oriented to a fault. Ivy meant the way she evaded change—staying in Oregon for college, for example—but Lou didn't see what was so wrong with wanting some consistency, some sustainability.

"I'm glad we're here," Catherine said, as if she could tell what Lou was thinking. "I feel like I haven't really seen you since districts."

It was true. When track ended, Lou started spending all her time with Ivy. Catherine hadn't said anything about it.

"You've been in California."

"I was there for, like, three days."

"Well, we're here now," Lou said.

Catherine bit at the skin between her thumb and pointer finger. She nodded out at the women racing, both of them muscular and faster than almost any human Lou had seen in person, except for maybe Catherine, though usually she was so far behind Catherine in races she didn't ever see her run. "I could beat them, right?"

"Yes," Lou said. "Do you want to go back to the house soon?"

"Not really. Do you?"

"I should check in with Ivy. They're probably done practicing by now. I told her we'd hang out a bit before they go on."

Two more runners took off, and Catherine seemed like she was watching them really closely, like she could track their form with her brain and know how fast they were going, whether they were running the right way. Running still just looked like running to Lou. She never paid much attention when her coach corrected her form, didn't know how to implement it when he did. She didn't know how to differentiate movements, posture, or whatever. Her body was so vague to her sometimes. She often forgot she was there. She didn't know when it was reacting to something until later. Her feelings were the same way.

Lou looked at her phone, and Ivy had texted her, asking where she was, if she wanted to hang out soon. Catherine glanced over, clearly read it, and stood up abruptly.

"Fine," she said. "We can go."

The show started after midnight. Everyone but Lou had been drinking for hours, and Catherine was so wasted that Lou and

Morgan had to tuck her into Morgan's bed with a short trash can beside her. Every sentence Catherine said sounded like she was reciting the last half of it backward. Lou wanted to stay and make sure she didn't throw up and choke—a paranoia engrained by every rock 'n' roll movie and DARE worksheet ever—but Morgan kept saying she was fine, and Catherine kept telling them to go away, and so Lou got outvoted and followed Morgan down into the basement.

Fortunato was tuning up, Tuck adjusting his snare drum, the crowd of drunk kids expanding. A couple of Morgan's roommates manned a card-table bar in the corner. They poured her and Morgan Solo cups of Sprite and vodka.

"Are you sure she's okay?" Lou asked again. "She seemed really out of it."

"Catherine? She's been drinking like that since she was a freshman. I'm done worrying about it. If she hasn't died yet, she's not going to now."

Which made zero logical sense. Could be said of anything, of anyone. The drink was so sweet Lou finished the whole thing in a few gulps, just so she didn't have to sip it any longer, then asked Morgan if she had ever been to New York.

Lou nodded at the stage. "Ivy's going there for college."

"We went last year with my parents," Morgan said. "My sister actually loved it, too, which is why it's so annoying that she, like, never stops making digs at me about why I want to move there. You couldn't *pay* Catherine to say that she likes anything I like, is a thing about her. But she's young. Young and lost. That's what I keep telling my parents when they call me to bitch about her. Like, she for sure sucks right now, but she's always felt things extra deeply. And I don't think they get that about her. Or they don't see how that's a good thing."

"So you think it's good?"

"Yeah," Morgan said, finishing her drink. "I really do. She just needs to keep running, and she'll learn to deal with it better. It's good for her to have something like that. Something she loves. Even if she won't admit she loves it."

Fortunato started to play. The first song was dreamy and slow; Ivy's guitar and singing were the centerpiece, but she was right, Tuck was very good, so keyed into what Ivy was doing that it was the first time Lou had ever really noticed a drummer adjust what they were doing, how subtle his shifts were with Ivy's chord progressions.

After a couple of songs, Morgan sidled up to a frat boy with thick arms in the corner near the bar and Lou was left standing alone with an empty cup. She pulled her Nikon out of her camera bag, relieved to have a purpose in this crowd other than to stare at Ivy without a real excuse.

There had been stutters of weirdness between her and Ivy lately that felt like they were getting longer and longer. Lou hadn't addressed it and didn't know how to. At first it felt like they were narrowing in on something, like shaving off distance times, but then it began to feel like an endlessly refreshing scroll through Tumblr, like it could have gone on forever, giving them split-second impressions of something close to the thing they wanted without ever being real.

Lou took a few photographs through the haze of weed smoke and the low-hanging pipes from the ceiling. Ivy was looking past her, in the direction of a group of girls near the laundry sink who were starting a game of flip cup. No one seemed to be paying that much attention to the band, even though they were good. So good that Lou felt overwhelmed by Ivy playing up there, by her left hand sliding up and down the fretboard, even through the lens of her camera. Maybe *especially* through the lens of her camera: the way it implied that Lou would be looking at all of this later, when it was over, and the melancholic underbelly of all her cravings showed itself again.

Lou's head swam, the vodka funneling into her all at once, and so she ditched out, climbing the stairs to the kitchen with cottony ears, gripping the railing. She filled her cup with water and drank it down and filled it again. In Morgan's room, she found Catherine awake but swollen-faced on the bed, curled away from the wall. She offered the water, but Catherine didn't take it. The show buzzed through the floorboards, all drums, no Ivy. Lou slipped her camera bag off and lay down on her side with her back to Catherine. Dark maple leaves swayed outside the open window. Catherine didn't ask her to leave, and Lou relaxed for the first time all night.

"I hate her," Catherine said, her breath hitting the back of Lou's neck.

"She's not so bad," Lou said. She'd been surprised by Morgan saying that Catherine felt things deeply. She'd always thought Catherine felt nothing, the way she could push through pain at the very end of a race, but maybe it was the opposite.

Catherine's hand slid over Lou's stomach and to the waist of her jeans, thumb moving back and forth. Lou's body responded or the vodka responded or the way it had felt looking at Ivy onstage responded, and she pushed her hips back into Catherine, letting her slip one hand down past the elastic of Lou's underwear and one under the elastic of her bra.

"It's okay," Catherine whispered. "She hates me back."

"No, she doesn't."

Catherine said something else, but her voice was so hoarse that Lou turned her head to hear her better, feeling like her body was rolling, and Catherine kissed her, hard. Lou didn't stop her, and for a minute, she disappeared into the bright, hot feeling of it, imagining Ivy onstage, her fingers on the fretboard, her mouth up against the microphone.

"I don't care that you like her," Catherine whispered. "We can still do this."

Lou froze. "What do you mean?"

Ivy's voice carried up through the heating vent, and Catherine glanced over at it, and suddenly Lou understood. Catherine hadn't been talking about Morgan. Lou pulled away and rolled off the bed, feeling like she might drop straight through the floor. Downstairs, the band stopped playing, and for a few seconds, everything was quiet.

When Lou went back down, Fortunato was just finishing a song. Ivy was looking down to tune her guitar, her hair falling forward, her eyes soft, all of it nostalgia for something Lou hadn't lived. Ivy started to sing, but then she stopped, and Tuck stopped with her. She glanced up and made eye contact with Lou.

"Um," Ivy said into the mic. "Actually, I want to do a different one." She strummed a few chords, and bent down to speak into Tuck's ear.

"Sorry, this is the first time we're playing this one," Ivy said to the crowd. She seemed nervous all of a sudden, glancing at Tuck, asking if he would count them off again.

The band restarted with a whisper, then a growl, Ivy's voice catching in her throat again and again. Lou saw streetlamps, like she always did, but now they flickered, seemed like they might go out entirely. Lou recognized the melody immediately, and her body felt like it might disperse, like a crowd leaving a stadium. It was a song Ivy had been fingerpicking around Lou all spring but always refused to sing.

> *See it in your eyes*
> *When you're dialing in a view*
> *You tell me please hold still,*
> *I'm trying to get a good shot of you*
>
> *And then you run through the brush*
> *flashing fear like a caribou*
>
> *Should I follow or am I*
> *just coming unglued,*
> *Lou Lou Lou*
>
> *Is there more to know*
> *Or am I left in the unknowing*
> *Scared of following through*
> *Scared of what I might be showing*
>
> *With the mountain at your back*
> *I know you see it too*
>
> *It's bigger than we both knew*
> *Please come on come on*
> *Lou Lou Lou*

Ivy finally looked at her when she sang the last line, repeating out.

When it was over, the room stilled, and Lou couldn't hear anything the people around her were saying. As the lights came on, her ears were too full, too muffled by what she'd already heard, what she had done upstairs, what it meant, and all she felt was sorry: Sorry that she didn't have a song, the words, or a firm hold on any of what she felt, which was so enormous, so physical, that sometimes it was like she was lost in the dense branches of a tree so high up she couldn't even imagine reaching the top, let alone looking down. Sorry that Ivy was so much, the most of anyone, already up there at the top, and Lou was just herself, climbing.

3

The morning after the show, they all sat around on the porch steps drinking coffee out of heavy mugs, the light sharp on the splintered boards and their bare thighs, everyone hungover except Tuck and Ivy, who couldn't stop talking about the show and the buildup they'd created once the crowd actually started paying attention. Catherine kept going back in to throw up in the bathroom, and Lou felt like her own body was whirring in that same direction. She wanted to tell Catherine she was sorry for what had happened, but Catherine wouldn't look at Lou long enough for even a reconciliatory smile. Lou was too afraid Catherine was going to confront her if she said anything directly and that Ivy would hear. She had no idea what to say to Ivy.

As the heat pushed everyone deeper and deeper onto the porch steps, Lou remembered a swimming hole their team had gone to after a state track meet. It was at the base of a waterfall.

The day had been dewy, emerald, cool. The shade had felt three-dimensional. She'd watched her teammates swim for hours, drinking beers and dunking one another in the icy water. Lou hadn't gone in, but it had felt like the idea of a perfect day, and it was what she imagined whenever she thought about coming to U of O for school in the fall. The promise of a future easy and beautiful and familiar. For a second, it felt like they might still capture how it could be in September, with a group of friends and an empty day ahead.

When she mentioned the swimming hole to everyone on the porch, asking if they wanted to go, Morgan got excited, knew the waterfall too. Even Catherine was game, so they all piled into Ivy's van and drove to the trailhead a few miles outside of the city.

By the time the forest shade on the trail opened up into a clearing of sun, illuminating a clear green pool, Lou had shed nearly every sticky layer. There was no one else there, just a smattering of crouching boulders, one of which Lou climbed up on to survey the landscape, camera around her neck. Down below, the others spread their towels on the rocky shore. Tuck and Catherine cracked beers. Ivy squinted up at Lou, hand over her eyes, and Lou took a photograph of the mossy canyon just behind her. She knew Ivy wanted to talk, but she didn't know what to say.

After a while, Morgan and Ivy waded into the water, pushing and splashing each other, sandals still on. The bottom was visible until about ten feet out, where the flat stones, green through the lens of water, gave way to a deeper pool.

Lou descended the boulder to wade around the shallows with Catherine, who wasn't being friendly but wasn't totally ignoring her. Tuck lay on his towel with a textbook, studying for a final. Lou tried to ignore Ivy and Morgan and the great big fun time they were having near the waterfall, which cascaded off a ledge thirty feet up. The skin on her feet tightened in the icy water. It was as stunning as it had been the day her team had gone, still lush and green through her sunglasses, but her stomach knotted from something, the edge of her hangover descending in full.

The waterfall surged off granite walls of violent-lime moss and thick meandering vines into a dark and boiling punch bowl. Water flung itself heavy and fast from the walls. Ivy and Morgan were both waist-deep by the time they left the green water for the black. They were confident swimmers, heading toward the edge where there were smaller rocks to perch on.

Through her lens, Lou watched them pull themselves up, and zoomed in on Ivy in a black sports bra and running shorts, Morgan in a bikini. She slowed her shutter speed and took a few shots, the waterfall blurring white. She couldn't hear them laughing anymore.

"How is it?" she called.

"Freezing!" Morgan shrieked, sounding farther away than she looked.

A few older people arrived together in the clearing and settled in front of a head-shaped boulder on the far end of the shore. Lou attempted to text her parents that she'd be home later, for dinner, but she didn't have service. She lay down beside Tuck, resting her head on her camera bag, going through the photos from the show. She was so tired. When she glanced up again, smelling the weed wafting over from the other group, Ivy and Morgan were balanced at the top of the falls, on a rock that jutted out like a platform. Their laughs echoed over the water.

Catherine wasn't visible, maybe gone to pee, and Tuck was deep into a chapter about famous sociolinguists. Lou had no idea what those were.

The showing-off started with Ivy, strutting around as if she were on a runway, hands on her hips. Morgan mirrored her. It looked very beautiful, all of a sudden, the sun bright, their bodies bare. Lou focused her viewfinder on them, zooming in. She couldn't hear their conversation over the sound of the falls.

She could see them turned toward each other. From this angle it looked like they were almost touching, and she thought, for one alarming second, that they were going to kiss. But then Ivy stepped back, took a running leap, and jumped. She gripped her knees in a cannonball and landed to the side of the rushing falls. Lou's breath caught when she didn't appear for a few seconds, but then she burst up gloriously, mouth open, wet black bangs in her eyes. She swam to the edge and made a gesture upward.

Morgan stood at the very edge of the rock, her hair so white it disappeared against the sun, and Lou took a picture of her. But when Lou looked back down at Ivy, she was still waving at Morgan, and it didn't look like encouragement. It looked like a warning. Suddenly Lou's heart was beating so quickly that it felt like she couldn't catch her breath to get any words out—and anyway, she was always the one calling out to be cautious when no one ever listened.

The dive itself was perfect. Lou had never learned to dive properly, despite years of swim lessons, but when she had watched her teammates' lazy dives from this exact same waterfall, she'd known their form was awkward, a little bent, inefficient. But Morgan's arms made a precise arrow as her body shot toward the water. There was only a hiccup of a splash. Lou's breath caught for those requisite seconds of a person's body rising to the surface. She imagined Morgan reemerging as triumphant as Ivy. The wet blond hair, the smile. The gasp of air. She willed it.

But the pool revolved in the same pattern it had before, each lick of water returning to its place, as if Morgan had never gone under at all. Five seconds, then ten. Thirty.

It was Tuck who burst Lou's silence. "Where did she go?" he said. So he had been watching too. Why hadn't either of them said anything before she dived? Under his breath, "Morgan?"

Lou stood now. Ivy was already swimming out and under the falls.

"Come back!" Lou shouted to Ivy.

"Where the fuck did she go?" Tuck said.

Catherine reappeared from behind one of the boulders. "You guys?" Her voice so small.

Everyone and their questions unanswered. Ivy going under and resurfacing, going under, resurfacing, coming up alone.

Tuck looked at Lou. "Call nine-one-one," he said. He darted around the rocks until he reached the deepest part of the pool and swam out to where Morgan had gone under, yelling at Ivy to get back to land, that she was turning blue. Two men from the other group followed him in and started ducking under the bulleting water.

It was Catherine who took off first, Lou fumbling for her and then Tuck's phone, both still without service, sprinting down the trail barefoot and empty-handed. Lou chased her but Catherine was faster; that wasted athletic talent catapulted her around the next bend, and Lou was incapable of keeping up on the rocky trail. But what could she do but run on, the green shifting and shimmering like a kaleidoscope, until she finally reached Catherine, collapsed along the side of the road without shoes, while cars started pulling over for them and everyone but her was calling for help and Lou was quiet, so quiet, holding Catherine and telling her lie after lie. *She's fine, she's fine. You're fine. I'm fine. She's fine.*

The medics in the ambulance tended to their bloody feet, the gash in Catherine's knee. There was less they could do for Catherine's hysterical yelling of her sister's name, over and over. Lou focused on the medic who was asking her questions as he extracted gravel from the sole of her left foot. His beard looked like her father's.

She kept asking if he had talked to Tuck or Ivy, if Morgan had been playing a joke, maybe holding her breath for a really long time down there, or maybe she had passed out, but maybe Tuck or Ivy or one of the other men had gotten to her, pulled her up. She knew she was barely whispering, but the medic didn't ask her to speak louder.

He asked how old she was, what her name was.

"Is that possible?" she asked the medic. "They could have pulled her up. That's possible, right?"

When he didn't answer, she could feel everything she'd consumed in the last twenty-four hours roiling in her gut. At the same moment she told the medic she was going to throw up, Catherine finally quieted and the ambulance stopped, turned off, and the doors opened to lights red and flashing, even when Lou closed her eyes.

4

In the weeks that followed, Lou did not google *drowned body* because the image results couldn't possibly be worse than how she had imagined Morgan thousands of times over. Hourly, mowing lawns or riding MAX trains or waking up in the morning, staring at the glowing planets on her ceiling, which now took on the disorienting shapes of boulders, Lou tried not to imagine that exact moment of Morgan's arrowed entry into the water, tried not to imagine her struggling to resurface beneath the crushing waterfall or what her body looked like after the rescue team finally found it and pulled it onto dry land.

This montage drew her tongue backward into her throat, and in order to make it shrink back enough that she could take even two normal breaths in a row, she had to turn on music and open the window and sometimes (though less and less) bike to Ivy's and lie down on the floor and get high and talk about normal things, like which guitar pedal Ivy wanted to buy off eBay and how Lou wanted to bike down the 101 someday—if she ever got over her fear of being sideswiped by a semi—and where Ivy wanted to tour and how maybe Lou could even meet up with them on her bike if they were playing in some little coast town in Oregon and wouldn't that be a really good time, as if they remembered what a really good time was and could ever be expected to have one again. After this, Ivy always asked how she was and Lou ignored her until she resumed her deliberately cheerful side of the one-sided conversation as if it felt normal to either of them. That Ivy had sung to her, what was or wasn't between them, belonged to another life. If Lou opened herself to that question, she'd have to open herself to more than she could possibly bear.

When she was by herself, it almost felt like she could skip past what had happened, like a song she couldn't stand, and her old life would resume.

Lou hadn't talked to Catherine since that day. Not once. Her parents had asked, of course, and she'd lied. They wanted her to bring over flowers. She ditched them in a neighbor's compost bin.

When Lou was a kid, her parents warned her constantly about sneaker waves at the coast. She learned never to turn her back on the ocean, or a rogue wave might just keep coming and coming and coming, knock her down and drag her deep into the heavy tide. When she was seven or eight, she hadn't been paying attention on her way back to her grandparents' house, watching the clouds instead of the sea, and it had happened: a sneaker wave had pulled her out by the ankles. Her mom had been the one to go in after her, dragging them both back to shore, sandy and wet and freezing. It was the closest she had ever come to drowning. *Why weren't you paying attention?* her mom kept saying. *You have got to pay attention.*

But this was the thing: Lou always paid attention. She was used to defending herself against accusations of paying too much attention, of pestering people with texts about whether they'd arrived at their destinations, of second-guessing a forecast ahead of a long drive, of triple-checking a lock. Now she spent all her time trying to mentally defend herself against the idea that she could have done *more*. She was the one who suggested the waterfall. If not for her, they would have just sat on the porch all day, hungover, stagnant, mad at each other maybe, but safe.

One night in late June, Lou and Ivy curled together on the floor of Ivy's bedroom in a pile of blankets, heads against the side of the window seat, watching YouTube videos on Lou's phone. Ivy and her dad and stepmom lived on the fourth floor of an apartment building Ivy said she suspected was made out of cardboard, painted to look like a diorama of a Tudor. Ivy's dad had grown up on the Warm Springs Reservation, in central Oregon, and her mom in Montana, where Ivy once said she wanted to take Lou, without saying anything further, and Lou had dwelled on it for several weeks, stalking geotags on Instagram, imagining them there together. It was the first thing Ivy had ever said about her mom. It was Tuck who told Lou, one night at a house show just before New Year's the previous winter, when Ivy forgot the lyrics to a verse midsong and locked herself in the upstairs bathroom, and Lou asked him if he knew what was going on with her. She still remembered how quietly he'd answered, how she had to lean in to hear him over a boy howling into a microphone in the living room. It was her late mom's birthday, he'd said. Ivy's parents had divorced when she was little, and they'd had split custody until her mom passed away, which was when Ivy had moved to Portland. She'd never told Lou how her mom had died, or when exactly, but Lou had also never asked. Asking felt off-limits. Invasive.

Ivy's bedroom was small and cozy, every wall and piece of the lofted bed papered over with photographs of the musicians she loved. Ivy had made it a life goal to educate Lou about music, which meant that for someone who didn't play and had no desire to, Lou knew a weird amount about vintage Stratocasters and Mustangs. She still liked Ivy's own music way better than anything Ivy had ever put on a playlist for her.

Lou turned on her side, resting her forehead against Ivy's soft bare arm. The bedroom floor shook or Lou shook or the ground the building was perched on shook. Maybe the Big One would arrive just when she finally feared something more. A dog whined in an apartment beneath them.

"Do you think about it all the time?" Lou said, so quietly she wasn't even sure Ivy could hear her. Her voice hadn't worked properly since Morgan had disappeared under the surface of the water. Like her warning was lodged in her throat.

Ivy's eyes were still fixed on the screen. She'd delivered Lou's Nikon in the immediate days after the waterfall, and Lou had shoved it deep under a pile of clothes in her closet, incapable of turning it on, even to erase its memory.

"I still can't stop seeing her dive," Lou whispered. "I mean, I actually can't stop seeing her body, either. Do you know what I mean? It's so *terrible*. Like, grotesque. But I can't shut it off."

Ivy paused the video. "You should talk to someone about it. It helps."

"Do you think we'd all be safer somewhere else?"

"Safer from what?"

"The earthquake."

Lou had read an article about it online the day before. How it would wipe them all out. The whole Pacific Northwest, but particularly Portland. She used to joke about it, as anyone would joke about the apocalypse without believing it was real, but now it seemed like a legitimate thing to fear. It felt absurd that no one else was really worrying about it—the only protection Lou had been offered were annual earthquake drills in school, ducking under their flimsy desks and covering the softest parts of their necks with their arms, as if their bodies could save their bodies from collapsing concrete. Yet they lived in the hills, the most vulnerable place they could be.

"Lou," Ivy said, gently. "Have you talked to Catherine?"

Lou shook her head.

"You'd feel better if you did."

But she couldn't. And she didn't want to feel better. Maybe Catherine wouldn't even care anymore about the kiss, about anything that had happened that night, but Lou knew that even if that *was* the case, her grief couldn't match Catherine's, couldn't even be considered alongside it. That was the thing she couldn't find the words to say. That she didn't deserve to feel overrun by this, to even talk about Morgan. Because she hadn't known Morgan. She had seen her hair fuse with the sun. She had watched a beautiful dive. She hadn't even seen her die.

Lou stared at a photograph taped to Ivy's wall, a black-and-white shot of the singer of a band she'd never heard of. The woman looked like the embodiment of a challenge, her short but shaggy hair, her tattoos and the boyish lean of her thin frame.

"Will you cut my hair?" Lou said, and Ivy finally smiled.

Lou followed her into the bathroom that Ivy shared with her dad and stepmom, who were both nurses. It was spotless, like no one lived there, with framed photos of hilltop barns on the white walls.

"Who took these?" Lou asked.

Ivy laughed. "Target. My stepmom bought them. They're all over their bedroom too." Lou didn't know very much about Ivy's stepmom except that she sometimes made them a pot of peppermint tea late at night after her shift, and that she'd recently repainted every room in the apartment except Ivy's room this snowstorm white. Ivy always seemed insistently neutral about her. But maybe her stepmom was just an insistently neutral person.

"I kind of like them," Lou said. There was something surreal about the red of the barns and the lack of animals or people or dirt, like the images were computer generated. "Is that bad?"

"Everyone likes them," Ivy said, as she pulled a metal stool in from the kitchen, positioning it in front of the oval mirror. "That's the point."

Lou sat on the stool, slightly hunched. "But I like them because they're disturbing. Like they're not somewhere you could ever actually go. Or if you were able to get there, it would spoil the whole thing. Because then someone would be there. And the emptiness would be gone."

Ivy gathered Lou's thick brown hair into her hands, part of it knotted, just under her ears, and they made eye contact in the mirror. Lou forgot what she was saying. She didn't know if she could actually stand this. Her head was thrumming.

"How much?" Ivy said.

"What?"

Ivy held up the scissors.

"All of it?" Lou said.

"So shave it?"

"Okay, maybe not all of it."

Lou focused on the barn closest to her, the one with the sloping roof, as Ivy chopped off the sides of her hair, then the back, with craft scissors only capable of cutting a few clumps at a time, rough and slow, more sawing than slicing. Lou's arms prickled as she tried not to watch Ivy in the mirror for longer than a few seconds at a time, tried not to note how she was noting the warmth of Ivy's side as she leaned in close to inspect her work.

Ivy didn't speak as she worked, walking around Lou's body in a full circle, until she made it back to where she'd started.

First it was a wavy bob. She looked like a lawyer on her way to sue the EPA. The opposite of who she wanted to be.

"We can stop here," Ivy said, inspecting it in the mirror. She ran her hands through Lou's hair again, brushing against the backs of her ears, and Lou thought she might pass out. "It's cute."

She didn't want cute. "Go shorter."

Ivy seemed pleased by this. She searched through the cupboard below the sink until she found a pair of clippers, then flipped them on and started shearing. The buzzing echoed through Lou's head, a sound that felt like it was always there made physical. She closed her eyes.

When Ivy was done, all that was left was the top, curly and wild. It hadn't taken that long for her to look like a completely different person: her face thinner and more intense, her jawline a sharp hook, her eyebrows less worried and more concentrated. It wasn't that she looked all-the-way-boy, exactly, but she didn't look like a girl. She looked visible.

Lou stood up and leaned toward herself in the mirror, feeling free of holding so still and free of being alone inside her head while Ivy touched her.

She shook her hair out. It was really short. Really fucking *great.*

Looking at herself, a small consequential energy ran through her. How quickly changing how she looked could change how she felt, who she felt herself to be.

She faced Ivy, with her back to the mirror. Lou was a few inches taller than her, and more aware of it than usual with this short distance between them, pressing her fists into the pockets of her jeans while Ivy ran a hand through her hair, arranging her bangs to one side, then the other. Ivy's scar looked different up close like this, and Lou thought of her falling off a bicycle as a kid, how she must have looked just like this as she flew over the handlebars, like it was too late to stop whatever was coming. Lou took a half step forward.

"Of course I think about it," Ivy said softly.

Lou could hardly speak. "About what?"

"Morgan."

"Oh."

Ivy gathered the hair out of the sink and into the trash can.

Both their clothes were covered in her hair, and suddenly Lou's neck itched terribly around her collar. She wanted to jump in the shower and wash it all away. She looked down at the trash can, where her brown hair spiraled in the bottom of the liner. It looked like an animal in hibernation.

"You want me to read this for you like tea leaves?" Ivy said.

"Tell me the future."

"The futures."

As if separating them. Ivy's for Ivy. Lou's for Lou.

5

The next day, Lou got scouted again. But this time all she could think about was Morgan and her dreams of New York. The afternoon walking around the U of O campus with the Ellis sisters was so vivid still, one of the only living memories of Morgan she had in her brain and so the one she revisited most, as if she could alter the events by pure magical thinking. The logic didn't make sense, but it felt as though if she had just agreed to model for Morgan, maybe they would have gone back to that long blue dress the next morning, instead of to the waterfall. If she hadn't been resistant, maybe they would have worked the whole day together, Lou helping her achieve some vision.

The image that came to her was of Catherine gripping a box cutter, about to stab the chest of a mannequin. That was when Lou could have pressed pause, could have made some perfect but honest joke to Catherine about how skin-crawling the dress made her feel, could have said that she wished they had gone to prom in matching tuxes, maybe not together, but as friends, as two people who got each other, and then turned to Morgan, told her yes, okay, she was game to model for her; she would try on anything Morgan wanted; she would try anything once. She wanted to be less resistant to everything.

Of all the sidewalk women, this scout had looked the most like a normal person, like one of Lou's teachers or coaches. She'd handed Lou a card that matched the logo stenciled behind the receptionist's head in massive block letters: PDX MODELS.

"Anne's with someone," the receptionist told Lou. "But I'll let her know you're here."

Anne was the agent's name. Lou had called the number on the card and spoken to the scout longer over the phone, and after Lou sent in some photos from her phone—all selfies she had taken for this purpose—the scout had referred Lou to Anne. Maybe for the first time, with her new hair, Lou felt like she understood what the women saw; maybe she wouldn't have to pretend to be some version of herself that she wasn't in order to be what they wanted.

Because it was raining out, and she'd parked several blocks away, her new hair was now a mess. She wore a pullover hoodie and hand-me-down jeans. She realized that maybe she should have worn makeup, or dressed nicer, but she matched most of the boys in the waiting room. And they were all boys.

Lou sat down beside one in a floral ball cap, who was flipping through a copy of *Vogue*. He smelled like her mother on nights out, and he was so handsome it was hard to believe people were actually born looking like that. She felt like a gargoyle next to him. A door behind the receptionist swung open and through it she saw another guy on the floor doing sit-ups in a pair of boxer briefs. He stood up, all six of his abs clenched, and a heavyset man with a DSLR camera around his neck led him out of the waiting room and into the hallway.

A young woman emerged from the same room and called out, "Harrison, get in here."

The boy in the cap, Harrison, stood and followed her into the room, the door shutting behind them. Lou watched the clock. Four minutes later, he was back, but now he kept looking at her. New boys filed in and rotated through the back room, some of them staying for ten or fifteen minutes, others ushered out in a matter of seconds. Lou began to bet on which would get the full fifteen, led from the room in their boxers by the man with the DSLR, and she was usually right. The waifish, the strange, and the long-haired did the best.

Harrison turned toward her, smiling. His energy was calm, quiet. She didn't want him to leave.

"I recognize you from somewhere," he said.

Lou never thought of her face as recognizable. It looked worried in the wrong circumstances—she was always being asked if she was okay—but otherwise it had served her well enough. Her eyes were a little far apart, maybe, and her mouth too swollen. Her ears had given her the most trouble, but now that they were out for everyone to see, unable to hide, she didn't mind their sticking out.

"Oh!" Harrison said, touching her knee. "At shows. That's where I've seen you before. You're Ivy's girlfriend."

She blushed, and looked out the window. "You know Ivy?"

"My band opened for Fortunato a few times last winter. She let me borrow her Strat for a show."

"I'm not her girlfriend."

"Oh. Then she's single?"

"What, are you . . . ?"

He laughed. "Oh, not for me. My bassist. She's had a crush on Ivy forever. But we figured, you guys, you know—you seemed like you were a thing."

"Yeah, I mean, I don't know. We're—" She picked up the copy of *Vogue* he'd been reading and flipped through it. *We're what, dude?* she heard Ivy say. It was as if everyone could see her life and how it was more clearly than she could, even this stranger in a waiting room. "—not."

"Fifty-seven," he said.

"Sorry?"

"Page fifty-seven," Harrison said, reaching over to stick his finger into the front of the thick magazine. She flipped to fifty-seven, and there was Harrison, in a Prada ad. He wore a suit, an overcoat, and shining black boots. His Afro was longer, and he looked much older than he did in person. She looked through four grayscale pages of him and a girl in an angular dress inter-acting in a doorway.

"Wow," she said.

"Are you signed here?"

"Not yet."

"Well," he said. "Do."

The woman came out again and nodded at Harrison. She held a card-size digital camera. "Fire escape," she said.

The boys in the room watched as she slid open one of the giant windows and she and Harrison climbed through it. The recep-tionist shut it behind them to keep out the rain.

Watching Harrison pose on the wet fire escape was the first time Lou ever saw anyone so aware of their body and its movements outside a context she was already familiar with, like dance or yoga or running. This was a whole new body grammar. He barely moved his legs, but his torso contracted and shifted, his arms framing his face, then loose at his sides, then flexed on the railing. A few times, he leaned back too far, and she winced in fear. What a thing to see: a model plummeting from a slick ninth-story fire escape, posing all the way down.

Another woman, older than the first, emerged from the carousel back room, where all the boys in their underwear were apparently deemed beautiful or not, and pointed at her. "Lou? You're my two o'clock."

Anne's office was chalky gray, the same PDX Models logo stenciled at eye level. Anne was probably Lou's father's age, but her hair was dyed a silvery rose. She wore a pair of round thick-framed glasses, but it was clear from her cheekbones alone that she herself had been a model once.

Anne sat down at her desk, and Lou took a seat in the leather chair opposite. Anne asked how old she was.

"Eighteen," Lou said.

"You look younger," Anne said. She crossed her arms, squinting at Lou with her chin tilted up, as if Lou's face were a shelf of books she was trying to choose a title from. "Hold on. Please don't take this the wrong way. But are you a girl, Lou?"

"Um."

Anne let out a soft laugh. Could someone have a stylish laugh? Because this woman did. "From the photos you sent, and your name, I thought—well, you're very handsome."

"I'm sorry—"

"Oh, please, don't be," Anne said, standing up. "It was my mistake."

Lou guessed that was it. Oh well. That was short-lived. She stood up and followed Anne as she left the office.

But Anne didn't guide her into the waiting room to deposit her, as she was expecting. Instead, she pulled a Polaroid camera out of the receptionist's desk and exited through the glass doors of the agency, leading Lou down a long white hallway, which was so empty and so long that if she had been following a strange man, not a woman, Lou would have taken a fast turn at the elevator and gotten the hell out. But there was something sure and commanding about how Anne moved, as if every direction any part of her body took was fully deliberate, like she'd never lead Lou on the wrong course without very clear intention. Her straight-backed walk down the hallway made Lou feel like they were striding out onto the tarmac to board their own private plane. Like Anne was really taking her somewhere. Lou had never paid much attention to anything about fashion, but even she knew how a model walked down the runway.

Anne opened an unmarked chrome door and led Lou into a small room with white walls and floor-to-ceiling windows. A reflector was propped in the corner beside a large parabolic umbrella, the kind Lou had used in photography class and then coveted.

The sole piece of furniture was a tall stool. Anne asked Lou to strip down to her underwear, and Lou didn't question it until she was standing there with her skinny legs extending out from her black boxer briefs and the fleeting embarrassment of her plain white bra, which was kind of ratty. If any of it was working against her, Anne didn't comment. The last time Lou had been this unclothed in front of a stranger was in the gynecologist's office, paper-smocked and freezing. But she felt comfortable, actually amused, being observed by Anne.

"Fantastic," Anne said, pulling a yellow tape measure out from her palm, as if she had conjured it.

Lou bit the inside of her cheek to keep from bursting out laughing.

"Let's get you measured and then see you against that wall there," Anne said, and it was quickly apparent that everything with Anne was a *let's*. The commands that followed included *Lou*, a gesture at friendliness, but were clearly instructions. Though Lou never would have admitted it, it was a relief to be given straightforward directions by an adult, particularly one as clear as *lift up your arms*.

Anne wrapped a tape measure around Lou's bra and wrote a number on a pad of paper slipped from her jacket. Her hands were soft and elegant. She continued on to the skinniest part of Lou's waist and finally, the largest part of her butt and hips, taking notes as she went.

"That's something we can work with," Anne said. "Now lean back."

The wall was cold against her skin. Anne took a half-dozen pictures of her with the Polaroid camera, and Lou tried to do what Harrison had done, moving just a little bit at a time. Posing. It felt goofy, but not entirely unnatural.

When prompted, Lou put her clothes back on and they took another round.

"Let's put your neck out," Anne said, "and pull that chin down. Hands lower. Lower. Bend your knee. Time your blinks. Good."

Lou mimicked the movements of Anne's body, as if playing a game of Simon Says. She felt exposed and too angular, but not as self-conscious as she would have expected, being on the opposite side of the camera. Anne didn't ask Lou any personal questions; she didn't seem to care about anything except for the pure aesthetic value of her. Meanwhile, Lou liked imagining how Anne was composing the shots. It was just so nice to be around a camera again.

They returned to Anne's office, and she laid the Polaroids in a long line across from Lou on the desk. Anne wrote down Lou's name on the bottom of a few of them in blue Sharpie, then 34"—24"—35".

Lou picked up one of the Polaroids and considered herself. The girl in the photograph was confident, cool, and yes, weird, but the kind of weird that stopped you on the street, not the kind that made you cross it.

Anne asked whether she could come in next week for a test shoot.

"Definitely," Lou said.

"Are you done with school?"

"Yep."

"What are your plans?"

Lou held up the Polaroid. "This?"

PART TWO

I

The morning of the celebration of life was warm, but the sky was low and gray. Heavy rain had slipped in and out all afternoon, and Lou kept dreaming up scenarios that forced Catherine and her family to cancel the party (flooded basement, electrical problems, sudden illness, excessive gloominess)— not that rain had ever canceled any party in Oregon. Lou had received an invitation in the mail from Catherine's parents. There had been a link included to donate to a scholarship for the University of Oregon's fashion program in memory of Morgan, but nothing personalized. Nothing from Mr. and Mrs. Ellis that said, *Our daughter drowned because of you.* Nothing from Catherine that said, *What the fuck, Lou?*

Ivy said they could go together, that maybe that would make it easier, and when the offer was still hypothetical, Lou thought it would. But when Ivy came to pick her up, Tuck was in the passenger seat, looking pale and too thin. Which made everything harder, how Lou's jealousy felt so petty in this context but unrelenting. Her brain felt staticky. Her panic thickened.

Lou got into the back seat and kept the window rolled down until her face was damp. It had been a week since she signed with the agency, and it would be six more before Ivy left for New York. Anne wanted her to build up her portfolio and comp card over the summer with test shoots. When Lou had asked what a comp card was, Anne had showed her a piece of cardstock with a model's headshot, measurements, and Polaroids. Like a business card, Anne said, something to give to casting directors and photographers, when the time came. It was hard to envision the time coming; Lou still hadn't said anything to anyone about the modeling. As far as everyone in her life knew, come September she was moving into the dorms at the University of Oregon, as planned. But there was no way she'd be doing that now. She didn't ever want to go back there.

It was dawning on Lou that Catherine's sister's memorial was the worst imaginable place to talk to her friend for the first time since the accident, but when Catherine answered the front door, it felt at first like nothing was all that weird between them.

"Thanks for coming," Catherine said, and looked at Lou more confused than distressed.

Lou could tell that she was drunk. There was a half lean she did sometimes at parties, where she held on to supports for longer than usual. She was holding on too tightly to the doorframe, staring at them.

As they hugged, Lou didn't make any excuses, but it suddenly felt possible that they could glide right past the last few weeks of neglect as long as no one acknowledged them. Catherine wore a black oversize men's sweater over a collared shirt, with creased slacks, her hair stashed under a beanie. She looked like an eight-year-old boy, tucked into herself. An already tiny person grown tinier, aging backward into preadolescence.

"Your hair," Catherine said to Lou, but didn't say anything further. It didn't sound like approval. She led them through the house, past a few dozen people milling around, all dressed in dark formal clothes, despite the summer humidity. Lou recognized some of them as graduates of their high school but didn't know any of them by name. A few said hello to Tuck, but he stayed beside them, following Catherine out to the stilted back deck, which extended into the woods. The patio furniture had linen covers over the cushions, and the house behind them was a white modernist box. Its enormous windows reflected all their dark-clothed bodies back at them.

There were fewer people outside, where there were silver tubs full of drinks, snacks, and a table holding the bleakest confetti cake in the world, with one slender slice taken out of it. Lou had forgotten how high this deck was, almost thirty feet down to the next tier of yard, full of boulders and ferns, and she felt nervous on the edge of it. She moved at least a full body's length away from the wooden railing, which was only waist-high. It didn't seem child-safe. Or drunk-Catherine-safe.

A large projector screen toward the back of the deck was running a slideshow of photographs of Morgan, most featuring Catherine beside her. Morgan shooting a layup; Morgan playing the flute at a concert. Morgan and Catherine at Haystack Rock in matching zebra-striped bathing suits; on their trampoline; at a birthday party; on Christmas morning; at a half dozen school dances coupled with boys in boutonnieres, including Tuck, none of whom she would ever marry. Morgan with her design projects; Morgan on a bike on the Brooklyn Bridge, looking so happy.

Lou felt nauseous as she watched Tuck take in the slide-show. He stared at it like he didn't know what he was look-ing at. When a photo popped up of him and Morgan on what was clearly freshman move-in day at the University of Oregon, Ivy slipped an arm around him, and his body slackened. He wasn't crying, but he seemed beyond that, like he had only just stopped. She didn't know how any of them were going to make it through the next hour. She wished she could say something to Tuck, and to Catherine, who was reclining on a spotless linen lounge chair, a little unsteadily. Something that would make any kind of difference to their pain. But she didn't know what that would be.

A video of a water-gun fight on this same deck played silently before them, while the speakers blasted Janelle Monáe. Kid Catherine shot kid Morgan in the face and opened her mouth in apology. Lou sat on the arm of Catherine's chair and leaned in. "'Screwed'?"

"I curated the playlist," Catherine said, with a half giggle. "My one job. My parents keep trying to get me to use the clean versions." She turned to rest her cheek against Lou's arm. "Have you noticed that they made this Fourth of July themed?"

It was only a few days past the Fourth, so Lou hadn't noticed anything unusual, but the cake was red, white, and blue.

"It's mostly inside," Catherine said. "It makes me want to puke. It was her favorite holiday, is their thinking. Like fuck you, maybe don't celebrate it without her, then."

Catherine stood up, swayed a bit, and gestured to her empty water bottle. She squinted at Tuck and Ivy as if seeing them for the first time, her eyes rimmed red and puffy. "Well, aren't you guys cute." She wandered off toward the house and Lou stood to follow her, but Ivy grabbed her hand and she stayed. It didn't take much.

"She's blacked out," Tuck murmured to them.

"How can you tell?" Lou said.

"My dad used to get like that, before he got sober. They stare past you."

Lou didn't know how to respond. There was a microphone set up beside the projector, and Catherine's father came out and began to mess with the amp. He wasn't getting anywhere with it, so Ivy went up to him and started assisting with the cords. She set up the whole thing in a matter of seconds. Catherine's dad tested the microphone, and people poured out of the house, onto the deck, gathering in a half circle.

"We're hoping that you all will share memories of Morgan," Mr. Ellis said into the microphone. "Catherine is going to start us off."

He walked back to the edge of the crowd and gestured for his daughter. The sun was going down. "Sweetheart?" he said.

"No, I'm not," Catherine said, loud enough for everyone to hear, as if she and her father were suddenly onstage in a play.

"Catherine." His tone sharpening. "*Please*."

Catherine flinched at the order, tucking a loose strand of bleached hair into her hat, but the sudden sternness seemed to revive her. She looked unexpectedly lucid as she walked to the mic stand, shoulders back, a ghost of her sister's posture.

"My sister," she said into the microphone, her voice reverberating off the deck and into the hills. "Morgan—"

Ivy touched her fingers to Lou's wrist, the slightest movement.

"My sister," Catherine began, "pretty much fucking hated me."

Catherine unclipped the microphone from the stand, hopped up onto the wooden railing, and hooked her feet around the balusters. She leaned back. Lou was afraid Catherine was going to fall backward off the deck into the rock-rimmed landscaping below. No one moved toward her.

Lou was the closest. "Catherine," she said. "Let's get out of here."

Catherine leaned back a little further. Her hat fell off, dropping like a shot bird down to the yard. "Why?"

"Stop!" Lou took a step. "Just come on."

"You want to know what Morgan really thought of me? Maybe everyone wants to hear this. Now that you're all listening. Morgan thought *I* was selfish. But I haven't done shit. It turned out that *she* was. *She.*"

Lou swallowed. "You're not selfish."

"Well, I can be," Catherine said, lowering the microphone. "Maybe I am."

Catherine's posture slumped, and Lou was too scared to move any closer to her, so she kept speaking quietly, carefully. "Let's go inside," she said.

"What are you even doing here, Lou?" Catherine raised the microphone up to her mouth again, as if she were going to belt a solo into it. "Just because we hooked up, you're never going to talk to me again? My sister literally drowned in front of you, and you can't ask how I'm doing?"

The crowd stood perfectly still. Before Lou could respond, Catherine slipped forward off the railing into an awkward cross-legged collapse, and her parents rushed her.

The crowd stared as Lou ran back through the house and outside again through the front door, pulse pounding, like they were all going to follow her in a mob. But no one followed. Not even Ivy. She was alone in the quiet so quickly that it almost felt like the party hadn't happened, like she was just gearing up to enter it for the first time.

Lou started walking along the shoulder of Skyline Boulevard. The rich old dudes who came up here to speed in their convertibles like they were in a car commercial were out, even in the rain, rushing up behind her, whooshing past, making the hair on her neck stand up, her face wet and hot and muddy. She couldn't think, couldn't do anything except see Catherine leaning backward off the deck, and there was something pulling her toward each car and each man behind the wheel that made her understand Catherine and what she needed right then, to feel like she was in control of her own death, to thwart it. Lou didn't wander off the shoulder into the center of the road, but she could have, if Aldenlight Park hadn't appeared so quickly, with its stand of Douglas firs, their giant bodies swaying in the dark.

She sank down on the wet grass beneath the trees and stared at the dark hill, willing Ivy's familiar slouching form to rise over it, with whatever indictment Lou might have deserved. But the willing didn't work. Alone here, Lou felt as stuck as the trees, like she'd always been here and always would be, until some heavy force took her down.

2

The next day, she heard from her agent. A New York modeling agency, Superb, wanted to sign her. According to Anne, it was one of the best in the industry. PDX Models would remain her mother agency, but Superb would represent her internationally.

"Internationally how?" Lou said to Anne on the phone.

"For the shows," Anne said. "For anything high fashion. For commercial work. The best work is either in New York or abroad."

"What if I stayed here? Is there work in Portland?"

"Do you want to stay here?" Anne said.

No.

When Lou came in to sign the paperwork, the waiting room was full of new girls. An open casting call. Some looked nervous, but others eyed Lou like she had something they wanted and they would steal it from her if they could. It was a perfect day outside. Most of the girls wore spring dresses, pretty and light, but they all wore heels. Lou wore her least-tattered Vans, which were still high on the scale of tattered. The receptionist was on the phone, but she mouthed, *Hey, Lou*, and signaled her back to her agent's office. A few of the girls watched Lou cross the waiting room like they were gearing up to trip her, but one in the corner in high-waisted jeans and thick eyeliner winked at her, and Lou blushed, closing the door to the hallway firmly behind her.

Anne sat at her desk, shades drawn to block out the glare from the window. She wore a black sleeveless blouse with a high buttoned collar and pearl snaps. Harrison sat across from her, his head freshly shaved, rubbing his hand along the base of his neck.

"Likely by August," Harrison was saying, his voice low. "Was what they said. But she's bounced back before, and honestly, last year, if you had told me that we'd have this much time, I wouldn't have—"

Lou knocked on the open door and they startled.

"Harrison's going to be joining us today," Anne said. "I thought we might go outside for the shots. We could all use the air, right?"

The three of them walked together to the waterfront. It was a warm day, the smell of algae and flowers in the air. Anne shot Lou first. Lou posed in her own clothes, a black T-shirt and cutoffs, with the Burnside Bridge behind her. She could sense Harrison watching her and wondered briefly if he was critiquing her technique. Her test shoots had all been alone in the empty room in the agency, Anne teaching her where to put her arms and how to stare at the lens without ever forgetting it was there. This was so public. It felt equal parts discomforting and exhilarating to be out in the open where everyone could see how she was changing, what she was deciding to do. She didn't want to run into anyone she knew, and also she wanted to run into everyone she knew.

When it was Harrison's turn, Lou sat on a graffitied bench to watch him. Harrison in front of a camera was just as enchanting as he had been that first day on the fire escape. He sat cross-legged in the grass. Stood up. Bent over. Slipped a hand behind his head. Every time she blinked, his body altered itself into another flattering position. It was like watching someone in a strobe light.

"Good," Anne said, zipping the camera back in her side bag. "Now Harrison's going to teach you how to walk."

"I know how to walk."

Anne shook her head. "No." She wasn't smiling. "You do not." She put her hand on Harrison's arm. "You walked for Tom Ford last fall. Who else?"

He listed off a dozen names Lou had never heard of but she knew were impressive by the hallowed way he said them. She widened her eyes and nodded enthusiastically, as she now did whenever anyone showed her a page out of *Vogue* that was supposed to represent a thing she should admire. She was starting to appreciate the photographs, the compositions, the *art* of the clothes and the design in editorial spreads, but on no level did she understand fashion, let alone speak it fluently.

Satisfied, Anne said that she'd see Lou back at the agency when they were done, that there was some more news she wanted to discuss with her. Then she turned to Harrison. "Stay until she doesn't walk like a librarian."

Harrison sat down on the bench and untied his boots. Then he pulled out two pairs of heels from his backpack. One pair he handed to Lou and the other he slipped onto his bare feet.

"Are you going to see Fortunato at that show next weekend?" he said. "My band's also playing a set."

"Oh," Lou said, her stomach dropping. "I didn't know about it."

Even before the memorial, Ivy hadn't been texting her to hang out as much. Lou had been busy with this. Ivy had been busy with Tuck, who'd moved back in with his parents in Portland. Ivy had said he was in deep grief over Morgan.

Harrison seemed surprised. "Did something happen with you guys?"

"Can I ask you something?"

"I have zero girl advice."

"Not that," she said. "Does Anne think I'm a huge nerd?"

"Oh, for sure. But in an It Gets Better kind of way."

From their conversations in the waiting room, and the amount of framed editorials of him on the agency walls, Lou knew Harrison had modeled for a few years, describing working in foreign capitals casually and generously, as if they were in her future too. Whenever Harrison described his experiences at Fashion Week in New York, it sounded like someone talking about drugs while on drugs.

"Why don't you live in New York anymore?" she asked him. Why would he come back to Portland if New York was so great?

What if she got there and she hated it? What if she gave up her life for nothing? For someone else's dream? Someone who wasn't even alive to see her do it.

Harrison didn't answer until he'd turned from her, walking with his arms swinging perfectly opposite his smooth steps. He wore skinny slacks, a bomber jacket despite the heat, and black four-inch-high stilettos that ticked on the concrete.

"My mom's sick," he said quietly. "So I came home."

She apologized, but he was already out of earshot.

Harrison walked a dozen yards down the esplanade like it was an invisible runway, then paused, slipping a hand into his pocket. Pivoting, he slipped his jacket off and held it over his shoulder, casually, handsomely, like he was alone on a stroll in some European city in another era. There was no heaviness to him, just elegant conviction. By the time he was back, two women were openly watching from the bench to Lou's right, overfull shopping bags at their feet.

He took a breath. "The trick is to walk like you know where you're going. Like you've already been there. Which is kind of the opposite of how you walk, no offense."

He declared it was her turn, but Lou stalled, adjusting the strap of her left heel, once, twice, three times, hoping the ogling women would leave.

"Well?" Harrison said. "Let's see it."

In addition to the two women, their audience had grown to a guy with a shopping cart full of rugs and several leashed animals (cats? ferrets? martens?) and a group of guys their age holding longboards and brown-bagged forties. One of them was filming. Lou felt the direction of their comments but couldn't hear well enough to know whether they were making fun of her and Harrison or just curious about the spectacle. She moved closer to Harrison, wobbling in the heels. "Can't we go—I don't know—somewhere else? Somewhere not so right here?"

"Why do you give a shit what they think of you?" he shouted suddenly, so loud a passing family on matching rental bikes collectively swerved. "Everywhere is right here. Most of it is worse. Lou, *walk*."

Walk. Yes. Okay. Lou took off down the waterfront, trying to keep her shoulders back, her legs in time, an imaginary jacket slung over her left shoulder. She paused where he had, picturing a crowd looking up at her from the end of the runway, examining her clothes, her stance, the image of her. She had never been watched like that. She tried to pretend she was Ivy, or at least alongside her. She tried to pretend she belonged on a stage.

"Yo," Harrison hollered, clapping at her like she was about to blow a lead in a race. So this was Harrison, excited. "Just for fun, try making it back in a straight line."

By the time she was back, having very carefully followed the edge of the concrete, mandatory scowl positioned on her face—not that it took much, what with all the public mockery—Harrison was bent over, cackling.

"Sorry, miss," he said, back to his calm tone, "but can you tell me where the reference materials are?"

"Did you script that? And what's your problem with librarians anyway? There are tons of graceful librarians. I'd be honored to be considered like them. I *love* libraries."

It only got him going more. After a few seconds, he managed to compose himself, then twirled his index finger at her. "Again."

Lou flipped him off and turned back to the pathway alongside the railing separating her from the deep and shining Willamette River. This time, with some defiance in her step, it was better.

Back in the agency, Anne was half-hidden behind her Mac. "Successful lessons?" she said wryly.

The delay between her question and eye contact was what made it clear that assigning Harrison as her walk instructor was more about giving him a task, a distraction, some authority, control over something. A straight line to walk. Which endeared Anne to Lou.

Lou sat down in the chair across from her. The leather was cool, and she leaned back, looking at the models on the wall, their poses elongated and sculptural. When talking to other models, Lou began to say *build up* in the same way that Ivy used to say it about her music, with optimism that her life and career would stack up into something beautiful and strong, like a cathedral in its earliest stages of construction.

"Harrison gave me a C minus," she told Anne, who laughed.

"So pleased you two hit it off. You'll have a friendly face in New York."

Lou thought of what he'd said about his mother. "Harrison's moving back?"

"At the end of the summer," Anne said. "At least that's what it sounds like now." She leaned forward, pushing her mandarin-colored glasses high on her forehead. "Which brings us to what I wanted to talk to you about today: Superb is having a shoot for some of their models in a few weeks in New York. They want to highlight some new faces ahead of Fashion Week."

At first Lou thought she was just informing her, like it was a fashion news bulletin she hadn't yet heard, but then she realized Anne meant they wanted to highlight *her*, and that was the first time any of this had felt real, that it wasn't just her rehearsing a play that would never be performed for an audience.

"They want you out there," Anne said. "As soon as possible really, so this would be a great chance for you to meet some people, get a sense of how it would actually be, if you want to do this. What do you think?"

Lou, she heard Harrison say, *walk*.

3

The only time Lou had been to New York, she was fifteen; it was the summer after she'd met Ivy, when Lou had just begun going to her solo shows, played mostly in record shops and college kids' living rooms, when they were always the youngest people in any room. Her mom had been invited to a journalism conference, and Lou took a few days off from her landscaping job to join her.

She and her mom had planned the New York trip together, though they had only one full day when Lou's mom wasn't busy at the conference: an afternoon at the Met (for the art, yes, but also because her mom had read Lou her own favorite book as a child, *From the Mixed-Up Files of Mrs. Basil E. Frankweiler*, at least a dozen times aloud at bedtime—"I think you're brilliant, Claude. New York is a great place to hide out. No one notices no one. . . .") and a pilgrimage to the Dakota to see the spot where John Lennon was shot, because that was the year Lou spent listening to endless Beatles albums on her massive head-phones, and her mom teased her that she always looked like she was in a recording studio, and that she couldn't be wistful for her childhood while she was still living it. Her mom's favorite Beatle was John and Lou's was George, and her mom always said that explained their differences.

The Met was infinite and lusciously chilled, and the sur-rounding fellow observers of art were as distinct as up-close brushstrokes, but they ended up skipping the Dakota because it seemed too sad and her mom wanted to make a happy hour with some other journalists. Lou took her own happy hour to pore over the lap-heavy photography books in the personal library of the reporter whose apartment they were staying in. The next morning, they woke up for their flight back at what her mom called an ungodly hour, but the light that morning felt a little godly anyway, and so they packed quickly and sat together on the grass in a small park a few blocks from the apartment. They had about twenty minutes before they had to catch a cab to JFK when the girl came up to them, asking if she could take their portrait.

The girl wore loose-fitting jeans and high-tops; she had long shaggy hair and dark eyebrows. She looked effortless approach-ing them, asking straight-up strangers if she could take their picture. She was *on assignment*, she said, a phrasing that perked Lou's mother right up, though she could have said she *had* an assignment.

Lou was disquieted by the thing that rose up in her, watch-ing the girl. It was the first time she had ever been really, genu-inely, climb-the-walls *attracted*. Not only did she want to be this girl, she flat out *wanted* her, like an alarm bell slamming through her, a fire alarm, the kind Lou had heard spat ink at you if you were the one bold enough to pull it in the halls. Lou was not bold enough even to look at this girl fully, let alone pull the alarm. But somehow the ink got on her anyway.

The girl was older than Lou but not older than college. Lou's mom told the girl, yes, *of course* she could. *What a joy it would be, to have you take our picture. This is my daughter, can't you tell?* The girl had said yes, she could absolutely tell, and Lou had been further mortified. *But you have to promise to send us a copy, someday.*

The girl promised.

Behind them, dogs had raced around, freed from leashes and morning commutes. The girl looked through her lens at them and talked to Lou mostly, back and forth for a few minutes while she adjusted her tripod and the settings on her camera. Lou realized how much easier it was to talk with the lens between them. It had struck her at the time as a real solution to something—craving shield, gaze shield, just straight-up shield; not that it was that straightforward for Lou later, particularly on the other side of the camera.

The girl had asked for an email address to send them the picture. It didn't appear in her mom's in-box for nearly six months. But the girl eventually fulfilled her promise. Lou's mom had it printed and framed, then hung it on her office wall.

That day in New York, her mom had watched Lou looking at the girl, and it wasn't judgmental, but it was knowing, which might have been worse.

"She was lovely," her mom had said after the girl left them.

Lou nodded, unable to say anything further, her cheeks burning, something in her body having turned on its side to face her directly.

"You know," her mom said thoughtfully, "that's how I imagine you someday. Just running around some city, taking pictures. Discovering new places, people. Won't that be nice?"

"I'm staying in Oregon for school," Lou said. She had long been set on it.

"Well, it doesn't have to be for school, that's not what I'm saying."

Lou nodded, distracted, watching the girl approach an older woman in the corner of the park. She stood back from her, setting up the tripod.

"Lou," her mom said. "You know you can tell me whatever you want, right?"

Lou didn't answer.

"Are there any boys you like?"

There were, and she didn't mind being asked that. The boys she liked were long-haired and a little weird and usually mute. The shyness made it easier to project whatever personality she wanted them to have. She liked her first boyfriend, a kid named Ralph who was the goalkeeper on the soccer team and memorized poems that he would recite only to Lou. She liked kissing him on dance floors, she liked the word *boyfriend*, how it implied she was a person who could get a boyfriend, if she wanted to.

"I liked Ralph."

"I liked Ralph too," her mom said. But she wasn't done fishing. It was obvious that wasn't the answer she'd been looking for, that it was only a tap on the curb as she parallel parked the question. She hesitated, straightened out her legs again. "Anyone else? Any girls?"

Lou said nothing. She felt like someone had turned her around blindfolded and let her go into dark and unfamiliar woods. She had never been more self-conscious than she was in that moment. Skinless. Afraid. It wasn't that she was afraid of liking a girl: her parents wouldn't care if she did; her older brother was gay, and her parents loved him and his boyfriend. It was that she knew exactly the girl her mom was really asking about, as if her mom had pulled something outside that was only supposed to exist in the surfaces of Lou's gut and eyes (not even in her brain; that would have been admitting something she couldn't conceptualize yet) and slid it across the table to her.

She meant Ivy.

But the girl with the camera saved them both in that moment. Saved them from the question she herself had prompted. Saved Lou from admitting that her mom knew exactly what she wanted. She circled back to them, asking if she could take just one more. "You guys look so perfect there. Just like that."

That was the photograph on the wall.

Her parents weren't happy about New York, about the future it seemed to imply—that is, not college, especially not college near them. Since Morgan drowned, it had felt like her parents were inspectors and she wasn't structurally sound. They kept suggesting she talk to someone, without saying who. Lou sat them down at the kitchen table, same as when she had yelled at them once for seeming unhappy together, when she thought that her mom might be cheating on her dad and they'd denied it—both the unhappiness and the cheating. This time, she was calm. She explained that she wanted to try this, at least see what it was like. They seemed confused and judgmental, but they didn't say they'd stop her.

Her New York agency booked the plane tickets, arranged for her to stay in an apartment while she was there. She didn't know if she would have to pay them back, but her agent didn't mention it and she didn't ask.

When Lou walked through the arrivals gate at JFK, a woman from her new agency was waiting with a handwritten sign that read *Lou, Superb*. Lou approached with a tentative wave, but the woman barely acknowledged her, thumb and gaze so engaged by her phone. The woman wore Gucci sunglasses and a slim black suit, her hair in a tight dark bun on the top of her head. She fiddled with an unlit cigarette between her left-hand fingers as she led Lou through the airport and out to the car at a clip, still texting, or emailing, or something, with her right. She didn't ask how Lou's flight had been. She didn't ask her anything. The woman still hadn't introduced herself by the time she parked the car, and it felt too late to ask who she was as Lou followed her into a ground-level apartment. There were photographs of greyhounds on the walls, a long brown leather couch, and a tall, full wine rack, light glittering onto the patterned wallpaper.

The woman shuffled through a stack of manila envelopes on the island and handed one to Lou. "There are directions to the shoot and the agency, a key, and your itinerary in there. I'll be down here if you need anything. We'll text you if any go-sees come up; we're hoping to send you to some after the shoot. Yukon will meet you at the agency."

Lou didn't know who or what Yukon was. The woman sat down on the couch, reengaged with her phone. When she looked back up, she seemed surprised that Lou was still standing there, envelope in hand.

"Where do I go?" Lou said, and the woman extended one elegant finger upward.

Lou tried all four locks on the door at the top of the stairs several times over—the key looked like one that went to a mailbox, not a door, but she didn't want to go back downstairs, or get between that woman and her phone. Thankfully, a few girls, who all would have medaled in high heels, climbed the stairs and joined her on the landing. They were all taller and skinnier than Lou. The tallest one rapped on the door and someone opened it for them.

"Don't bother with the keys," she said, glancing over her shoulder at Lou. She sounded cheerful about it. "None of them work. But someone's always here."

The apartment was more like a space station than a home, especially compared to the woman's downstairs. Bare hanging bulbs, fashion magazines stacked on the long kitchen table, nothing on the walls, a sofa a weirdly far distance back from the flat-screen television. Five doors, each leading to bunk beds, stacked suitcases, and very tall, thin girls talking to one another, talking on cell phones, on video chats, in English, German, French, Swahili, Mandarin, in other languages Lou had never heard before. There were no boys. The girls looked startled when they first saw Lou, like she had wandered into the wrong locker room.

The last room was empty, thank God, and Lou dropped her backpack onto the bed. The bottom bunk creaked when she sat on it, like it wasn't actually load-bearing, which, judging by the size of the other girls, seemed likely. She pulled out her itiner-

ary. The shoot was in a few hours, so she had some time. Anne
had sent her with her first pair of heels, skinny black jeans, and
a top that seemed more net than shirt. Lou wore a sweatshirt
over it, even though the air was soupy with heat.

She'd brought her Nikon, a last-minute decision after digging it out of the back of her closet. For the first time since
Morgan died, she turned it on. All her old photos were still on
it, and she started flipping through them, zooming in, zooming
out. She lingered on one from the night at Aldenlight Park,
before everything changed: Ivy, leaning against a Douglas fir.
Ivy was grinning like Lou had just said something hilarious
(Lou loved to make her laugh like that, even if it wasn't always
intentional), and her hand was indistinct in movement, pointing out something, or someone, just beyond them.

Lou waited outside the tall brick building until people started
arriving with equipment, one by one. The city light was hazy,
the air humid. Eventually, there were six models, including her,
and a few people from the agency who were running things.

Inside wasn't a studio like Lou was expecting but someone's
apartment, which felt cozy, lived-in. There were mugs in the
sink, a pair of sheepskin slippers by the door, a fireplace with
a large cactus potted in terra-cotta in its center. It felt like the
owner might walk in at any second and ask what they were all
doing there.

She sat with the other models around a dining room table,
and they talked to each other with the amount of English that
they had between them. All of them seemed just as nervous as
she was. She had expected everyone to be as self-assured as Har-

rison, so it was easier to hang out with these girls, ask them how long they'd been modeling, where they were from. Siberia, Senegal, Tallahassee, Belize, Singapore, Wales, and Portland, Oregon. Where was that? America. Above California. Ah.

One by one, they were shepherded into the breakfast nook, which had been set up with a tall stool and a wide mirror. The table held varying sizes and colors of blow-dryers, makeup palettes, and hair clips. Two men circled Lou, one with a pristine red beard, the other with a shaved head and large wire-rimmed glasses. Pristine Beard buffed her nails, picking at her cuticles with tiny tweezers. Wire-rim started handling Lou's hair like it was escaping from him. He pulled out some trimmers and asked her if she minded if he fixed whatever someone had done to her, and Lou smiled, imagining Ivy behind her, the two of them laughing at themselves in the mirror over her uneven but confident chops.

"It's growing out kind of weird," Lou said.

Wire-rim raised an eyebrow, lit a cigarette, and said something under his breath in French. Pristine Beard painted her nails with a clear gloss that made her fingers feel like they were being suffocated, and then a silver polish. After he moved on to the next girl, and the hair stylist released her, Lou went to the bathroom to pee and washed her hands without a second thought.

When she returned to the kitchen, Pristine Beard was leaning out a window, smoking a cigarette. He stared at her fingers, the polish damaged and chipped, and gasped. "What the fuck?"

She apologized, face boiling, but he had to do it all again, and by the time he was done, it was her turn with the photographer and she was suddenly so panicky she could barely stand up.

The photographer called everyone *cara*, dear, in a warm way, like she had known all the models and their families for years. The other models—people kept calling them *new faces*—had seemed tentative at the table, talking to one another, but every one of them had relaxed once they were in front of the camera. They had all shot in the living room, but when the photographer put Lou beside the fireplace and looked at her for a minute—taking a few shots, adjusting settings—she soon stopped. She was looking at Lou like Lou was withholding something, but Lou didn't know what to give her. Anne had always told Lou what to do. She'd never had to direct herself before.

"We'll be back," the photographer said to the room. "Come with me, *cara*."

The photographer took Lou up to the roof alone. It was beautiful up there, the city noise softened by their new distance from the street and the shuddering trees in wide wooden planters around the perimeter, all pruned to the same size and shape. Finally Lou felt like she was breathing real air.

The photographer was in her forties, Lou guessed. She had long black hair, streaked with gray, and wore leather sandals that clicked as she walked. She spoke with the slightest accent, Italian, or Spanish. "By all means, take the shoes off, *cara*. If that's the problem."

Lou slipped off the heels and did feel better in her bare feet, freer. She ran her hand along the newly shaved back of her neck, velvet stubble like the day Ivy had cut it. She could see the Brooklyn Bridge. She imagined Morgan riding a bike across it.

The photographer asked her what was wrong and Lou really did want to describe to this woman exactly what *was* wrong, if she could have named it. It felt like she was really asking Lou what she felt to be wrong and not why she wasn't moving her body so the photographer could do her job and go home. Lou wasn't moving her body because she felt very alone and very far from the people she loved, and it could have gone either way whether that made her feel free or scared.

When Lou started to move, none of the poses probably appeared to the photographer as anything other than a body doing a normal body thing in front of her, but with each one Lou envisioned them somewhere else, and it was five minutes, maybe it was ten or thirty or maybe it was hours they were up there: Lou diving off, Lou a fault line, Lou at fault. The photographer moved around her like Lou held a center of gravity that only she was witness to, and every movement was certainly smaller than she perceived, but who was there to tell her they weren't as large as she felt?

When it was over, when the photographer lowered her camera, they looked at each other without anything between them.

"We got it," the photographer said, like they had made something together. Something good.

4

Lou stayed through everyone else's turn and walked out of the apartment alongside the photographer, helping her carry some reflectors and lights, lingering when they got to her car. Lou asked if she'd been doing this a long time.

"Ten years, give or take. For money, if that's what you're counting, far less. Though I'm not." She nodded at Lou's camera bag, which she still used as a purse. "Do you shoot too?"

"I used to, more."

"You live in the city?"

"Not yet."

She told Lou that New York was the best place in the world to make art and gave her her card. *Sienna Vece Photography*. It felt different than receiving a card from an agent. Like it could get Lou what she actually wanted. "For some of us," Sienna Vece said, "it feels like the only place."

And for the first time, Lou felt like it could be, for her. She imagined walking to a park to meet Ivy, with her camera and a coffee and a whole afternoon ahead of them to go anywhere, be anyone. A whole sea of time, a whole decade, a whole life.

The next couple of days were busy with measurements and Polaroids at the agency, and go-sees, which turned out to be meetings where a few people turned her around in a bathing suit and heels in semipublic places. Once in a hotel lobby, passing businessmen eyeing her without apology. Even there, she managed to keep the feeling from the rooftop photo shoot with her, that pure batch of promise. The days were so packed and overwhelming with new things that she was too tired to really worry about why Ivy hadn't texted her back since the memorial, let alone worry about the things she'd normally worry about—the gap between the subway platform and the train, whether one could fall down into it; the sturdiness of overhead scaffolding; the probability of the businessmen from the lobby following her and cornering her in an alley. New York felt like enough distraction for her brain that she was really just focused on the people in front of her, watching them carefully, mesmerized by the way she could slow down just by letting people move fast around her.

Yukon turned out to be the first and only name of her new agent, one of the tallest people she'd ever seen in real life who didn't play for the Blazers. They had beautiful long red hair and bright eyes. Yukon sat her down in a conference room after the Polaroids, talked to her about plans for Fashion Week castings, and told her she'd need to be in New York by the end of the summer if she was serious about doing this.

When she agreed to move out in a couple of weeks, at the

end of August, fingering the photographer's card in her pocket like a talisman, she thought of the girl in the park, circling back to Lou and her mother for one more shot. Seeing a thing, *people*, so clearly that they saw themselves that way, too, if only for an afternoon.

The Fortunato show Harrison had told her about was the night she got back from New York. It was at a four-story Victorian punk house in Northeast, with electric-blue trim and a long line of pride flags. All the Goodwill furniture was shoved to the walls, and Fortunato was already playing before giant bay windows when she pushed her way into the high-ceilinged living room. The room was wood-paneled, foggy with smoke and hot breath, loaded with bodies. She was glad she was late. No one noticed her enter.

At first, it felt like if Ivy caught her eye, Lou would combust or implode or shatter, and so she watched the crowd watch Ivy instead, pressing her body against the people in front of her, who pressed their bodies closer to the band. But by the third song, Lou couldn't keep her eyes off Ivy, the shape of her hands on the fretboard, her eyes skimming the crowd without ever landing. Ivy's bangs were shaggy, and her hair was tucked behind her ears. She wore a white pocket tee and loose-fitting jeans. When Ivy noticed Lou, she stopped mid-lyric, as if she'd forgotten the words. Tuck kept playing, but Lou could hear him, even unmiked, ask if Ivy was okay, if she wanted to stop. Ivy shook her head and picked the verse back up right where she'd left it. It was so intimate, the way Tuck was looking at her, trying to read her, that Lou wanted to take his picture.

After that, Ivy's voice carried up and down and followed Lou through song after song until she felt sadness and want like a punch in the ribs. She couldn't keep her eyes from Ivy's neck, that mouth, those hands a blur through the blur of the crowd. Her desire greening like a slow bruise.

After the set, Lou squeezed through the crowd to a kitchen with peeling wallpaper, where she found Harrison, drinking a tall boy of Rainier beside an island, squinting against the fluorescents. He wore his floral ball cap and overalls and was talking to two leggy girls in shorts who were sitting on the countertops around the sink, kicking their heels against the cupboards. Harrison hugged Lou hello and introduced her to the girls, his band. While Lou tried to figure out which one of them was the bassist who'd had a thing for Ivy, a guy emerged out of the pantry and handed her a drink in a Solo cup, but Harrison took it away and dumped it in the sink.

"Fuck off," Harrison said to the guy, who did.

"Careful," he said to Lou. He opened a beer for her instead. She loved him for everything.

"When are you guys on?" Lou said.

"Next," Harrison said, glancing out at the porch, which was when Lou noticed Ivy through the window, chin to knees on the steps. Tuck was perched on the railing over her shoulder. The porch was cast with pink light, a two-person sunset, flooding only their shoulders. "We should actually go set up."

Lou nodded, watching Tuck press his foot into Ivy's shoulder. Ivy looked up at him, smiling.

"I know what I've said about girl advice," Harrison said, nudging her toward the back door. "But maybe go talk to her."

The bare bulb above Ivy and Tuck was wrapped in red cellophane and tied with a ribbon, like a hazardous birthday gift. A corner of the wrapping had melted away. Approaching them, Lou felt like there was hot light inside of her too, something she'd swallowed and swallowed and swallowed, searing her in spite of the misting Portland rain wetting everything slowly, softly, infuriatingly.

Ivy didn't stand up to greet her. She seemed so calm that suddenly nothing made any sense. She smiled between Lou and the splintered railing like they were strangers she wanted to introduce, as if she hadn't been ignoring Lou's texts for the last week. Her gaze settled on the railing, for sure the better conversation partner. Lou had never really seen Ivy drunk before, but maybe she was now. There was something distanced in her eyes that was so unfamiliar and disorienting that Lou stood there for a few seconds just holding the beer Harrison had given her, not saying anything.

"What's up, Lou?" Tuck finally said.

"Ivy, I want—" She could feel the beer, or adrenaline, in the way that she was able to push through her usual feeling of wanting to retreat. Why was her natural way of being in the world like walking backward up a hill? "I need to talk to you about something."

Suddenly, Ivy looked directly at her. "Go for it."

Tuck was trying and trying to light a joint and not getting anywhere with his matchbox, and he seemed relieved when Harrison appeared.

"I thought you guys were on?" Lou said to him. Maybe he had arrived to rescue her.

"Our drummer lost her sticks," Harrison said. He looked at Tuck. "I was hoping you might have an extra pair?"

He was definitely there to rescue her. His glitter shone, and Lou could have kissed him.

"Sure," Tuck said. "Got some in the van I can grab." Ivy threw him some keys, and he jogged down the steps.

"Wait, how do you guys know each other?" Ivy said to Lou and Harrison.

"We have the same agent," Harrison said.

"As in secret?"

"Modeling." He looked at Lou. Then his face changed. "Fuck, I totally forgot! How was New York? Your Superb comp card is amazing."

"Where did you see it?" Lou said.

"Instagram."

"I'm on their Instagram?"

"You're like the whole feed."

"*You're* modeling?" Ivy said to Lou. She said it like Lou was throwing plastic into the ocean, or killing endangered birds, or going off-trail.

"What?" Lou said. She blushed. Half a dozen boys were standing in the middle of the street, blocking traffic, yelling at one another, and she hated them, the way they grouped themselves so easily, taking up space somewhere they didn't belong, with no regard to the loudness of their voices. She couldn't even stand in the middle of her own life.

"What do you mean, what?" Ivy said. "You've never once let me, or anyone, take your picture. You wouldn't even take your self-portrait. You didn't like it when we had to draw ourselves in the mirror in art class."

Harrison laughed. "My friends and I have a place in Bush-wick, if you're interested, Lou. There's an extra broom closet you could sleep in. I'm subletting my room right now, but I'll be back there soon."

Tuck came back, holding up a pair of drumsticks. Harrison looked relieved to take them and head back in inside. Tuck read whatever was happening correctly and followed him in. Which meant she and Ivy were finally alone.

"Bushwick?" Ivy said. The boards of the porch were rotting, and when Ivy leaned against the uneven pillar, Lou wanted to pull her back so the roof of the porch didn't come crashing down on top of them. But she tried to control that part of her brain that was always afraid everything was going to fall apart without her vigilance. It was an anxiety barometer, a needle rising, rising, rising in her. "Bushwick as in Brooklyn?"

"I'm maybe moving there," Lou said.

"Maybe, or you are?"

"I am." This was coming out all wrong. She felt cornered, even though she had wanted to tell Ivy.

"But you're going to U of O," Ivy said, like Lou had lied to her, when Ivy had never expressed any feelings one way or another about Lou going to school there. Suddenly she did sound upset. Really upset.

"I changed my mind."

"Because of Morgan?"

"No," Lou said. "I mean, yeah, kind of. I don't know. Honestly, because of you?"

"I'm not moving to New York anymore, dude."

Lou's heart stopped. "But what happened to NYU?"

"The whole point of going to New York was to find people

who were actually serious about making music with me. And I realized, why would I give it up if I have it here? After everything that's happened this summer, I don't want to waste any more time. The album's almost done. We're planning a tour. Tuck's not going back to school. And I want to be where he is."

"So, what, you're staying for him?" It was like a bad joke. Lou was supposed to be the one staying. Ivy had always wanted to leave.

"Tuck's my best friend," Ivy said slowly. Every syllable of it loaded with: *you are not*. "And, Lou, until just now, I thought you were going to be here, too."

"Well, I thought *you'd* be in New York. That's been your plan, forever. And if you were serious about music, why wouldn't it still be? It's the best place to make it. The only place." She heard the photographer's words come out of her mouth in a straight line and wished she could reshuffle them and pull them out in a different order.

"If I was *serious*? Are you fucking kidding me? I used to think you were the only one who really got it. And now, what, you're some totally other person?"

"What are you talking about?"

"I'm talking about, what happened to the weirdo who made me watch footage of whales suffocating? What happened to buying all that slo-mo photo equipment so you could capture *moss* growing? And now you're *modeling*?"

"I like it," Lou said. As she said it, she realized it was true.

"Fine," Ivy said. That distance reentering her gaze, like she'd slid a piece of glass between them. "If you like it, then go do it."

And for a full second, Lou did feel like she could say something, the actual something, whatever form that took, whatever

shading-in it required. Her breath tumbled forward in antici-
pation, like tripping off a too-high curb, but then Tuck reappeared, holding out a beer to Ivy, and in that split second her
mind interrupted itself.

"Let's go watch their set," Ivy said to Tuck. They weren't
touching, but the energy between them was that of a unit,
something bigger than a couple. Two people who were going to
stay and *make* something together.

Lou and Ivy didn't talk again after that, but a few days before
she was supposed to get on a plane to move to New York, Lou
finally called Catherine. It was eleven at night. She'd been on a
night walk in Forest Park, roaming around the shadowy trails
where she and Catherine used to go running together under the
evergreens, which she knew was reckless. She knew there was
always the off chance she'd get murdered whenever she did this
past dark, but by then, it was worth it to avoid her parents, who
wouldn't leave her alone about her choice to defer her enroll-
ment at U of O. They didn't understand the modeling. *What
happened to ecology?* her poor dad kept saying, as if that made
any sense anymore. He was a science teacher. He should know
that ecology was all about how to keep things from dying, or to
understand why they died in the first place. Lou didn't want to
have anything to do with that.

She'd brought her camera with her on the trail but didn't
take any pictures. Suddenly, she had the feeling that someone or
something was directly behind her, lurking in the ferns, speeding up as she did, but it felt like if she turned around to look
whatever or whoever it was in the eye, it would incite some-

thing, make it worse. It was a feeling she had in her emotional life all the time. When she made it back to her car, she locked the doors immediately.

She hadn't talked to Catherine since the memorial, but she suddenly desperately needed to see her. She pulled into the Ellises' long drive. All the lights on the house were off. She wondered if Morgan ever sat in this spot, with a boy in the car, or just watching her family from a distance for a minute, like Lou did sometimes, before going inside.

"What's going on?" Catherine sounded sober. Awake.

"I'm in your driveway."

Catherine was flat on her back on the trampoline, staring up at the trees or the stars. The trampoline was netted in, which made Lou feel safer, even lying down, like there was no way she could roll off any edge. Maybe she should just net herself in at all times. She placed her camera bag on the plastic edge and rolled into the center so she was beside Catherine, careful not to touch her, holding her knees so she took the shape of an egg.

"I'm sorry for not being here sooner," Lou said. "I really fucked up."

There were so many apologies running through her, whole tributaries of them, but this was the one that felt the clearest, the strongest. It felt so good to apologize, even if it was unforgivably overdue, like something in her fusing itself back together.

When Catherine asked how she was, Lou told her. Told her everything. The modeling, and Ivy, and Ivy and Tuck, and New York, and how she loved Catherine, she really did, but not like that, and she should have just said that the night they hooked up, instead of bailing.

Even without looking at Catherine when she said this, it was the closest Lou had felt to anyone lately. And how miraculous: that you could hand something that felt so heavy over to someone else and they would take it; that to them, it was so light, compared to whatever they were carrying, it was practically nothing. Normally, she'd be embarrassed, talking about herself so much. But she just felt like her head was entering a lightness, the aftermath of a headache she hadn't even known she'd had. The cedars swayed their feather branches overhead.

"What should I do?" Lou knew it wasn't really a fair question to ask Catherine, but it also felt like Catherine would be honest with her, because she was always honest with her. And maybe she wanted to be told whatever Catherine wanted to tell her. Maybe she wanted to see Ivy the way Catherine did. As self-serious and standoffish. As an enemy.

But that wasn't what Catherine said. She said this: "My sister had the same boyfriend for almost all of high school. Seb. He was a year ahead of her. They got together like literally the first week of her freshman year, because she was in advanced math. Seb got a full ride to play soccer at a college in Colorado, and he really wanted Morgan to go with him, like everyone thought they'd get married someday and Seb would be a hot stay-at-home dad and Morgan could bread-win or whatever. But they didn't have a fashion program at the college he chose. So she didn't go. She, like, really really loved him. I think Tuck really loved my sister, and she still really loved Seb, and that was always a problem with them. Maybe Tuck's moved on to Ivy now, I don't know, not that it matters anymore. But Morgan told me that if she'd followed Seb, she would have been so unhappy that she wouldn't have been a good person to love anyway. Morgan was so certain she'd fall in love again, after college, when she got to New York. But she didn't get to do any of it."

"Have you ever been in love?"

"Don't flatter yourself, man." Catherine laughed, but she sounded a little self-conscious. "But no. I don't think so anyway. You'd know, right?"

"What did you mean at the memorial," Lou said, "that Morgan thought you were selfish?"

Catherine didn't answer right away, but when she did, her voice was heavy and stiff. "I came out to her in eighth grade. I told her, you know, not only do I like girls, but maybe I'm not even a girl myself, I don't know. And she told me not to tell my parents."

"Oh."

"I mean, maybe she was trying to protect me. I've thought about it a lot since, obviously, but like, my older sister who I totally worshipped as a kid tells me not to tell my parents something, and so I don't. And they still don't know, not that I even really know either. I mean, I haven't really let myself think about it. That's how much it fucked me up. Morgan and I never talked about it again. I wanted to, that weekend. I thought it would be the right time. Because I always told myself I'd do it before I went away to college. Before we were at the same school again, because like, what, she's not going to somehow see me dating girls, or being the way I want to be? So that weekend was it. That was my chance. I wanted her to actually get it. I wanted to actually get it too."

Lou felt like a terrible friend that she hadn't known any of this, that maybe she and Catherine were having parallel experiences, or at least categorically similar ones, without being able to talk about it. She also felt glad that they had been drawn to each other without knowing fully why.

Catherine was quiet for a while, then asked if she was actually going to New York.

"In the story, am I the boyfriend, or am I Morgan?" Lou said.

There was a yell in the dark, and Catherine and Lou both bolted up. Two kids hopped off the top of the wooden fence and ran toward them, giggling. Lou couldn't tell they were girls until they were right up close, at the edge of the trampoline. There were no lights on in the yard or the house.

"Can we hide here?" one of the girls said. She was small, maybe sixth grade.

"Are you hiding from something bad or something good?" Catherine said, laughing. "Should you be out this late?"

"Shhh, Catherine," the girl said. "It's a game."

The other voices got closer to the fence. Bushes rustled.

Catherine laughed, loud, and the girl shushed her again. "Don't worry, we'll distract them." She pulled Lou up and started jumping. They jumped higher and higher, yelling nonsense, yelling just to hear themselves. The voices of the other kids grew louder, while the girls hid under the deck.

"Nothing to see here!" Catherine started shouting, and the kids on the other side of the fence skittered on.

Lou jumped so high, she thought she might go over the edge of the net. She landed on her back and bounced back to standing, the way she remembered from when she was little, the curve of her body like an astronaut's.

Catherine kept jumping, and the girls climbed on too, and

Lou remembered her camera. She grabbed it off the edge of the trampoline, saved it before it hit the hard edge of the springs. She clutched it to her and watched them. The air smelled like soil and roses and pine. It was too dark, but she took their picture anyway, all of them midair, hiding in plain sight.

5

Afterward, she drove to Aldenlight. It was three in the morning. She texted Ivy a dark picture of the still branches overhead, without expecting her to answer.

Are you still there? Ivy texted back.

Yes. Please come.

Lou's stomach hurt, and her head was pounding with nerves, waiting for her. She couldn't stop picking at her calluses, from all the raking and digging she'd done that summer. She'd peeled three clean off before Ivy walked up and sat down beside her. She left a foot between them.

Something ran across the field in front of them, a cat, or a coyote, it was too dark to tell. It disappeared into the blackberries, with no concern for thorns.

"Why didn't you tell me about Catherine?" Ivy said.

"Because I like you," Lou said. She could only say it because she was staring off at the city, not at the girl next to her. She was just talking out into the night air. And because this was her last chance. "I like you, not Catherine, not like that. We did hook up, but it didn't mean anything. It was barely anything. I was just worried about her, and I went up there, and I don't know. It happened. I wish it hadn't."

"Here's the thing: saying literally *anything* about the song, or honestly just about how you feel, would have been better than saying nothing. You know how much that sucked? To have that be met with total silence?"

"I didn't know what you wanted me to say."

"That's the point, Lou. I don't want you to have to ask me or say what you think I want to hear. Just decide what *you* want to say and say it. It's easy."

"No, it's easy for you."

Ivy shook her head. "You didn't even tell me about New York."

"I did!"

"No, Harrison did. You wouldn't have even said anything, if he hadn't."

"But I want you to come with me. Did you cancel any of your school stuff? Even if you did—undo it. It can't be that hard. Tell them you made a mistake."

"You're not hearing me, dude. It's *not* a mistake. The band is the most important thing. And you should follow your thing. Even if it's modeling, which I really don't get, but you sounded excited about it, talking with Harrison. Just because I don't get it doesn't mean I want to get in the way of it."

She said it as if Lou was directly asking to get in the way of hers. Which she wasn't, because, if anything, Ivy could make *better* music in New York, she could meet lots of new people there, drummers way more experienced than Tuck, musicians who could teach her a lot.

Or maybe Ivy was right. Maybe Lou just wanted to be her most important thing. She wanted everything, or nothing.

"Please," Lou said.

"Why did you wait so long?" Ivy said, the grief in her voice echoing out, and there were a thousand answers but none of them were clear or satisfying or enough, and none of them would change what was happening. None of them would make her choose Lou. And that was fair. Lou knew it was. But somehow she was still asking to be chosen anyway.

That was it. Lou didn't remember Ivy leaving, but at some point, she must have, because Lou was sitting alone when the sun came up. And it was stunning, the sun, too bright, right there behind Mount Hood, yellow and orange, too bright, the whole sky, the city, burning, too bright, like the mountain had finally erupted, the thing Lou had feared most as a child, coming to pass right when she was finally going to leave.

At the end of the week, Lou went alone. Packed alone, her parents hovering in the doorway of her bedroom, as if they expected her to change her mind at any minute, recant, stay. She didn't see Ivy again before she left, didn't say goodbye. Her plane took off the runway, and when she looked out the window, blinking back her fear at the swooping up, the trembling wings, the red towers blinked back.

PART THREE

I

The American girls were young. Some were accompanied to the castings by mothers so unlike Lou's own mother, who had stopped accompanying Lou to the school bus stop by the time she was six, that it was difficult to identify their roles at first, and Lou assumed they had been hired by the agencies as chaperones. The mothers read books or iPads in waiting rooms and hallways and spaces set aside in warehouses, while staying attuned to their daughters, passing them snack bars and concealer and high heels out of boxy purses. Lou would have lost her mind if her mother had paid such close attention to her needs, but at first, she liked to talk to these women, the only adults in the room who had time to talk. The mothers told Lou they were just off flights from Idaho or trains from New Jersey or living in the Upper East Side condo of a friend of a friend for the castings leading up to Fashion Week. Their daughters—the girls she walked shoulder to shoulder with toward the table of casting directors, who picked out the ones they liked, arranging them in a line for comparison—appeared to be the kind of girls Lou always felt one step removed from in high school, or who just flat out scared the shit out of her. But the mothers were warm and familiar, soft-bodied and sneakered where everyone else was all hard angles and skinny shoes. They asked her about herself. All the other adults were there to look at her, to decide whether or not she was what they wanted.

The first casting was two days after she arrived back in New York. This time, she took the subway to the model apartment in Bushwick instead of a car. The greyhound woman hugged her hello. The key worked.

She was sharing a room with seven other girls for the duration of the castings and New York Fashion Week. Then came Milan, London, Paris. From the first week of September to the middle of October, she would be walking, if she was lucky. After that, according to Yukon, she'd return to New York and do print work, high-fashion editorials, commercial work that paid the bills. She planned then to move in with Harrison and his roommates in Brooklyn, but for now, the space station was hers again. The very spendy space station it turned out. When Yukon told her how much it was costing her to stay there, she thought they'd added two extra zeros.

Her bottom bunkmate, Mari, she remembered from the Superb new-faces shoot. She had braids almost to her waist and an easy smile, like she was always about to tell a joke she knew you'd like. Mari's father was Nigerian and her mother was Welsh, but Mari sounded Californian. She was so thin that Lou was reminded of a giant sunflower, the kind that could barely keep their heads up in her father's garden, but she was always snacking on something that Lou had been told models weren't allowed to eat. In a pdf handbook Yukon had sent her when she signed with Superb, there was a full page devoted to good foods (almonds, vegetables) and bad foods (cheese and carbs and fruit, everything Lou liked).

At six thirty the morning of her first casting, Lou was wide awake in the living room reclined on a sofa, already nervous and half reading a novel Ivy had given her once, when Mari walked in through the front door holding a cardboard drink carrier of coffees, eating a bagel with lox. She was wearing a denim jumpsuit with a tie waist and bright white sneakers. Her braids were in a bun on top of her head.

Mari kicked off her sneakers and untied her waist, then handed Lou one of the cups. Before Lou could say anything, Mari took off the lid and splashed cream from a container in the fridge into Lou's coffee, as if they were old friends who knew each other's drink preferences. She led Lou out to the balcony, so they could talk without waking anyone up.

"I've been up since four," Mari said, sliding the glass door shut behind them. "Couldn't stop thinking: *What if I flew all the way to fucking America and I don't book a single show?*"

Lou hadn't even thought to be nervous about that, but now she was. She hadn't realized it was a possibility. But of course it was. She could easily fail.

There weren't any chairs, so they sat with their backs to the brick, facing a wrought iron railing. Below them, dock doors were pulled up noisily, men shouted; there was the scent of cigarettes and hot metal. A woman watered yellow flowers in a window box across the alley from them the whole time they talked, and Lou wondered if she was eavesdropping.

Mari was twenty-one, and, until recently, studied cello at an Italian conservatory, which she'd quit for her modeling career. She lived part-time with her girlfriend in Rome, but she was in New York for Fashion Week, her first one. Her parents were so upset that she'd dropped out of school to start modeling that they'd stopped speaking to her.

"They'll get over it," Mari said, picking at her bagel. "It was the same when I told them I was queer. They just need a three-month reset, and then they'll be apologetic. And I'll be gracious."

"What does your girlfriend think of it?" Lou said.

"She thinks the idea of it is sexy. Or so she tells everyone. But she's also afraid I'm going to stay here forever, or meet someone else and leave her. Which is ridiculous, because we're poly, and I'm always meeting someone else, even when we're living in the same place. I don't know. She's a violinist." Mari said it as if that detail alone explained the whole situation. "Do you have anyone back home?"

She made it sound like they were in a war. "Not really," Lou said. She used to want to talk about Ivy all the time. Not about how she felt about her, but just about who Ivy was in the world, what she wanted, how she was going to get it—like Lou had some stake in it. Now it felt like talking about her in the open air would spoil something, fruit sitting too long on a windowsill.

"Well, there are loads of beautiful people around," Mari said, as if she wasn't one of them. She crumpled up her bagel wrapper and stood. "What're you wearing today?"

Lou looked down at her T-shirt with its stretched-out neck, already stained from the coffee dripping out the side of the lid. "Not this?"

"No, babe," Mari agreed. "Not that."

Lou met Yukon at the agency before the first casting. Yukon had a faded Midwestern accent that thickened whenever they were excited. Lou recognized its long vowels from visiting her dad's family in the Twin Cities, where her brother lived now. When they'd met the previous month, Yukon told her they'd left their tiny Wisconsin farm town and moved to New York at seventeen to try to make it as a designer. They came out. Changed their name. Grew out their hair. Bought a new wardrobe from scratch. Successfully became the new person they'd self-prophesized. But they were terrible at sewing, imprecise and lazy. They'd made their way to agenting after being hired as an assistant at another smaller agency and worked their way up, wanting to be around fashion however they could. Yukon called themself a fashion lifer. *If you want to be a lifer too*, they'd said, *do everything I say*. Which at the time sounded less like a promise and more like a sentencing.

Yukon greeted her with three cheek kisses and then led her to a large walk-in closet in the back of the agency. They selected an outfit for her, shuffling hangers, holding skirts up to her waist, hemming and hawing over different pairs of shoes. Lou was relieved by the simplicity of what they finally settled on: slim black pants, a flowy short-sleeved shirt the color of sand, and black loafers.

"You can't fuck this combo up," Yukon said to her. "So wear it to everything." Then they handed her a pair of four-inch high heels. "These you can."

"I'll practice."

"Wait," they said. "What kind of underwear are you wearing?"

"Um." She showed them the waistband of her boxer briefs.

Yukon held up a finger and disappeared around the corner of their cubicle, returning a few minutes later with an unopened five-pack of nude thongs.

"Oh god," Lou said. "Seriously?"

"Never leave home without one."

Lou took the pack from them and pulled out a thong, holding it up. It was a triangular string, with a tiny tab of fabric.

"Two," Yukon said.

"Pardon?"

"I changed my mind. Never leave home without two."

By the time Lou reached the correct subway stop and found the correct gleaming glass building, she was so nervous that the odds of throwing up into her tote were very high. But at least then she'd have an excuse not to wear the heels.

A young woman with an iPad checked her in. Lou got in line in a hallway and tried to pretend this was the dentist's, with very hot dentist clientele. She kept touching her hair, to reassure herself it was clean. It was grown out from when the hairstylist at the new-faces shoot had cut it, and it looked kind of good, skater good, and kind of like she'd jabbed a fork into an outlet. But there was nothing to do about it now. If Yukon thought it was fine, it was fine.

When her name was called, she slipped on the heels and then walked into the room, stopping in the back, near the woman with the iPad. Mari had explained it all to her that morning. The table of people at the end of the runway were casting directors: two women and one man, all three of them in glasses with clear frames. Lou still felt residual embarrassment for having worn the same striped rugby shirt as a popular boy on picture day in sixth grade and wondered if these casting directors ever had that feeling, or whether they invented that feeling and were thus immune to it.

The man gestured for her to approach.

"You are a girl, yes?" he said, speaking with a French accent. He raised two perfect eyebrows at her from behind his glasses until she nodded. "We want a casual walk. But fierce too, yes? Like you are late for something very cool."

Fierce she could do; she pretended she was Catherine at the beginning of a race, with all that swagger. She didn't know if she looked like she was late for somewhere cool—if she had ever been anywhere that was the kind of cool he meant in her life—but she didn't trip. She looked straight ahead as she walked, and did not roll either ankle, as feared. When she paused at the end, she felt a jolt of something, looking out at the three of them: like she was really who they thought she was, that suddenly she had expanded to take that expectation in.

The man nodded when it was over, but the women did nothing. Not even a glance at each other, or another word to Lou. It wasn't that she expected cheers, but she did expect something, even just a dismissal. It reminded her of all the times she'd done that to others, most particularly Ivy. Though at least her silences had been driven by fear, not existential boredom.

They called the next name. The woman with the iPad directed Lou to a backdrop near the exit where someone took her picture. She handed them her comp card, and that was it. No one asked to see her portfolio, which was full of pictures Anne had taken of her in Portland. It would have been nice to show it to them, show an actual piece of herself to someone besides the mothers. But that wasn't what she was there for, she kept having to remind herself. She was there to shed pieces of herself. Not regrow them.

Lou changed back into her loafers and exited into the sun, ready to sit somewhere quiet, alone. She felt spent, hot-faced with the aftershock of nerves. She didn't know if the casting had gone well. But it turned out there were nine more addresses and casting times in the email from her booker, two of which she was already late for, so she didn't have long to dwell. She started to run for the subway. There was a train car full of girls just like her when she reached it, gripping screens open to Google Maps and the handrails, barely keeping their balance as the train lurched away from the platform.

2

Most of the castings that week were two-hour waits for a ten-second walk, then a full-body photograph against a plain wall or backdrop. She started to recognize a lot of the girls waiting in line beside them, in addition to the mothers. It turned out they were just girls. Goofy girls. Serious girls. Some of them so ethereally beautiful that she thought about asking them to run away to Paris with her, like she might've the first time she met Harrison. She ran into Mari at roughly half the castings, and Mari's friends in line became her friends in line. Somber Eline, a Norwegian soccer goalie who had been bound for the Olympics before blowing out her knee, who would dish on international women's players if people got her very high, which Lou did back at the model apartment, with gummies she'd forgotten she had in her carry-on. Jia, a former ballerina from Singapore trying to support her nascent hip-hop career with modeling, who shared endless playlists with them. Thayer, who'd grown up in Sri Lanka and Vancouver, Canada—the one Lou most wanted to run away with—who wrote on her laptop in the common room at night and sometimes read aloud what she was working on, if you asked, and the whole room listened to dialogue from the play about the fashion industry she was writing, some lines of which had come out of their mouths only hours before.

Then there was Keeley Dot, a teenager from Alabama who was probably the funniest person Lou had ever met and, according to Mari, on the cusp of being very, very famous. Keeley Dot made friends with everyone, mostly by telling incredibly dirty jokes and asking people their favorite brand of vibrator. She had no filter, even in front of her mom, Connie, who didn't bat an eye. Connie was one of the first moms Lou had met, in the Superb office in Midtown. She was mayor of a suburb of Mobile and the only person Lou had yet seen her agent Yukon intimidated by, when she asked for a glass of water and was handed a can of seltzer.

Rushing from one casting to the next was like Google Maps roulette. Lou was late for every single one, chest pounding, breath tight, stuttering apologies, but it didn't ever seem to matter to anyone. It turned out that the way castings were scheduled, it wasn't humanly possible to be on time, so she surrendered to the feeling of being late. The castings were in warehouses or dance studios or in the buildings that housed the labels themselves, runways set up down the center of large conference rooms. She never knew where she was going to end up. Often, even if she was late, she ended up waiting in tiled hallways like she used to in high school, leaning back against lockers, cross-legged with her brown-bagged lunch. Mari brought a whole pizza to the

Vera Wang casting, and they split it straight out of the box. She'd sign in and then wait for her name to be called and then wait for the directions, which started to feel like learning viral dances, with their particularities in the smallest of movements.

"Pop your hip."

"Pop your shoulder."

"Less jaw, baby boy."

"More jaw, baby girl."

"Next."

"Paul, can you fix her?"

"Again but slower."

"Again but faster."

"More fierce."

"Less attitude."

"Next."

"But can you follow the directions?"

"Next."

"Yes, thank you."

"Next."

"Try to make it more effortless."

"Next."

The callbacks required more undressing. She had never hated anything like she hated wearing a string thong. The night before her first callback, she spent half an hour hovering over the toilet in the model apartment's bathroom, trying to figure out how her pubic hair was ever going to fit beneath the tiny triangle of nude fabric. The answer was probably to rid herself of it entirely, but that made her squeamish. Just how far up her ass was the string supposed to go? Did the boys have to wear them? Should she pretend to be a boy, just to keep her pubic hair?

The looks—she had stopped calling them outfits after one aggrieved stylist corrected her—were often more sculpture than clothes. She got very good at letting other people button and zip her, which she hadn't even been good at as a child, distrustful of the ruffles and flares her mom defaulted to. She'd once been so unwilling to let her mom help her take off a prom dress in a dressing room, she'd ripped it clean in half. But her movements turned ginger around these pieces, as if they were a painting she'd been tasked to move. Because they were beautiful and handmade, but also because Mari told her some of them cost $50,000 or more.

At one callback, one of the American mothers asked Lou where she had grown up, and for a second she genuinely couldn't remember. Oregon was a dream, and maybe she had always lived in this place, always lived enveloped in this much movement, with this many strangers surrounding her, touching her: bringing her body forward out of whatever the past had been, like a figure emerging from clay.

When she wasn't working, she was looking at Fortunato's Instagram and listening to every piece of their music she or the Internet had. Their EP, the shows that were on YouTube, the clips they were tagged in on Instagram and Twitter. She walked from casting to casting with their songs playing, letting them drag her to the ground, into the sewers, into the open manholes on the streets, through the grates, to the molten center of the gaping earth. Fortunato's album dropped on the fifth day of castings. The song with Lou's name in the chorus was the last track.

On her first listen on the way home one night after a casting, she had to stop to get ahold of herself in a park: sinking down on a bench, placing her head between her knees, and letting herself sob until she was empty. No passersby asked if she was okay, and she was grateful to be in New York right then. Someone had probably sobbed on that bench an hour before her. Which made her cry harder, the idea of some other person being as clueless as she had been: *waiting* when she should have *spoken*.

She left her headphones on, back in her bunk bed, while she swiped through the same photos on their feed. She didn't know who was taking Fortunato's pictures, but they weren't as good as hers. They were on tour, in Olympia, then Seattle, then Vancouver. They posted shots of communal meals and friends in lavender fields and clips of the hot movements of shows. Looking at Ivy like this, the way she fit into her band, into a world that wasn't Lou's anymore, made her fear that maybe she preferred Ivy this way: at a distance, onstage, in a photograph, in her headphones. When she'd been faced with how Ivy actually felt, she had done nothing. From afar, she could want and want and want and never have. She could make a shelter of it. Burrow down.

Fortunato's spaces were warm and green and lived-in. Lou's were bleached, cold, fleeting, set up for function only, everything collapsible.

3

Her last callback was the next day. The casting directors were sorting models as they came in, girls to the left, guys to the right, and they pointed Lou to the right without asking her name or agency, and she didn't question them. Lou in a sea of boys. She wore her loafers to walk. It was the best one she'd done. For the first time, the casting directors asked to see her whole portfolio.

On her way back out, someone grabbed her arm from behind, and she turned, so tired of being touched by other people that she almost elbowed whoever it was straight in the stomach.

But there was Harrison, glowing Harrison, glorious Harrison, wrapping her in a hug. They had different New York agencies, so she hadn't seen him yet.

"My petite librarian," he said.

Seeing him flooded her with relief and giddiness and something heavy too. She felt like she was wearing her own clothes again. She hadn't been hugged by anyone who knew her since leaving Portland.

"Come home with me," he said to her.

The word *home* meant something different in his mouth, and she started to cry again and he didn't ask why.

Harrison's apartment was full of boys, just like the casting, but they were the cleanest boys she'd ever seen in her life. There were six or seven of them, a few cooking something elaborate for dinner, with cutting boards full of crusty bread and cheese and olives and another full of beets. There were boys spread out across the living room and a piano against one wall, where someone was tinkering around, while the wall of mismatched speakers played Frank Ocean.

Lou wanted to ask Harrison about his mom, but his presence in New York seemed like an answer, and she couldn't quite get the words out in a manageable way. If he was in the city, she must have died. There was no way around it.

"Are you okay?" she said.

He poured her a mug of wine. The mug was printed with an image of the Doug Fir Lounge, a venue back home on Burnside that Ivy had always wanted to play, that sometimes had all ages shows. "Not really."

"I'm sorry, Harrison."

He nodded quickly, like she'd said something he agreed with but wanted to move past. "Last season, after her second diagnosis, I worked myself into the ground. And I'm grateful for the work now, because I'm broke as shit, but I just honestly don't know if I can do it this year. New York's one thing, but I don't know about London, Milan, let alone Paris. If it's worth it. I just don't feel like myself, at all. My brothers are falling apart without her, back home, and it's only been a month. My dad—I don't know. I feel terrible that I can leave and they're stuck there, with all her things, thinking about how she's gone every second. Some days, it's not like I forget, but I have this feeling in the back of my mind like I could call her and she'd answer. It's like I can trick myself, for just a fraction of a second, if I don't think about it head-on."

"What was her name?" Lou said softly.

"Coral."

She held up her mug. It wasn't anything, nothing like enough, but she felt the name catch in her throat anyway: her sorrow for Harrison and the missing of her own mother, the idea that someday, hopefully a long time from the present, but inevitably someday, she too would be gone. "To Coral."

Harrison toasted her.

The boy at the piano started to sing, plinking out a melody that sounded like "American Girl," which Ivy had once called a perfect pop song. She was always on the hunt for them. Told Lou perfect pop songs were about the mix of longing and irresistible movement.

"*Something that's so close,*" the boy sang, his voice gentle and sad. "*And still so far out of reach.*"

Maybe she'd break in half, right there.

Instead, she got drunker and drunker on the wine in her Doug Fir mug. She felt like she hadn't eaten in weeks. The boys fed her cheese and crusty bread with beet spread and wine and more wine. In the bathroom mirror, as she gripped the edge of the sink, her mouth was dyed a vibrant pink. But in that moment it didn't matter; her castings were over, the callbacks too. The following day, she was supposed to find out which shows she'd booked. She feared that after all that, she hadn't booked any, that she had failed completely after making such a big deal out of coming to New York.

She fell asleep on Harrison's shoulder, and when she woke up, the party was still going on around her. A familiar feeling. She was always the first to cave at sleepovers.

"Did you see Ivy when you were home?" Lou said. She felt safe enough to ask it. So tired she felt high.

"Not since that show we played. Tuck and I have been texting though."

Lou's stomach clenched, remembering when she'd seen Tuck at the celebration of life, the lost look on his face as he stared at the photographs of Morgan. Morgan, his ex-girlfriend. His dead best friend. "How is he?"

Harrison craned his neck at ceiling, as if there was a long answer inside of him that needed help going down. "I think he gets the grief, you know?"

Yukon called her the next morning, ecstatic. Lou was back in the model apartment, nothing on the walls. She had fallen asleep in her one casting outfit. She pulled off her bra without taking off her shirt—a trick she'd perfected in middle school gym, eyes glued to the lockers and not the girls undressing around her—as Yukon let out a long string of shows she'd booked, including being selected to close the most anticipated show of the season. She'd already heard from Harrison that he'd booked it too.

"It's the best possible news, Lou. Your life's about to change," Yukon gushed. They were insistent on this front, as if anyone could possibly predict anything.

Lou realized there was a part of her that had wanted to fail so she didn't actually have to do this. She took three deep breaths into her cotton T-shirt. It expanded out, then deflated.

Lou got sick that weekend. It felt like just a head cold at first, and she knew how to weather that, knew how to drink liquids and take the meds her parents told her to buy from the pharmacy down the street. But after a couple of days, it began to feel like she was in the deep end of a swimming pool, about to surface but unable to.

Her senses went out one by one. First smell, then taste, then her hearing, which felt like divine punishment for all her wallowing in Fortunato songs. She moved her body once every six hours, it felt like, and no one called her except her parents, and she didn't tell them how bad it was, did not want them to tell her she would have been better off back home. Her dad had returned to school that week and was telling her about his new students while she pressed her phone to her ear and turned the volume all the way up. It felt like if she could just pop her ears, everything would return to normal, so she extended her jaw again and again, until it was sore, like she was on an airplane. It didn't work. There was no release.

The only thing in the fridge was other people's leftovers, a jar of pickles, and a tub of vitamins. Lou hated pickles, but she bit into one anyway, and it was novel to be able to without revulsion. Here was a pickle shape, in her hand; here she was, taking a bite out of it without gagging. Here she was, alone in New York City, as far across the country as she could possibly be from the people who loved her. She went to bed that night with an escalating earache and the distant taste of vinegar in her mouth.

Lou woke up to dried blood on her pillow; then when she pressed her finger into her ear, which was distantly ringing, there was blood there too, as little as a papercut. There was relief in that ear, but not the other. In the other was pain like something just before a siren.

She woke up Mari and asked where to go to the doctor, and Mari called them a taxi and took her to urgent care, rubbing Lou's back, telling her it would be okay, her ear throbbing like someone had drilled directly into it.

The doctor confirmed what WebMD had fearmongered, for the first time in Lou's life. Her eardrum had burst. It would take a month or more for it to heal. She'd take a large antibiotic pill twice a day, along with painkillers and ear drops. No swimming, in the meantime—as if she knew where to go swimming in New York, as if she ever wanted to go swimming again. She thought about calling Yukon but really couldn't hear now, so she composed a long text to them instead, explaining that she couldn't do the shows.

But then she thought about a conversation she'd just had with Yukon about exactly what she owed to the agency. It turned out she was in debt to Superb for her plane ticket, her fees for the new portfolio, not to mention the nights at the model apartment. If she didn't do the shows, she would only be able to afford to stay another few weeks. New York was a money hole. She had to start working.

Lou deleted first the text to Yukon, then all her Fortunato playlists. She didn't want to listen to anything except the echoes of the subway stations, the models talking in their bunk beds, her own muted breath: only the sounds that permeated in.

4

At the shows, she learned to walk on different surfaces—water, glass, stone, carpeted stairs, slick plastic, bunched fabric. No runway was ever the same shape, ever as straightforward as an out and back line. She walked in an infinity symbol around a garden; in a rectangle around a pink-walled warehouse; in an oval within an enclosure that looked like a fish tank, orchestra musicians suspended on the glass above them.

Her face was put on and wiped off four or five times a day. She came to loathe the cold glue of false eyelashes but love a makeup artist rubbing moisturizer into her cheeks and forehead before beginning. Her skin cracked around her mouth and eyes after the first day's shows. She stole her roommates' lotion, just a dollop at a time, until she finally asked Mari to take her to buy her own, and they spent several long hours in a Sephora trying to make Lou's face look like a girl's face. It didn't work. She looked like a boy wearing makeup, which neither of them could explain. Even the professional makeup artists couldn't accomplish it. She usually ended up in the same looks as the male models. Clean. Natural. Blank. She'd never minded being mistaken for a boy, but she'd never wanted to be a boy either. She liked her androgyny and liked other androgynous people. But she liked it even better now, in this heightened form, and the designers and stylists did too.

Her hair was so dry from all the heat, the straightening, the curling, the lights, that she wore a hat anytime she wasn't at a shoot. Her fear of the stylists and makeup artists and designers subsided, if only because she was focused on trying to hear what they were saying, instead of focusing on what they thought of her. She walked for Vera Wang, Oscar de la Renta, Tom Ford, Ralph Lauren, Carolina Herrera, and a half dozen others. She walked herself up the stairs to her bunk bed. She walked back to the pharmacy for a bigger bottle of ibuprofen. She walked through the park, for a field of green, to stare without being stared at. Sometimes when she walked home at night in the dark, she called Catherine, who was already in summer training, blasting all her old times out of the water. Catherine talked to Lou about pronouns, how she thought she was fine with the ones she had for now, how she/her with Catherine's vibe and aggression confused everyone in a fun way, in an interesting way, although maybe, she admitted, she was just scared of announcing a change. She talked about how she wanted to start testosterone, now that she was away at school, but didn't want to disqualify herself from future races or her spot on the women's roster. Lou talked to her about the rabid raccoons that were supposedly infesting New York City and how she had a profound fear of them but also a profound desire to see what

rabidity looked like in person. Catherine told her she was fucking weird. Lou walked up the stairs to her bunk bed and fell
asleep within seconds.

The opening walk and the final walk were the most important. One set the tone for the collection, the other was the last
impression, the image the audience was left with when they
reentered the bright world. Closing the show was a huge deal,
Yukon and Harrison and even Mari pressed on her, and she
started to believe it.

The show was in the American Museum of Natural History,
in a room of preserved animals that she tried not to look in the
eye. The most important place to look was at the photographers
at the corners or ends of the catwalk, depending on its shape.
The runway for this show was a triangle, and the photographers waited at the first turn. A not-small part of her wished
she was standing there instead, the photographer waiting to get
the perfect shot of the clothes in motion and not the model
who might trip, who carried the show on her shoulders and
back.

Backstage, it was her and that sea of boys again. But the photographer was the same one from her trip earlier in the summer. Sienna. By now, Lou could hear again in her left ear, the
one that had burst, but not her right, so she walked up to her
and said hello, nervously explaining who she was, assuming the
woman wouldn't remember.

"My rooftop friend," Sienna said, smiling. "Of course I
remember you, *cara*."

"I'm glad it'll be you out there."

"Have you gone out to shoot anywhere, since you've been back in New York?"

Lou blushed. She knew Sienna meant her own photography, not as a model, and she wished she had a better answer for her. "I haven't had time."

"Soon, then."

Someone with a clipboard ushered her away to get her makeup done. She sat in the folding chair while her makeup artist, who she knew from the Vera Wang show, told Lou how her daughter's piano recital had gone. It was funny to have a normal conversation at an event so dramatic in essence. They could have been small-talking anywhere, but the woman was applying something from a compact onto Lou's cheeks and forehead just before she was going to go be scrutinized by thousands of people, including celebrities and fashion royalty, and maybe, so the rumors went, Beyoncé.

Her look was posted on a board, with a photograph that had been taken at rehearsal. She wouldn't have recognized herself if she hadn't been last. The stylist helped her into the clothes, which were so much simpler than anything she'd worn for the women's shows. So far she'd worn capes with shoulders the size of two-by-fours and a coat that reminded her of the artificial turf she'd installed one summer in her landscaping job. The suit for this show was beautiful, made out of silky lilac fabric that she wanted to nap in.

Harrison appeared behind her in the mirror and kissed her gently on the cheek.

"My petite librarian," he said. "Don't fuck it up."

The energy was that of just before a high school play. Everyone rushing around, telling each other how good they were going to be, how fantastic they looked. She'd been a stagehand one year for *Oklahoma!*, when Ivy and Tuck had been in the pit orchestra, but never thought she'd be the star of a show like this. Adrenaline pulsed through her as she did her first look, against a backdrop where the models lined up preshow for a horde of photographers, all clamoring to get a good shot, to be posted on all the fashion sites the next day. Harrison posed with her, slipping his arm around her waist, then her shoulder. He was wearing a look that he might have worn in the day-to-day: long brown trousers, a patterned turtleneck, and a watch cap. Other boys joined, a long line of them, everyone shouting at them to get their attention, the boys and Lou acting like this happened to them every day, even though no one knew their names.

Their marks were labeled with printout numbers. Harrison was number three. Lou was number fifty-nine, last in line. She checked her phone one last time, and there was a notification for a text from Ivy. Her ears throbbed as she stared down at her phone screen, but she didn't have time to open it before a stylist grabbed her by the elbow and rushed her to a rack of clothes, swapping out one scarf for another, in a brighter shade.

Heading back to her spot in line, the designer intercepted her.

She was younger than Lou expected and dressed plainly compared to the extravagance of the models. Lou had never been starstruck before—even when musicians who were famous in the Pacific Northwest came into Ivy's coffee shop and Ivy got all weird and gooey-eyed and hid behind the espresso machine, Lou was always oblivious until afterward. But when the designer looked into her eyes, Lou's heart started hammering, and she felt swept up in the energy of everyone else who had been side-eyeing the woman all afternoon, gravitating toward her one at a time, in some kind of prearranged order, like they had an audience with the queen. Lou tried to imagine the designer as Morgan—like this was the moment she had moved to New York for, this exact interaction—but the woman had her own calm and removed energy that felt like the opposite of Morgan's determined friendliness. The air was too harried to focus on what Lou could even say to the designer, now that she was standing there.

"You look perfect," the designer said, taking Lou's hands in hers.

Lou thanked her, and the words floated away as soon as they came out. The designer moved like she was going in for a hug, but it turned out she was just fixing the hem of the suit, making a last-minute adjustment.

When the designer released her, Lou felt like she might pass out and whispered it in warning to Harrison, on her way to the last mark in the lineup. The look in his eye said, *Don't.*

One by one, the models in front of her exited backstage and started down the runway. She kept her eyes glued to the back of the head of the model ahead of her in line.

Then his turn came and he left her there. And it was just her alone in a lilac suit.

As she walked out on the runway, just out of the corner of her eye she could see people holding up their phones, filming, but she kept her gaze straight ahead. She felt like it didn't take any effort to walk forward anymore, like she could have kept on like that forever. She didn't have to look behind herself. There was no one there. She walked like a boy with the world in front of him. Like she was owed a clear path and a crowd in awe.

By the time she rounded the corner and returned behind the curtain, everyone backstage was clapping and cheering. The energy was manic as the models made one final fast walk around the catwalk. The designer came out behind Lou, and the crowd erupted for her. Lou wished Catherine and her parents could have been there for that one singular sound.

Backstage, Harrison hugged her and everyone was smiling and congratulating one another, like they had all won an Oscar or an election. She didn't feel owed the congratulations when other people had been working their whole lives for this moment. All she had done was get there on time, sit still, and walk without tripping.

Someone helped her take off the clothes, and when she was back in her own jeans and shirt and loafers, she walked out the side doors, into a different part of the museum, even though she knew she would have to return for her things and the brigade to the after-party. She descended a staircase onto a floor welcoming her to the Hall of the Universe.

Lou stopped before a meteorite, named for the Willamette— the river or the valley, she didn't know, but the word suddenly looked foreign to her, out of context. The Willamette meteorite looked like a massive gray skull with too many eye sockets. The sign said it had been found in Oregon, near present-day Portland, and was the sixth-largest iron meteorite in the world.

She and Ivy had once watched a meteor shower together, on her parents' roof. *Fusing lighter elements into heavier ones.* She wished she could do the opposite. Her hands were shaking as she opened the text from Ivy.

It said, *We're in New York.*

5

The after-party was at a bar but there was no bouncer checking IDs, and Harrison dragged her in anyway, yelling, "This bitch closed the show!" to no one in particular. Lou was just thinking about Ivy's phrasing of *We're in New York. We.* This *we* arriving in New York together, wandering around New York without her. Why did Ivy's *we* make her feel more alone than she ever had? She hadn't responded to the text. She didn't know what to do, or what Ivy wanted her to do.

Lou and Harrison slid into a booth with Mari and their friend Thayer, the model-playwright, who'd come from another after-party. Mari kept leaving to take phone calls, looking more and more upset each time. Harrison was telling the others how good Lou had been, not that he had technically seen her walk, so all he meant was Lou hadn't tripped. But they echoed his praise anyway, until Mari's phone buzzed and she stood up yet again to take the call.

"Who keeps calling her?" Harrison asked Thayer.

"Her girlfriend," Thayer said. "Mari posted something she's upset about, with some famous model."

Thayer showed them the Instagram post. Harrison knew the model, but Lou had never heard of her. Harrison followed the fashion world like her brother followed the NBA. He knew everyone's stats, even those who played for other teams. "Is Mari hooking up with her?"

"Actually, no," Thayer said, raising an eyebrow. She was known for her eyebrows in the industry, and they were, in fact, incredible. Thick and severe. Lou didn't know if she had ever envied another person's eyebrows, but Thayer's were a whole vibe. "In my opinion, she's not the one Mari's girlfriend should worry about."

"Are you?" Harrison asked.

Thayer laughed. "Hell no. Mari and I would decimate each other."

"But you'd be so cute together," Lou teased. "Even decimated." She didn't know Thayer very well, but there was something so open about her that it made Lou want to be open too. Besides, she was a little drunk. And the *eyebrows*.

Thayer grinned at her. "You think?"

"At least put it in your play."

Lou got to the bottom of her drink, ice clinking against her teeth, and Thayer offered to get her another one. She had been planning to go back to the apartment after the first one, but she didn't want to be alone yet.

"Sure," she said. "Thanks."

When Thayer left for the bar, Harrison took a long sip of his drink and leaned against Lou.

"Is *that* maybe happening?" he said. His eyes were cheerful.

"What?"

"Never mind," he said, with a close-lipped smile. Then he glanced around, seemed to realize they were alone, and took a long breath. His expression changed, like he knew what he had to say might ruin her night, if not her life, and she could sense what he'd been holding back.

"I already know," she interjected.

"You do?" Harrison said. He looked surprised. "About Tuck?"

"Ivy texted me that they're here."

When she said it aloud, it became real: Ivy was here.

She was in the city.

Here.

Or almost here.

Harrison nodded. He said the next part really fast, as if try-ing to get it over with as quickly as possible. "And also I told Tuck they could crash with me."

She imagined Tuck and Ivy in the spare room that Harri-son had promised to save for her, when one of his roommates moved his stuff out of it and Lou was back from the European shows. The roommate had stayed there mostly on weekend vis-its to his boyfriend, and they'd just broken up. Lou had already been thinking of the room as hers. It would be a way better deal to live in Brooklyn and pay a normal rate for her own room than to share a model apartment in Manhattan for five times that.

"But honestly, I thought your flight was leaving earlier, that it wouldn't even have to be something you'd have to deal with. Their show's the night you leave for Italy. So I figured you'd be on a plane leaving the continent, and you wouldn't have to overlap with them at all."

Mari reappeared. "Overlap with who?"

That was when the photographer, Sienna, walked up to the booth, holding a long-stemmed wineglass.

"Hello, friends," she said, kissing Lou on both cheeks. She smelled like summer, but a summer from another place, like an orchard, not this crowded bar with weed and cigarette smoke wafting in from the patio.

Mari looked delighted to see her. "*Tesora*," she shouted, embracing her. A triple kiss. All without spilling the wine. "So glad you could join us."

Sienna was younger than Lou had realized, maybe in her early thirties, less intimidating when she was squeezed in a booth with them—or maybe she just looked less intimidating without a camera in her hands. She congratulated Lou and Harrison on the show, and she and Mari drifted closer and closer as the night went on. Mari clearly stopped responding to her girlfriend, and just like that, Lou understood who Thayer had been talking about earlier.

Sound was still strange for Lou, with her unruptured ear remaining clogged, and so the night was hushed and beautiful. The bar was stuffed with models and celebrities Lou half recognized, who she'd have to google later to tell her mom about. When the designer slipped through the crowd like an apparition, Lou remembered the cheering for her earlier, the forceful wave of recognition for her art, the way it built through the space like people were realizing as they applauded the depth of what she had done. An understanding of her and her work dawning on them all at once. Lou had known she wanted that for Morgan. But she realized she wanted it for herself too.

Lou decided over and over not to leave, until it was so late that there was no way she could text Ivy back, could meet her anywhere. Besides, she was having too much fun with Harrison and Thayer.

Thayer was telling them about the show she'd walked that evening, for a young designer who'd wanted dogs in the show. "And listen, I love a dog," Thayer said. "Love a dog in the right context. But these were the wrong dogs and the wrong context."

"Wait, what happened?" Lou said.

"Oh my god," Harrison interjected. "I already saw the video, but tell Lou—"

Thayer snorted. "One took a shit in the middle of the runway. And like, what was that poor girl supposed to do? Scoop it up? Stash it in her clutch?"

Lou couldn't stop giggling. The cocktails or the adrenaline or just the hilarity of Harrison and Thayer and their stories and how it felt to suddenly be in this lovely world, with these lovely people, and to feel so at ease.

By the end of the night—or the beginning of the morning, really—she didn't think beyond her exhaustion when Harrison offered for her to come stay at his apartment, in his bed. They took a taxi back to his place, already hungover and so tired that every joint in her body felt like a dam bursting.

"It's a queen mattress," he promised, like a lullaby. "Pillow top."

It was only when they arrived at Harrison's apartment, walking past the spare room's closed door, that she remembered that Fortunato was in there, sleeping.

In the morning, after the densest sleep of her life, Lou walked out into the hallway and paused, trying to listen. The door to

the spare room was open. It was empty. Daylight streamed
in through the little high window. But when she entered the
kitchen there was only Harrison, sitting with a steaming cup of
tea. He was staring out at the fire escape, absently pulling at the
tea bag's string.

"Are they here?" she said. Her voice was hoarse, and her head
began to pound.

Harrison startled. He looked really tired. "They left to get
coffee. I'm going to meet them in a few." He paused, assessing
her. "Do you want to come?"

Lou had to get on a plane to Europe in twenty-four hours.
"Maybe later."

Somewhere in the city, Harrison was meeting Fortunato for
breakfast at a diner. Somewhere in the city, Ivy and Tuck were
sitting at a table, sipping coffee, telling Harrison all about their
tour, unloading every detail Lou had only been able to guess at
from Instagram. Lou watched the whole thing over and over in
her head, but she still couldn't make herself get off her bed and
leave her apartment.

Mari was packing her bags for Italy; she and Lou were
booked on the same flight. There was no sign of Sienna, and
Lou didn't ask what had happened between them. They were
supposed to stay with Mari's girlfriend in Rome when they
got in. She wasn't sure she wanted more information. She was
afraid of having to keep secrets. She felt like she was keeping
enough from herself as it was.

"Am I hot?" Lou asked, half to Mari, half to the ceiling fan.
"Like attractive?" It wasn't a question she'd ever asked herself

before. She didn't think about her body like that, or had never had the right context for it before.

Mari's hair had been redone for a show, and her braids were turquoise and shoulder-length. She wore a sports bra and cotton gym shorts. Mari was hot. "Not like that."

"Help me be hot."

Mari sorted through her suitcase for a minute, then tossed Lou some denim shorts and a crop top. Lou changed, and Mari arranged her for a while, futzing with her hair, before she stood back, admiring her work.

"Better," Mari settled on. "But hotness is never about the clothes. It's the confidence, one hundred percent. Don't tell anyone I told you, or we'd be out of a job."

"What's your girlfriend like?"

"Very organized. Very good at sex."

"How did you know you wanted to be together?"

"I guess I just want her in my orbit. Even when it's harder when she is. She understands the orbit, and she is in its path on purpose. Now, tell me, who are you doing this for?"

Somewhere in the city, Ivy was walking down a street, with her slouchy shoulders and her messy black hair and her hands gripping each other behind her back, which she did when she was a little nervous.

"Someone from back home," Lou said.

"You love them?"

"I don't know," Lou said. It sat between them for a minute, the air condensing, before Mari left to make them a snack.

6

The park where she met them in Brooklyn wasn't anything like the parks back home. It was crowded and loud and open and so hot that it felt like another country. Portlanders were always huddled into any available segments of shade in parks, as if the direct sun was too unfamiliar to reckon with, but New Yorkers lounged in it, set up with coolers and Bluetooth speakers blasting reggaeton and pop and hip-hop, kids running full speed through the basin of the concrete fountain as water spouted up. Lou spotted the Portlanders under a tree. Harrison and Tuck reclined on a sheet, with Ivy in the grass beside them, picking at the dandelions.

Lou blinked and Ivy was still there.

"I did a shoot here once," Harrison was telling them, when Lou walked up, wearing Mari's clothes, pretending to be a confident hot person. He'd texted her their location, asked her to *please come*. "For a swimsuit company from the Netherlands. It was fucking weird but it paid well. I just remember there was this inflatable duck they kept trying to get me on top of, in the fountain. I never saw the pictures from it. So I must be in a Speedo in some Dutch magazine somewhere, full-on straddling a duck."

They all laughed, but Ivy stopped when she noticed Lou standing there.

Lou didn't know what to do with her hands, so she put them in the back pockets of her shorts, then took them out, then put them back in again. She'd thought about texting Ivy beforehand, but she hadn't known what to say. She'd assumed Harrison had told them she was coming, but now she wasn't so sure. "Hi."

Tuck and Harrison both acted happy to see her, but Ivy didn't. She just stared at her like Lou was blocking the view of someone she'd been waiting for.

Lou's whole body felt tight and wired, like she might start crying or running at any second. It had taken her an hour to get out here on the subway, and it suddenly felt like a huge mistake. She should have stayed on the bunk bed. She should have curled up in Mari's suitcase and let herself be checked straight through to Italy.

Two dogs were growling at each other a few blankets over. Lou sat down cross-legged beside Harrison, who put his arm around her, and Ivy glanced between them. Lou concentrated on listening to the boys talk about some band they both knew back home, who'd been named *Willamette Week*'s Best New Band, but she couldn't stand it for very long. She was the only one sitting in the sun.

"I'm, uh, really thirsty," Lou said. "I'm going to go find something to drink."

"Same," Ivy said.

Lou felt like she might throw up. She was hoping to just disappear into the throngs of people and never return. Harrison gave Lou a questioning look, but he and Tuck stayed where they were. Ivy followed her toward the perimeter of the park, where the crowds thinned out.

Ivy kept looking her up and down, not like she was checking her out, but like she was trying to determine if Lou was injured.

"What?" Lou said.

"You look different," Ivy said. "Like a lot."

"Bad a lot?" She was hoping Ivy would say, *No, of course not, a lot amazing, a lot hot, a lot new, the kind of a lot I have a lot of regrets about*, but Ivy just gripped her hands behind her back. So she was nervous.

"How's the tour been?" Lou said.

"I feel like I'm finally doing what I'm meant to be doing. I just feel like myself again."

It was hard to feel hurt over that. But her phrasing was so general. It wasn't how Ivy talked with her. Lou was used to her eager images. To clarity. Not the automatic crap of *feeling like myself again.*

"How's all"—Ivy paused, like she didn't quite have the vocabulary for whatever Lou was doing—"this been?"

"Good, also." Lou felt like a hypocrite. She didn't have anything better to offer? It was like they were stuck in a waiting room or a reunion that neither of them had asked for. Except they both had. They didn't have to be here.

Ivy talked more about the people they'd stayed with on tour, which, of course, Lou knew all about from her Instagram stalking but didn't admit. Everything felt so vague between them that Lou wanted to shake them both.

"Why didn't you tell me you were coming here?" Lou said. She'd interrupted whatever Ivy was saying about the band they were opening for on the East Coast leg of their tour, a thread she'd completely lost track of, because she so badly needed to know the answer to this question. "I mean, before yesterday."

Ivy stopped walking. They were beside a giant swimming pool, compressed with people, blue shining through the cracks. "Are you taking photos again?" she said, as if she hadn't heard her. "Your own, I mean."

"Not really," Lou said.

Ivy shook her head. "You should. You'd be happier."

"I haven't wanted to."

"I didn't know if I wanted to see you here," Ivy said. "To answer your question."

"If you wanted to see me, or if you wanted to see me here?"

"Both, honestly."

"That's fair," Lou said softly. "But I'm glad you did. And I'm sorry."

The first breeze she'd felt in weeks rustled through the trees above them. For a second, it felt like they were in a different park, on the other side of the country; a park where they used to know each other, where they used to be, if not *together*, at least mistaken for being together.

But Ivy was getting back in a van in the morning and Lou was getting on a plane and then they'd both be gone, and who knew when they'd see each other again? It could be years. Or easily never.

"Can we go somewhere?" Lou said.

———

The marble lions out front were exactly how she imagined, and Lou asked Ivy to take her picture with them, on the steps of the library.

"For my parents," Lou said. "So they think I'm still learning. They're very obsessed with me going back to school at some point."

"You're clearly learning," Ivy said. "Just not what they'd hoped."

The New York Public Library was actually the one place in the whole city that her dad seemed excited she would get to visit. He was very much a woods-and-bodies-of-water kind of person, and not a landmarks-and-loud-streets guy, but her parents had met in a library, and they seemed to bring him nostalgic peace. She wanted to send him some evidence that she was thinking of him, even if she hadn't returned his last few calls.

Lou smiled in front of a camera on purpose for the first time since she'd arrived in New York, possibly ever, just because she was suddenly so happy to see Ivy standing there on the sidewalk in front of her, even though it had only been a few weeks since they'd sat in Aldenlight Park, miserable and out of time.

"You're like, a real model now, huh?" Ivy said to her, deadpan.

Lou couldn't tell if she was teasing or still remote. On the subway, they'd avoided each other's gaze in the dark glass. Ivy had been on her phone, even though she didn't have service, and she'd always hated being on her phone, didn't think anyone should have phones. Every time a girl who looked like a model got on the train, Lou had winced, hoping she didn't know her, wouldn't have to transform into the person she'd become here in New York in front of Ivy, any more than she already had by wearing this ridiculous crop top.

Lou leaped off the steps of the library with all her limbs out,

in a jumping-jack move their PE teacher had called *I'm a star!*
They had to declare they were stars as they jumped, their bodies
the exclamation point.

Ivy finally laughed. "You didn't say it."

So Lou did another and shouted, "I'm a star!" and she did
feel like one, for a second, even more than she had at the end
of the runway or the after-party. Like all it took was an enthu-
siastic declaration.

It was cold inside the building, and the marble floors and
high ceilings made it feel more like they'd entered a museum
or basilica than the brick box of the library Lou had gone to
as a child, with its low fluorescents and dirty purple carpet and
drive-through book drop. But the smell was the same.

They wandered the floors and floors of stacks, and Lou tried
not to follow Ivy, tried to make it seem like she was just going
wherever she wanted to go, but she thought about what Mari
said about her girlfriend being in her orbit, and maybe it was
okay to submit to that idea once in a while. Maybe that was the
whole reason she was in New York in the first place.

"My parents met in the Central Library," Lou whispered.
They were on the edge of the reading room, chandeliers and
massive pastel ceiling murals overhead. The Central Library in
downtown Portland was beautiful enough, with its rose-print
rugs and wide stairways, but this was so much grander. "Which
makes sense, I guess. Harrison calls me the librarian."

"Why?"

"Because I'm bad at runway."

"Not from what I've seen online."

Lou didn't know how to respond. It felt wild that Ivy might
have been following her Internet trail just as closely as she'd
been following Fortunato's, but also warm and so sweet she

didn't know what to do with herself. She imagined Ivy in the passenger seat of the van while Tuck drove them across a flat cornfield, looking at photos of Lou, going backward in time, and she took Ivy's hand. It felt so natural that she didn't even realize she was doing it until Ivy clasped her fingers tightly. They gazed up at the pastel clouds in the reading room. The mural reminded Lou of something deep within herself, a daydream of something from when she was younger: something ancient, someplace she wanted to go but never thought she'd really reach.

They met the boys back at Harrison's apartment in Brooklyn. Harrison and Tuck had picked up dumplings and beer, and the four of them ate on the roof because the apartment was too hot, with its rasping AC window unit.

Just before dusk, the boys went back downstairs for more beer and never returned. She and Ivy were stretched out on the blanket off Harrison's bed, sweatshirts bundled beneath their heads. It had been an almost perfect day. Lou's right ear had finally popped, or the pressure had lessened enough that it no longer felt full. She could hear more distinct sounds, which meant she could think more clearly too. She was thinking about what Ivy had said at Aldenlight, about why she had waited so long.

"You know that game we used to play in gym?" Lou said. She'd been thinking about this because of her *I'm a star!* on the steps of the library, like that had been a portal back to who she'd been when she first saw Ivy. A dweeby kid in gym class. "With the mats and the scooters?"

They'd called the game Islands. It only came out in ninth-grade gym class when their teacher was exhausted from coaching and set up a progression of blue tumbling mats from one padded wall to the next, an elementary school throwback. They were given a plastic four-wheeled scooter and a warning not to ride it like a skateboard. They had to get down on their knees to move from blue island to blue island, pulling their classmates along with plastic jump ropes. They couldn't touch the bare gym floor or they had to go back to the start. Ivy had been a new kid that year, shy and smart, winning all the solos, essay contests, and band chairs. But they were playing that game the first time Lou really noticed her. Ivy had kicked off first and got stranded in the middle of the wide gym floor, laughing in between the first two mats, trying and failing to propel herself without anyone else around to help. Back then, Lou had never met anyone their age who so clearly did not care what other people thought but was still fundamentally kind to them anyway. She still hadn't.

"We always made you go first because you were so good at it," Ivy said. "You'd stay on the first mat and help every single kid make it to the next one, even if your team lost."

"I used to think that I had to make sure every single person got where they wanted to go first," Lou said. "And to make sure they got there safely. Before I let myself have what I wanted. Before it felt okay to have it. Isn't that ridiculous?"

"It's a slow way to get what you want."

She had missed the way Ivy was looking at her. Like they both noticed each other in the same ways, understood what was good about the other one, what could still be good. Quiet and sure, Lou slid her hand behind Ivy's head, inching her fingers through her hair, then to the fold behind her right ear. Ivy's mouth hovered in front of her. There was no sound coming out of it, no singing. Lou kissed her.

Ivy's face up close, the heart shape of it, her eyes wide, her mouth.

Ivy's mouth.

Lou's Ivy.

The Ivy.

For a few seconds, everything felt right, like what she had been waiting for had become clearer, truer, more necessary, no hesitation, no walking backward up any hill, only running downward.

"It could be like this all the time," Lou said softly.

Ivy pulled back, and everything seemed to roll away, the hill itself collapsing. "But it's not," she said.

For the short walk back downstairs—Lou's arms full of bottles and takeout containers, having made an excuse about needing to clean up, just to be able to catch her breath fully, to not cry on a blanket on a rooftop on a perfect night—it seemed overwhelmingly likely that Tuck and Ivy were now on tour and in love and perfect for each other, because there had to be a completely reasonable reason for why Ivy *wouldn't let it be like this*, other than that Lou really wasn't who Ivy thought she was: not an artist at all but just a person with her eyes open. Tuck, on the other hand, was exactly the kind of person Ivy wanted to make something with, maybe a whole life. Which, in Lou's opinion, was completely reasonable, because Tuck was a sweet, good person who had a brilliant and subtle sense of rhythm and seemed to understand exactly what Ivy needed and when she needed it. He'd been a good friend to Morgan. A good friend to Ivy. A good friend to Harrison too.

But back in the apartment, Harrison and Tuck were tangled up on the living room sofa, and it took Lou a second to register just what they were doing, until she could absolutely register it, until she realized she had been *extremely* wrong, or Catherine had been extremely wrong, or maybe neither of them had been wrong and things had just changed while she was looking in the wrong direction. She dropped everything in her arms.

Harrison and Tuck bolted up, and they were all frozen for a second.

She was going to Rome the next day. She suddenly felt like she might laugh, like pastel-cloud laughter could spill out of her forever and it would never be enough. An eternal fountain. An ancient need. She apologized to the boys and cleaned up the cans and food and took off like she was late for a casting, when, in fact, there was nowhere on earth she needed to go, no one on earth who needed her anywhere. She let the heavy door to the building slam behind her.

Out on the street, she looked up at the rooftop of the brick building, as if Ivy might be standing there, looking for her too. But she couldn't make anything out in the dark. For the first time, Lou didn't want Ivy at a distance. Didn't want her up there, onstage. She wanted her right beside her, in frame.

The saplings shook in the breeze. Lou reached up to touch a leaf between her fingers. It needed water. As soon as she turned the corner, the streetlights came on all at once.

PART FOUR

I

It was the dead of night in Rome and Mari's key didn't work. Mari's girlfriend wasn't there, or wasn't answering. The key looked like it belonged to a medieval groundskeeper. The door too, enormous and wooden, inside a building that might have been built in the 1500s. It looked like an abbey, or the way Lou imagined one to look from the animated version of *Robin Hood*, the one that sent her into a prolonged archery phase in second grade.

"This is just unbearably classic," Mari said. She sounded so tired she was almost laughing. Lou felt nauseous with jet lag. They'd both been awake for twenty-two hours, after their flight got delayed at JFK in endless one-hour increments, which meant they sat at the gate an extra day. Lou had finished the only book she'd brought, then fell down a deep Internet hole on how all the polar bears would be dead by the time she was forty and just how more fucked-up the climate and therefore society would be by then, not to mention how little anyone in power was doing about it. She'd doom-scrolled until they boarded, then stayed awake the entire flight thinking about how they were producing approximately one ton of carbon with just this flight, and how she'd have to take another flight to Paris afterward, and then infinite flights after that, until she single-handedly destroyed the ozone layer, killed the Great Barrier Reef, and burned the droughted West Coast to ashes.

Mari was still messing with the key. She handed it to Lou, and Lou was so tired that she felt certain she was inserting it upside down but kept trying anyway, fiddling with the handle, then kicking the door itself. The wood was so dense that it barely made a sound.

"Where the fuck is Rosana?" Mari said for the third time.

"Don't you guys all eat at midnight?" Lou said. "I'm sure she's just out or something."

"Or she dumped me. And didn't tell me."

"Let's get a hotel." This was starting to feel more and more appealing, especially since Lou harbored a vague and mostly unwarranted fear of sleeping in strangers' living spaces, ever since she'd gotten lice in the third grade at a sleepover birthday party, hosted by a girl who didn't even talk to her at school, and then had to spend a long summer with her parents alternating turns picking through her hair with a nit comb.

"What if she changed the lock?"

"Mari. There is no way she changed this lock without the permission of the Italian government. Or a crowbar."

Just as Lou was about to throw the abbey key down the stairs and make the decision for them, a scream and a long string of Italian echoed out from behind them in the dark hallway. A tiny woman rocketed at them, jumping into Mari's arms; Mari spun her around, laughing. Then they were making out. With fervor. When they wrapped it up, Mari's girlfriend opened the door for them without a key and Lou felt like her body was disintegrating. At least if she were a pile of debris on the floor she wouldn't have to go to the shoot the next day.

Lou slept on the sofa and woke up in the morning to sex sounds and the smell of coffee. There were croissants and espresso waiting on the table. She appreciated the snacks but would have preferred a little volume control from Mari and her girlfriend.

She had half a day to herself in Rome before an editorial shoot later that afternoon for *Vogue Italia*, booked solely based on the hype of the New York shows. It would be her first editorial, which meant she was officially a player in the big hot-girl leagues, as Harrison put it. Editorials told a story. They weren't just there to sell clothes because a lot of the people looking at them usually couldn't afford the clothes, but they were there to sell a look, an aesthetic, a person. The idea of a lifestyle. The idea of a person. That, Lou related to.

She'd actually heard of the photographer, which meant that he had to be extremely famous, and when she'd told her mom about it on the phone, before leaving New York, her mom sounded impressed. *Wow, Lou*, she'd said. *Take notes*. The highest compliment from her journalist mother. During her first week of shows, where crowds and crowds of people lined up outside the venues to get in, Lou had become acutely aware that what she was experiencing was interesting to other people, which made her feel nervous, as if she would screw it up in some way and let everyone down. According to Mari, the famous photographer was known for being a very handsome and talented dick. *Don't have sex with him*, Mari had warned, as if Lou would ever be tempted. *He'll definitely ask.* But she said it as if it was better than him not asking, which turned Lou's stomach. She decided not to think about it until it was happening, so as not to ruin the day in Rome she had to herself, the first in weeks.

It was eight in the morning, the latest she'd woken up since leaving Portland. Lou dropped a sweater and her wallet into her JanSport, still stained at the bottom from an ink pen explosion in history class, and gratefully slipped on her Vans. She didn't bring her camera. She didn't want the distraction of feeling guilty about not using it.

She shut the abbey door behind her and exited into a very dark and cool hallway, which looked tenfold less creepy than the night before, when she had been hallucinatorily tired. She hadn't connected to Wi-Fi since leaving New York, and even though it meant she was going to have some very expensive data coming her way for Lyft rides in Milan, it was a relief not to have it now because it meant she wouldn't have to think about how Ivy wasn't texting her and she wasn't texting Ivy.

Being in New York had felt like she was one step away from Morgan the whole time, like Morgan was looking over her shoulder, expecting Lou to live up to something, to take advantage of being in the city and not read Jane Austen novels on her bunk bed whenever she had a free night, wishing Elizabeth Bennet and her friend Charlotte had just run away together instead of marrying such aggravating dudes. Being in Rome, she felt closer to a new self, like she could watch the people wandering by and even if she couldn't understand what they were saying, she recognized herself in them, in the snippets of their pain and pleasures that she saw in ten-second intervals. The woman and her daughter playing beside the newsstand, the girl jumping onto her back, then sliding down, over and over, like her mother was a human firepole. The Italian couple so engaged with what the other one was saying, arms wrapped around each other, that they almost walked into the back of a delivery truck. The man screaming into his phone, holding his small son's hand tightly as they crossed the street, then bending down to retie the boy's shoes when they got to the sidewalk. She drew them all in her journal. The prior entry in her journal was from months ago, sketched in the coffee shop where she used to hang out while Ivy worked. She'd drawn Ivy with an expression on her face like she was smirking at Lou, even though she was still talking to a customer. Sometimes it felt like there were two halves of a person. The person themselves, wandering around the world, having their own thoughts, and the people everywhere else having thoughts about them. She wanted to capture the second one, in her drawings, in photographs.

Lou walked to the Pantheon but didn't get in line to go in. The wide pillars out front were bathed in pink and orange light. There were a thousand tourists holding selfie sticks, following flags around like children at a crosswalk. But there were also people just living their lives, late for appointments, tired of the company of the people they were with, falling in love. She couldn't understand what most of them were saying to each other. The tourists' obvious discomfort at not being able to communicate in restaurants and at train stations, unable to ask for the most basic thing, felt familiar to her. It made her anxieties feel less weird, more of an experience that everyone had, in this context. Being nervous and not looking like everyone else was just what traveling was. She could imagine staying abroad. Maybe she could live in Rome and go to school, like Mari had. She didn't understand why Mari would want to give that up for modeling. Lou didn't hate the industry so far, actually liked it more than she expected to, but it didn't feel like she was making all her own choices. It felt like she'd stepped into the path of a very elegant avalanche.

Eventually, she found her way to a famous park, up on the side of a hill, where she could see the whole city. She saw a bride and groom taking their wedding photos at the church down the street. Then another couple on the lawn in the park, a photographer just a few feet away, directing them. Soon, she realized the park was almost entirely her and just-married straight couples. They rotated around her. One couple by the streetlamps, another by the view, another still by the bushes of flowers. The women were all in white. The men were all in gray. Lou didn't know if she wanted to get married. She hadn't grown up imagining it. For most of her life, marriage equality wasn't a thing, and she didn't know herself well enough to know who she'd want to marry one day anyway. In any case, it didn't feel like a cornerstone, or an aspiration. She wondered if it did to Ivy. She doubted it. Ivy would marry her guitars, if she could.

Lou couldn't think about the kiss on Harrison's rooftop, so she was choosing not to. She couldn't think about Harrison and Tuck either, what that meant about her, that she was so in her own head about Ivy that she couldn't see what Harrison might be struggling with, or wanting. He was flying from London direct to Milan, so she wouldn't see him until the following week.

She'd been seeing posters pasted to the sides of buildings

for the retrospective of a photographer she'd heard of, and she finally made her way to the art museum by midafternoon. The museum was quiet and unpopulated compared to the ruins. Most of the photographer's work was self-portraiture in precipice: the artist in her claw-foot bathtub on the edge of a cliff, the artist stepping off the wing of a plane, the artist gripping a tree branch, her fingers loose.

Lou had a photo of Morgan just before she dived off the rock. She knew it was there, on her camera's memory, but she'd never looked at it. She remembered taking it. She thought about what it would be like to have someone else look at it, to know it existed, to tell her it was as terrifying to see as Lou knew it to be. She bought a postcard of the artist and the tree branch in the gift shop for three euros and tucked it into her backpack in its brown paper sleeve. She didn't know who to send it to. Maybe she'd hang it on her own wall, if she ever had her own wall again.

The *Vogue Italia* shoot was in an old movie theater that had been converted into a music venue, a marquee across the front of it advertising an American indie band that Lou knew. It was the first time she'd been to a real photo shoot, the kind where someone was paying her. An editorial was a whole spread. Nine pages. The shoot was supposed to take place over two days. Mari told her the first day was always hardest, that her nerves would die down once she met everyone.

Her nerves didn't die when she met Pete Webbs, the famous photographer. Everyone on the shoot deferred to whatever Pete Webbs wanted. The hairstylist and makeup artist talked to Lou about him like he was a genius, but as far as she could tell, he was just a bearded British guy in jeans and a baseball cap. He didn't look anything like the other fashion people she'd met so far, who were usually dressed like they were going to the wedding of their lives. Pete Webbs was dressed like a dad at a baseball game, and he talked about the models like they were children up to bat. Unathletic children. The models were kept separate from one another, rotated into the lineup from a lumpy sofa in the corner.

Lou was up first, which meant she didn't get the chance to see how the other models did anything. The clothes didn't fit right. The first look was a dress, a ball gown really, and it looked wrong on her. Her shoulders looked knobby and her waist refused to be a waist and Pete Webbs kept asking the stylist to fit things tighter and tighter, sometimes with heavy metal clamps with red noses, like the kind used to jump a car.

"That's as small as it'll go," the stylist said to him. Lou could barely breathe, but she didn't know who to tell.

"She still looks incorrect," Pete Webbs said, directed at Lou more than at anyone who could actually do anything about it. Lou was the last person in the room who could do anything about her incorrectness.

She didn't know what to say. She didn't want to say sorry. She especially didn't want her voice to shake if she said it.

Pete Webbs told the stylist to pick out a different look, to swap hers out for another model's, and when she was in a wide-legged pair of slacks and lace-up heels, with a sheer white tank over her bare chest, he seemed more satisfied. Lou was certain her nipples were visible through the shirt, but she didn't say anything. She didn't want to go back into the jumper-cable dress.

At least she could breathe in this. The makeup artist wiped off an hour's worth of work and started over. This time it was simpler, just concealer and mascara, a nude lip. He worked fast and released her back to Pete Webbs.

A mic stand was set up onstage and Pete Webbs positioned Lou behind it. Blue lights focused on her, and the air smelled like flat-ironed hair. The floor was covered in thin canvas. Pete Webbs asked if she knew how to hold a guitar.

"Sure," Lou said. She could pretend, anyway. He handed her one, gingerly, like he didn't trust her. She could tell it was extremely expensive. Probably not anywhere near as expensive as any of the garments she'd worn in a runway show, but it clearly meant something personal to Pete Webbs. It was an offset shape, with a gold-glitter body and a flecked pickguard. She wondered if she could get away with taking a picture of it for Ivy, then remembered that she wasn't talking to Ivy, that she couldn't just text her pictures of guitars, even very beautiful ones. Maybe she could steal it for Ivy, and then Ivy would want to be with her. She smiled, and Pete Webbs thought she was smiling at him, so she felt like she had to say something. "What kind is it?"

"It's a '65 Eko," Pete Webbs said. He didn't ask if she could play. She put her fingers on the fretboard, in the shape of an F chord, and cupped her right hand in the shape of a U, but he told her to grip it in a fist instead and hold it out like an offering.

Then he told her to fall to her knees. He mimed the movement but didn't fall himself. Stopped himself just before he might have, like he was doing a skate trick. She tried to do it halfway, like that, without actually falling.

"No," he said. "All the way down."

Lou gripped the guitar neck tight, but underestimated her distance from the floor and landed hard. Pain shot through her knees. Her legs were shaking when she rose to stand, her eyes watering.

He gestured at her to do it again.

"I can't," she said.

He seemed irritated but directed her to some other poses, had her lunge forward, like she was trying to step over a wide creek. Each time, he asked her to go a little farther, until she was nearly doing the splits, her muscles straining. The guitar grew heavier in her hand.

"This isn't working," he said to one of his assistants.

"Should I try something else?" Lou said. But they were both looking at the camera, not at her. The assistant scurried off, and Pete Webbs seemed to remember she was there.

He asked where she was from, with a friendlier tone. She could tell he was trying to warm her up, but she didn't want to be warmed up. Her knees ached. She really didn't want to cry. She could feel the other models watching.

"The States," she said.

"Which part?"

"Portland, Oregon."

"Oh yeah," he said, like she'd finally done something right. "I love Portland. Lived there for a few years in my twenties, but I got out before it turned into something else. You know how it is now."

She didn't really. She didn't know how it was then either.

Pete Webbs asked her to pretend to sing, and her mouth felt rubbery and foreign, like it had been numbed at the dentist, as she opened it while not making any sound. How did a singing mouth look? She couldn't remember if it was round like an O or just open like a scream. Everyone was staring at her, with the camera clicking, with Pete Webbs trying to get her body to look like the exaggeration of a musician's body, when the only musician's body she wanted was all the way across the Atlantic.

She kept trying to envision Pete Webbs as her good-natured agent Anne, taking her picture on the waterfront, but she couldn't get out of her head long enough to imagine him as anyone other than who he was. A guy who could see her nipples, who seemed dissatisfied with all her movements but couldn't tell her what to change. She had no idea why he'd chosen her for the shoot, or whether it had been someone else's decision. Maybe she looked different in person.

The room was overly air-conditioned, and she looked out at the empty seats, which started a few yards back from the stage, trying to imagine how Ivy felt at a microphone: able to amplify her feelings like that, to fill every square inch of air in a room with them. For a second, there was a real crowd in front of her, and Ivy was in it and Lou knew exactly what she wanted to say.

"Portland, lean into that mic," Pete Webbs said.

She leaned in.

"Closer."

She could smell the metal of the mic. She grazed it with her lips.

"Close as you can get," he said. "Like it's your boyfriend's cock."

Lou let go of the guitar.

Everyone in the theater froze, and one of the boys holding a light reflector cried out in Italian as it hit the cement.

It slipped so easily out of her fingers, this guitar that was as old as he was, and it wasn't like the word *cock* was really that shocking, coming out of this guy's mouth, but one second, she was holding it with a firm grip, and the next, its neck was broken, the strings loose and wonky, the body of it at her feet.

Lou knew she should have felt terrified that she'd snapped the neck of a vintage guitar, the centerpiece of the shoot, but the way Pete Webbs was staring at her, angry, red-faced behind his beard, she only felt angry right back, holding his gaze as he asked what the fuck her problem was.

"Sorry," Lou said, with a shrug. She walked off, leaving the guitar on the floor, and left out the back double doors of the venue, empty-handed except for her green JanSport, suddenly starving. It was dusk outside, the sky purple and gray. The windows on the buildings were lit up from within, steamy and yellow, and she could see bodies inside, through wooden shutters, cooking dinner or sitting at laptops, cats dozing on windowsills, and she wanted to start shouting and banging on their windows, disrupt their peaceful evenings, sprint down the street like she was hot on somebody's heels.

2

Back at the apartment, Mari's girlfriend, Rosana, had made an elaborate Italian meal that Lou shoveled into her body. She soaked up olive oil with the crust of her ciabatta. She complimented the pasta, which was hand-rolled, eggshells lined up in a neat line on the kitchen countertop. Rosana and Mari seemed hours into a fight that Lou was just wandering into. They might have actually been years into the fight; there was an elliptical feeling to what they were saying that reminded her of her parents' arguments, like the air had been filled over and over again with the same words, no one quite hearing each other, no one changing their mind or logic.

When dinner was over, Lou overheard them arguing in the kitchen, which was so small, she couldn't enter it without one of them leaving. She waited in the main room, dirty dishes in hand. She felt like she was eavesdropping at the top of the staircase, like she used to do as a kid when her parents had conversations after she and her brother went up to bed.

"Do you see the pattern?" Mari was saying. "How you deny you're going to and then do this *every* fucking time."

Her girlfriend would answer her in Italian and Mari would respond in English.

"I don't *want* to live here, love," Mari said. "I don't want to go back to school. I'm sorry, but it has absolutely nothing to do with you."

Rosana said something else that Lou couldn't understand.

"You said I could sleep with her! You can't give permission in the moment and take it back a week later. That's not how this works. What would you say if I told you to stop seeing Brio? What would you say if I was suddenly so disgusted by the idea of you and her?"

Mari came storming out of the kitchen clutching an uncorked bottle of wine and almost ran straight into Lou.

"Sorry," Lou said. There was nothing she could have been doing except eavesdropping. "I was just—"

"Wishing you could get the fuck out of here?" Mari slammed the wine down on the table, but it didn't spill. "Same."

Mari wanted to go to a show at the same venue where the shoot had been, which made Lou feel like Pete Webbs was lurking in the crowd the whole night. During dinner, Yukon had texted her a string of questions about why Pete Webbs had banned her from the second day of the editorial shoot, and Lou hadn't answered any of them. What was she supposed to say to *Lou, just what kind of property did you destroy?*

For once, she didn't feel any guilt. Her only regret was not smashing his camera too.

Instead of listening to the band, she and Mari stood in the back while Mari shouted the backstory of her relationship with Rosana. Mari and Rosana had met at the conservatory where Rosana was still a student, their first semester there. They'd played in a quartet together for a couple of years, which had been Mari's favorite part of school, before she got scouted. But Rosana planned to audition for orchestras in the spring. They were supposed to do it together.

"The odds of us even ending up in the same one were basically zero anyway," Mari said. "The odds of me getting a job were low to begin with. I was good enough to get into a conservatory because I was forced to practice literally every free moment of my entire childhood, instead of playing outside with my friends, but I'm just not that good compared to everyone else who wants it more than me. At least with modeling I know that I'll age out, so this is the time to do it. I just want to do whatever the fuck I want. I don't want to practice anymore. I want to have my time back. And Rosana's never strayed off that path. She's so regimented. It's suffocating."

"Does she like it more?"

"She loves it," Mari said. "That's the difference. She's always loved it, while I just loved pleasing my parents."

"Is she mad about Sienna?"

"No, or at least, she shouldn't be. She gave permission. There are rules, and I was following them. Rosana has another partner here. I've told her, if you want to live with someone so badly, move in with her. But she wants me. Because I'm the one she can't have anymore."

Lou got them more drinks. She slid her passport over to the bartender, who looked at her fourteen-year-old self in the picture very skeptically before handing over their drinks. The band wasn't anything like Fortunato, but she felt comforted by the familiar landscape of the show, the unfocused gaze of the singer, the sticky floors, the chatter of the crowd, even in a language she didn't understand. Which was why when Mari kissed her against the wall, so stapled with posters that it was soft, cushioned, Lou was startled. She was used to standing alone at shows, not having moves made on her. She'd never been kissed by anyone taller than her before. Even the boys had been shorter. Mari was extremely good at it, but she pulled back, grinning, clutching Lou's cheeks with her hands, like Lou had told a hilarious joke and now she would get a prize.

"You may look like a boy, but thank the lord you kiss like a girl."

"What does a girl kiss like?" Lou said.

Mari laughed. "Babe, as if you don't know."

She and Mari took a train to Milan the next evening. Lou tried to offer her snacks from her bag, but she wouldn't take any. They hadn't said goodbye to Rosana, just let the heavy abbey door slam behind them. She wondered if they broke their rules at the concert, if Mari was using her to break them. Lou didn't feel skilled enough at balancing people to be in Mari's full orbit. On the train, Mari seemed distant and hungover, curled away from Lou toward the window. The kiss had been like a game, something they were bound to try eventually, and Lou knew Mari had probably already forgotten it, but she was still a little afraid something had gotten messed up between them. Kissing Mari had none of the heat of even kissing Catherine, despite the

skill, and it was much better to have Mari like this, as a com-
panion, as someone she might have told about the Pete Webbs
shoot—how anxious she felt in its aftermath now, that it had
somehow screwed everything up—but wasn't able to, because it
felt like complaining about it would be petty and overdramatic.
He'd said one suggestive thing to her, so what? He hadn't hit on
her, not like Mari said he would. But she still felt like she had
been dumped out of the back of a moving truck, in the way no
one on the shoot had intervened or acknowledged that what he
said was fucked-up.

Before they parted ways in Milan, Lou bought a caprese
sandwich from a vendor in the train station and slipped it into
Mari's purse when she wasn't looking. Mari kissed Lou on each
cheek, then saluted her goodbye.

In Milan, something had changed from New York, where she'd
had fifty castings and no indication of whether she would book
anything at all. Now designers wanted her without ever seeing
her in person, based purely on her reputation from the New
York shows. Yukon emailed her a new long list of fittings, some
of which were at exactly the same time, but they didn't mention
the Pete Webbs shoot again, as if they knew Lou wasn't going
to give the full story. Or maybe they didn't want to know it.

All the same girls from New York were there—Thayer and
Eline and Jia and Keeley Dot all hugged her hello, telling her
how excited they were to see her again, even though it had only
been a week since they were all in New York together. The press
had deemed Thayer and Mari and Keeley Dot the girls of the
season, the ones who had booked every huge show, and Lou

wasn't a *girl* of the season exactly, but she was a *something* of the season. She was extremely alarmed at what happened now when people googled her, which Yukon suggested she do, as well as set news alerts for her own name. She was also alarmed at just how many times her name appeared on modeling forums with speculation about who she was and where she'd come from—let alone Vogue.com, let alone Instagram, where she seemed to have a very devoted following of tweens posting disturbingly suggestive things about her. Her dad started texting her pictures of herself walking in shows asking, *Is this you?*

Sometimes it was, sometimes it wasn't.

The shows in Milan blurred together. There were a dozen more than in New York, crammed into every second of the day. She woke up at four in the morning, had call times by 7:00 a.m. and after-parties until 2:00 a.m., only to wake up again a couple of hours later for a new full day. Time meant nothing, except spacing out her snacks and meals and caffeine intake. She walked almost thirty shows over the course of a week. Lou's model apartment was nicer than the one in New York, with more than one bathroom and heavy curtains on the windows, but none of her friends were staying there. Lou didn't understand how she could have just met so many people and done an admirable job at it and now she had to meet even *more* people.

The only night that was any good was when she finally found Harrison, at an after-party for the Missoni show. She dragged him away from the noise and Negronis, and they walked through the darkened streets together. As soon as they were alone, she became worried about whatever information he might offer about or from Fortunato. She asked him how he was, intending to avoid the subject altogether.

"Tired," he said. "Milan is always a low-key nightmare. A beautiful one, for real. But like Da Vinci took ecstasy and then dragged you around behind him like a rag doll."

They stopped at a corner store, where Harrison bought them both blue Gatorades.

"What're you, a soccer mom?" she said. She felt self-conscious as soon as she said the word *mom* to him, but Harrison just laughed.

"Hydrate, bitch."

She uncapped the Gatorade and took a long swig. It tasted amazing. Like the inside of an ice cube.

"I'm sorry I was such a nerd in New York," Lou said. "I left because of Ivy, not because of you and Tuck."

"You did look like a huge homophobe," Harrison said, and this time Lou laughed.

"What's going on with you guys?"

Harrison sighed. "I don't know, man. We ran in the same circles in Portland for a while, before he left for school. I always thought he was cute, but straight. But we started texting after his ex died."

Morgan, Lou wanted to say. *His ex, Morgan Ellis.*

"And I don't know," Harrison said. "Guess he's not so straight."

"He dresses straight."

Harrison hooted. "Look who's *learned* something! Drag him."

"Have you guys talked?"

"I told him I'd be out of service. I don't know. I don't want a relationship. I couldn't handle one right now. I'm like scraping myself up off the ground, and I don't need to scrape anyone else up either. But I also really like him."

"He doesn't seem like the kind of person who would need you to do that."

"Everybody needs it sometimes," Harrison said.

"He's a great drummer."

"And smart. And calm. And interesting."

"You're smart and calm and interesting. Does he want to date you?"

"He's acting like it. Also, Lou, who says *dates*? You're legit middle-aged."

"Fine, does he want to smoosh you?"

Harrison laughed. "He already did, baby."

They walked for a while before she said, "I was there. When his ex died."

Harrison looked over at her. "That must have been really horrible."

"Yeah."

He shook his head. "Ivy's talked about it, a little bit. How fucked it was because of everything around her mom too."

"I don't know," Lou said. "She never talks about her mom."

They were passing a group of American tourists, all young-ish men. They wore three-piece suits and matching baseball caps, and Lou wondered for a second if they were part of an MLB team or just a very stylish bachelor party. One of the men blatantly checked her and Harrison out, with a full up and down, without breaking stride or his sentence about real estate investments.

"Ivy's been a good friend to me, since my mom died," Harrison said. "It's a sucky thing to share, but it's better to know someone who's been through it."

They approached a lit-up basilica, with its Gothic steeples. Even though it was four in the morning, tourists were milling around, taking selfies. It was a cool night, and everything was washed in an auburn light. For the first time it felt like fall, like they were out late after a football game, not that Lou ever really went to football games. Lou asked Harrison if he ever felt like he was living in a dream.

"It's not mine," Harrison said. "Is it yours?"

"What's your dream?"

"Does anyone know?"

"Ivy does."

"Maybe you just think you know hers. Maybe you're assuming you know what it is. Like, take my mom. I'd always thought it was her dream to be a poet. She worked for the city for her entire career, in water management. But she studied poetry in school and read so much of it, and she was always scribbling things down. She never showed anything she'd written to anyone. But one day I asked her. She and my dad had told us just a couple of days before that the cancer was back and that it was terminal. And I asked her if she regretted that she hadn't published her poetry. She had no idea what I was talking about. And I was like, you're always writing. What are you writing, if not that? She said she was just making plans for her garden. And of course, I knew she loved her garden, that she spent all her weekends working on it—I just never thought of it as a dream. It was the best one in the neighborhood. It still is. People would stop and take it in, and she'd just keep working. And one day we were sitting out there together on the porch, when she couldn't work on it anymore, and she told me her dream was to go to the Boboli Gardens. She showed me this whole album of photographs she had of it, in her office. Like an entire scrapbook of famous gardens. She told me she'd read about them in a book as a really little kid and that she regretted that she'd never gone while she could. And I told her I would take her. Even though, obviously, she couldn't leave the house at that point, let alone come here."

"Here?"

"Well, Florence. Basically here."

"Florence, Italy?" She realized she'd yelled it when some people crossing the street looked over at them. "Let's go tomorrow."

"We have to walk the Gucci show tomorrow."

"Then after."

"We have to go to Paris after Gucci."

"Why else are we in Europe, if we can't go to the Bo—" She tried to wrap her mouth around it but was afraid of adding too many extra syllables.

"The Boboli Gardens."

Lou liked how it sounded, like a hot-air balloon, or a fancy girl's name, and it made her think of Harrison's mom, Coral, writing it out in cursive in her scrapbooks, imagining a place oceans away from real life, a dream to live within on the harder days.

They took the train right after the Gucci show, even though Harrison had told her their after-parties were legendary and that the year before, someone had famously gotten their mouth stuck to the dick of an ice statue of Michelangelo's *David*, and then an entirely different person got stuck to its nipples, as if that detail would make Lou more likely to want to go.

Lou watched the countryside go by as the sun came up and Harrison slept. She watched the rows of sunflowers, the clotheslines of suburbs and rooftop satellites of small towns, car blinkers at the train crossings. She felt happy as they pulled into the stop for the Firenze SMN station, the passengers rising all at once to grab their bags from the overhead racks. Ready to capture her own energy.

The gardens were up on the side of a hill, on the edge of the city. It was just barely light out as they walked the road up through the neighborhoods, to the fort above the Palazzo Pitti, which Lou had read about on the train. It was bought by the Medicis in the sixteenth century and, at one point, served as one of Napoleon's headquarters. The fort and the palace weren't open yet. There was a tall fence surrounding the gardens, with a top of rusted spades. The front gate was locked. A white sign in multiple languages stated the operating hours. It wouldn't be open for another few hours, right around when they had to get back on a train to make it to Milan to catch their flights to Paris.

"Shit. Who closes gardens?" Lou said, gripping the front gate. Beyond it was a drawbridge over a pond, and long hedges. It didn't look that extraordinary. In fact, it looked kind of plain, but Lou didn't want to say that.

"We got really close," Harrison said. "We're basically in there."

"No," Lou said. She walked around the long side of the wrought iron fence, where a hedge was blocking it. She was the reason they were here. She would get them in. Even if they were the world's most underwhelming gardens. She'd never heard Harrison give up so quickly on anything. She refused to let that moment be now. "Follow me."

"You're scary like this."

"It's a *public* garden," she said. The side of the fence looked a little like a ladder, with even spaces between its bars. She scaled the edge and balanced at the top of it, where the arrows of iron poked up. It wasn't really that high. Surely others had done it and not been arrested for it. She jumped down and landed on her feet, but half in the hedge.

"My agent's going to kill me," Harrison said, as he gripped the fence and followed her. They emerged on the other side with scrapes on their arms and legs. Lou wiped blood from her cheek.

"This is why makeup was invented," she said.

"This specifically? For breaking and entering into gardens?"

They spotted a security guard a few dozen yards away, and they ducked down behind a statue of a man on a horse. He didn't have a gun on his hip, because this wasn't America and what were people going to steal from a garden?

Lou felt the same kind of excitement rising up that she had as a kid, playing hide-and-go-seek in the dark. "When I say run, you have to run. Just keep moving. We'll get to the edge. I have an idea."

The security guard went around a corner. Lou took off her shoes, to move faster, and the grass was wet and cold under her feet. She stashed the shoes in her backpack.

"Run," she said.

They both took off, laughing hard, especially when Lou slipped on the way, catching herself with one hand instead of wiping out. Somehow they made it around a corner, away from the guard, and then they were in an open patch of grass alone, with thick hedges on either side of them, like they'd entered a labyrinth.

Lou had her camera out, adjusting her shutter speed and aperture for the light, and she told Harrison where she wanted him, near the modern sculptures that were clearly on loan from somewhere. They looked brand-new, in colors that didn't exist whenever these gardens were conceived of. There was one of a fucked-up-looking angel that she liked the best, made out of electric green plastic, and she placed him underneath it.

"Okay," Lou said, and took a breath. "Now do—I don't know, whatever it is you do."

Harrison looked at her like she'd totally lost it, but after a second, he seemed to understand what she was asking. He knelt down like he was asking the green angel for something, but in such a way that it didn't seem like an angel but something even bigger than that: a pond he'd come to the edge of, a place of a long rest. He bent his head and stayed like that for such a long time that Lou almost knelt down beside him.

When he stood back up, he started to pose, but more slowly than she'd seen him do in the past, like every gesture was standing in for something else. He leaned against the angel, like it was a bus stop shelter. He held his hands up to it, like it would pour something into them.

The way he moved was luscious to take in as a photographer. He seemed to be able to predict where she wanted him before she gave him any directions. It wasn't like with Pete Webbs, the way she felt manipulated, ineffectual, unnatural. She was a pair of eyes, but she was a pair of eyes who saw something true, something that didn't belong to her alone, something she wanted to give to everyone else on the planet—point to it and make them see it too. Here was a boy in a garden. Here was a boy in a garden his mother had always wanted to see. Here was a boy in a garden seeing it for her. Here was a boy in a garden who knew that wasn't enough.

By the time they were finished, the gates were open. Tourists flooded in, and Lou and Harrison walked out, as if they'd entered with a ticket like everyone else. They got back to the train station early and waited on a bench for the next train back to Milan. Through the big windows, a group of skateboarders did kickflips off a long row of planters. A small child chased pigeons pecking at pastry crumbs until they flew away.

Harrison looked at the pictures from the gardens on her camera and kept saying how good they were, and Lou felt warm and heavy with pleasure.

"Can I use these for my portfolio?" Harrison said. "I'll credit you, of course."

Later that night, she uploaded the photos to her laptop and sent them to him, not expecting him to actually do anything with them. But he posted one on his account the next day and tagged Lou. The photo got thousands of likes and hundreds of comments complimenting the shots, their composition, Harrison's beauty, but none of it felt as good as the way Harrison had praised it, as someone who really knew what he was talking about, as someone she trusted. It was funny sometimes, how photography didn't feel like a real thing to her, an art worthy of praise or particular attention, because it was something that everyone else also did all the time. Sometimes she wished she could have been a photographer in the days before every single person carried around a camera in their pocket, but she also liked the challenge of finding an image that no one else could have taken, even if they were there. She liked seeing more, noticing everything, and choosing the one thing to document. Ivy had once said that it bothered her how people were always looking through their phones at stuff and not just looking at the thing itself, like that was the only way to know what they were seeing was real, but Lou understood it. It was kind of like saying *I'm here, I was here*, over and over again. People wanted to document themselves, especially if no one else was going to. With her own photography, she was usually looking for something else, something apart from her, a documentation of a feeling, but not necessarily a feeling someone would want to remember if it was their own life. The ache that they didn't want any-one else to see. The photo she loved the most of Harrison at the Boboli Gardens she took when they were outside the gates again, heading back to the train station. He wasn't looking at the camera, or at her. He was looking over his shoulder at the entrance to the gardens, like he didn't want to leave the dream of someone he loved behind.

3

Catherine FaceTimed her the next morning, when Lou was waiting to board her flight to France. She just happened to be connected to Wi-Fi, to check on the list of castings for Paris shows that Yukon had sent, emailed along with a suggestion of the best place in Paris to get macarons and a note implying she shouldn't actually eat the macarons herself but should instead ship a box of half bergamot and half rose petal back to New York for Yukon. *If they're out of bergamot,* Yukon texted, *scratch all of that and go for two dozen of the cake batter.*

Lou could tell Catherine was fucked-up as soon as she answered the call. Drunk and crying. It was two in the morning in Oregon and pitch-black, but Lou could make out that she was in a car. Catherine kept swinging the phone around. She saw a steering wheel. Catherine was in the driver's seat, but the car wasn't moving. She listened for the engine but couldn't hear anything under Catherine's heavy breaths. It took Catherine several tries to tell her that she might get kicked off the Oregon track team.

Lou felt nauseous, hearing her say it. "For what?"

"I don't know, it was going well. It really was, all preseason. I just got offtrack." She laughed at her own joke. "Fuck."

Again, Lou asked what happened, and Catherine was so quiet that Lou could finally hear the engine running. But then she started to talk.

Catherine had been at a party a few nights before. She was flirting with this girl, who was a sprinter on the team. Things were going well. The party wasn't even that out of control. No one was drinking very much, not even Catherine. She'd had a few beers, smoked some weed, took some Adderall, or maybe some Molly, she wasn't exactly sure, but that was it. There were a lot of people from the team there, but when the neighbors called the cops and everyone else escaped out the back, Catherine and the sprinter happened to be in the bathroom. She seemed more pissed that the neighbors were other college kids who had a grudge against them, for some rager they didn't get invited to, than the fact that her friends had left her behind to get caught. Lou didn't exactly follow—Catherine went down a tangent about the grudge for a long time before ending up at the point. She'd almost been charged with a minor in possession, but one of her coaches bailed out her and the sprinter, to protect the reputation of the program and keep it out of the local news. The sprinter had blamed Catherine, and now the coaches were talking about how if she didn't clean herself up, she'd lose her place on the team. Apparently Catherine already had a couple of strikes against her but didn't expand on the details of why. Now the sprinter wasn't talking to her, and her teammates were pissed at them both for getting caught.

"I wish Morgan was here," Catherine kept saying. "She would fix this. She knew exactly what to do about stuff like this."

"I know," Lou said. "And you're right. But can you turn off the car? You can't drive, okay? It'll make everything worse. And I don't want you to fucking die like your hero. It's a cliché, okay? It's not what you're meant for."

"Nobody's *meant* for anything," Catherine said.

But Lou heard the car turn off. "Go back to your dorm, Cath. But keep me on the phone, okay?"

The car door opened. She watched the campus go by in dark pixilation. She could hear yells in the distance. Catherine's face, against the trees overhead. The leaves hadn't fallen yet. It was the last week of September. Catherine entered a bright fluorescent lobby, then a stairwell, then a long, tiled hallway. Finally, she unlocked her door and put Lou on the desk beside her bed.

"I'll stay here, okay?" Lou said. She had her finger pressed against her ear, trying to drown out the warnings about unattended luggage, and the other passengers, who were antsy for their flight announcements. A toddler was screaming in a language she didn't know.

Catherine took off her shirt and pants and got into bed. Lou felt like she was so close, she could have curled up beside her, rested her head on the stuffed pig that Catherine was clutching. It was the first time she really wished she could be back home, if only for a few hours. Maybe she should have gone to U of O after all, just to prevent nights like this. It would have done more good than pretending like she was helping Catherine by living out her sister's New York fashion dream.

"You have to keep running," Lou said. Her head felt tight and full. She didn't know what else to do, except stay on the phone.

"You sound like my sister," Catherine said. She was already almost asleep. "You never told me what's going on with you."

Lou didn't hang up until Catherine had been passed out for thirty minutes, turning away from the camera, bare arm over her face. Lou texted Tuck next. She didn't even have his number, so she had to ask Harrison, who didn't ask what she wanted it for. She wrote the message before she could second-guess herself, or second-guess what Tuck would think of her, after her disappearance in New York, which felt like years ago now. Or even what he would think of her and Ivy. She texted him as the friend he might have been, if things had gone differently.

Hi, it's Lou. I heard from Catherine, in Eugene. Do you still talk to her parents? Do you think you could just let them know that she needs some help? I don't think they'd want to hear from me.

Tuck texted back almost immediately, even though it was the middle of the night. *Yeah I do actually. Thanks for the heads-up. I'll talk to them.* A few minutes later, another text appeared from him. *You should talk to Ivy.*

He didn't give any further explanation, and she didn't make any promises. Part of it was that he didn't say why, and she hated imagining what was being said about her when she wasn't around. The other part was just being angry that she was so distant from Ivy that Tuck was having to play go-between for them, when obviously that was exactly what she was doing with Catherine.

Lou thought about calling Ivy, but the time difference stopped her. She put her phone on airplane mode and left the Internet behind. She was freezing. An older woman in a fleece jacket across the gate smiled at her, or smiled at whatever was happening in her earbuds, and Lou was reminded of her mom, how she looked on the back deck on summer evenings, gazing out over the trees.

A chime sounded over the PA system and then an announcement in French, then German, then Spanish, then English, *If you see something, say something*, then more that she didn't recognize, translations cascading out. Her departure gate had changed, but she didn't stand up right away to find it.

4

In Paris, Lou and Harrison had a long conversation about how there were two types of people: those who frequently imagined their own violent deaths and those who didn't. She and Harrison were both in the former category. She decided there were two types of models too: those who imagined falling face-first off the runway into the lap of Anna Wintour or Rihanna or LeBron James, and those who didn't.

It happened at the Chanel show, which she'd actually been really looking forward to, rather than being scared out of her mind, because it was taking place in a courtyard of the Louvre. She was walking last again, this time in the wedding dress, the crowning piece of the collection. Yukon had been ecstatic about Chanel and what it meant for her career, the jobs she would book, the prestige of it, for both Lou and themself. Suddenly, Lou was an asset to the agency, not someone they had to teach how to dress.

But she was coming off walking three other shows in the same day, call times starting at five that morning, and her internal clock was so fucked-up that despite being hypervigilant about being on time she still managed to be more than an hour late. She scrubbed at her face with a makeup-remover wipe, running for the entrance, where a large man with a headset ushered her through. When even security was worried, she knew she was in deep trouble.

She hadn't had anything to eat that day, and she felt like she had as a kid when she passed out a few times on field trips, always if she hadn't eaten breakfast and her class had to walk around somewhere, her vision darkening, waving in and out like a bad signal. Since modeling, she'd begun to take advantage of her body functioning despite a lack of sleep or regular nutrition. Normally Mari kept her fed, whenever Lou forgot or didn't have time, but she'd been light-headed all morning, and she couldn't find the catered tables of food people could normally snack from.

When she arrived at the backstage area at the Louvre, off the courtyard in a marble side room, she was rushed by a team of makeup artists and hairstylists and a watcher, who was supposed to triple-check that the look was on-brand for Chanel, as if anyone was trying to thwart it. They all dragged her to a chair and moved around her in a frenzy. The first model was already walking. People were screaming at her in French, like she'd hit someone with a car. A stylist grabbed her, and she stripped, pulling on the enormous wedding dress. It looked like a white intestine. The heels weren't anywhere near the tallest she'd worn. They were wedges, even. The stylist pulled her up to standing.

"You're going to make it," the woman said to her, with a thick French accent.

"*Merci*," Lou said, over her shoulder, already jogging to her place in line. The dress on its own was massive, but it was when someone stopped her for a headpiece that she knew there might be a problem. It was gauzy and extensive. It looked like a wedding veil mixed with something a medieval princess would wear just before getting her head cut off.

The runway was raised, laid over the cobblestone courtyard, rimmed with lanterns. A scene so beautiful, Lou felt like she was looking through her life into something else. Maybe it could be her dream, after all.

Lou smiled, just before going on. She'd made it.

But the veil didn't flow behind her, like she imagined. It clung. It felt like trying to walk with a shower curtain sticking to her bare arms and legs. She tried to breathe, tried to stare straight ahead as she walked. Anna Wintour wasn't in view, but several members of the royal family were.

It happened just before the photographers. She was walking normally—fine, good even, maybe the best she'd ever done, which wasn't the highest bar in the world, but was still something, considering she was almost forty shows in. But then her vision swayed and she was plummeting, as quickly as if she'd let go of a ledge.

Sometimes, when she imagined her own violent death, there was a moment where she prevented it. There was a moment when she tackled the guy with the gun in the movie theater, or made it to the red EXIT sign before the blaze overtook her, or spun the wheel at just the last second before the guardrail. There was no saving herself in that moment. She put her hands out, which met free and empty air, and fell straight off the runway.

It wasn't very high off the cobblestones, which meant that she landed half in the lap of a woman wearing a pristine white suit. Lou, on her wedding day, falling into the bride. She landed awkwardly, over the woman's back, like a circus trick. She rolled off the woman, who gasped, gripping Lou's wrist like she was a child who had misbehaved. The other models in front of her kept walking, but her friend Thayer had just pivoted on her way backstage, and hopped off the runway.

"Are you okay?" Thayer said. Her hair was arranged into a sculptural brown wave down her back. She wore a silver floor-length gown with a shawl and pearled gloves, which she took off and placed carefully on the edge of the runway before taking Lou by the hand. Lou didn't know if she was bleeding, but by the concern on Thayer's face—iconic eyebrows raised—the odds were high. In fourth grade, Lou had once had the wind knocked out of her after leaping from a swing set and landing on her back, and her whole class had gathered around her as she wheezed out a sound like an airless accordion. While she knew this was, in the scheme of her life, much worse, the look on Thayer's face was just how her best friend had looked then—like she was both glad Lou was okay and so grateful it wasn't her.

Thayer kept asking if she was okay and Lou kept laughing and couldn't stop. Her laughter was nervous and painful but it kept coming as Thayer apologized, as if she was the one who had dive-bombed off a platform in a courtyard of the Louvre during a show in Paris Fashion Week, and not Lou.

Everyone around them was filming. Lou knew even as they pointed their phones at her that this was what everyone would remember: that she had somehow ruined the designer's whole show, that every other model who had waited for this debut would blame her for stealing the attention away, derailing everyone, going viral for something so inept, so ridiculous.

Lou gathered the headpiece back up. Her shoe strap was broken, a possible reason for the fall in the first place. She wanted to hold the shoe up, prove to everyone this was all the fault of a weak seam, not her blood sugar, or clumsiness. Instead, Thayer helped her to her feet, barefoot now. Lou wished she could get back up there, finish her walk, but there was no way she could without the shoes. She didn't know the protocol. No one had ever told her what to do if she fell. It was so out of the question.

Thayer helped her backstage. She carried Lou's veil and the security guys let them pass, as if it had all been a part of the show.

"Thanks," Lou said. "This is horrifying."

Thayer nodded. She knew as much as Lou did just how horrifying it was. "You're bleeding?"

"Shit," Lou said. "You're right." Her elbow was scraped, and both her knees, from the cobblestones.

A stylist appeared, grabbing the veil out of Thayer's hands.

"I'm sorry," Lou said to the stylist. But no one was paying her or Thayer any attention. People were talking into headsets, but no one was accepting her apology. She found her way to a quiet corner, where she sat down in a chair and inspected her elbow and knees. She felt like a kid who had wiped out at a sports game, but with no hovering parents, no concerned coaches. Just herself and Thayer, who was still standing there.

"It would have been better if you'd really injured yourself," Thayer said, smiling. "Then at least there'd be sympathy."

"Yeah, why couldn't I have broken an arm at least? Or bled more?"

"Do you want to get out of here, before things get worse?"

"How could they get worse?"

"Well, we're trending," Thayer said, holding up her phone.

Thayer's ex-boyfriend met them at a bar in another arrondisse-ment, after they'd changed back into their own clothes and fled the Louvre, like art thieves. Diego, the ex-boyfriend, had been at the show to watch Thayer, but didn't mention the fall until Lou brought it up. He told her it wasn't that bad. He was so kind, Lou almost felt like apologizing to him for disrupt-ing what was an otherwise once-in-a-lifetime experience. She thought it was nice he was there. It felt like proof that people could be friends with their exes. Maybe she could be friends with Ivy again someday, or at least adults who knew each other.

Diego wasn't a model. He was a normal-looking person, with a bright smile and curly hair, who lived in Paris year-round. He was a writer, like Thayer, but he wrote essays and articles for his university's paper, not plays. He had the same interview style of conversation as Lou's mom.

"How do you like modeling?" Diego asked her, after he'd paid for her glass of wine. "Have you been doing it long?"

"I liked it until an hour ago," Lou said. "And it's my first season."

"Do you think you'll do it again next year?"

"Not after today." She was half joking. In truth, Lou hadn't given it any real thought. She had parachuted to this point in her modeling career. It was hard to imagine deciding to get back into the plane, let alone jumping again, but it also seemed like it would only get easier.

"Olympians fall all the time, don't they?" Diego said. "Why can't models?"

Lou shook her head. "It's not the same."

"It was pretty astounding," Thayer said.

Lou liked how she said it: *astounding*. Like it had added to the art of everything, not detracted from it.

"This wine is really good," Lou said. She was drinking in order to not look at her phone, because she was very scared. Her intention was to get drunk and then ask Mari or Harrison to look for her. She'd already missed several calls from Yukon, which couldn't be good. They never called her, only texted or emailed. "Like, it tastes good."

Thayer laughed. "Does it usually not?"

Not the Liquid Popsicle wine Catherine brought on camping trips. Lou had another glass, and she felt melty and nice, sitting next to Thayer, their knees pressing into each other. Thayer wore a black fisherman's sweater and skinny slacks, and Lou had on a green hoodie and jeans, but she didn't feel out of place in this catacomb bar in Paris, mostly because Thayer seemed so relaxed that Lou didn't question that they both fit in perfectly.

At some point, Diego started flirting with another woman in a long lace skirt on the other side of the room, and Thayer got closer and closer to Lou. The signals that in the past had been lost on her were suddenly very clear. Thayer wanted to be kissed, and so when they left the bar to get some air, Lou kissed her up against a vine-covered wall in the alleyway. An ivy-covered wall, it occurred to her. This was different from kissing Ivy, less terrifying, but it was soft and warm and easy. She felt like there was a small flame inside of her, a flame she could feel the outline of. Thayer rubbed her thumb just under the hem of Lou's hoodie and Lou slipped her hand to the warmth of Thayer's back, beneath her sweater to a thin, soft, tucked-in shirt. Somewhere on the other side of the world, Ivy was waking up on the morning of another show, and maybe she was meeting fans who loved her music and wanted to kiss her, and maybe Lou needed to stop pretending they were together, that they ever had been.

Lou and Thayer went back to Lou's apartment, found an empty bedroom, and locked the door before anyone else got back. Lou knew it was a dick move, but she'd had it done to her in New York. It felt heady and strange to be kissing someone she didn't know well but was extremely attracted to. Her body hummed as Thayer took off her shirt and peeled down her jeans, then lay there, looking up at Lou. Lou asked what she wanted, and Thayer told her. Lou didn't know what to do, but she knew how to follow directions. She could put her mouth there and there and there, and she could move her tongue like that and that, and she could do everything that was asked of her, especially if she was asked like that, and it turned out she could do it all well, like *really* well. Thayer smelled and tasted delicious and Lou was so hungry, and as soon as it was over, she wanted to do it again.

Harrison took her out to breakfast the next morning. He said he wanted to talk to her about something, and she assumed a pep talk was coming, a big old pep talk for the girl who had destroyed her burgeoning future with a single sticky veil and an empty stomach. He was the first person to show her the footage.

"Wow," Lou said. Her body didn't look as awkward midair as she thought, but her face burned just thinking about the moment of going down, combined with the moment of going down on Thayer, and how now she was just sitting there, eating a croissant like everything was chill and normal.

"You're a legend," Harrison said, but he sounded concerned.

"Is my career over?"

"Have you talked to your agent?"

"I'm too scared. Will you look for me?"

Harrison held out his hand and she placed her phone in it. She closed her eyes while he scrolled. Silence. When she opened them again, he was staring at her phone, mouth ajar.

"You're booking *everything*."

Lou leaned in to look at her phone, heart pounding. "What? How is that possible?"

"They noticed you."

"Who's they?"

"Whoever's cool," he said.

She listened to the nine messages Yukon had left her, each one getting more excited as the requests for her grew, as she started booking things. Big things. Bigger than the Pete Webbs shoot. The most immediate news was that there was a shoot in Tokyo that Yukon wanted her to fly out to as soon as Paris Fashion Week was over, shot by a famed Japanese fashion photographer. All five of her remaining shows in Paris were safe, except for one, which had pulled out, citing the distracting press. But otherwise, she was blowing up, booking shoots months in advance. It didn't make any sense.

The thing that was more surprising than the bookings was how much the Internet loved the video. Not because she had tripped. Because she was laughing. Comment after comment about the laughing. The Internet adored it. They thought she was a different person, someone who reacted to pain with joy.

Which apparently meant they couldn't see the fear in her eyes.

In addition to the laughing, they also loved Thayer. Thayer, the only person who had helped her. The Internet loved her and Thayer and the perceived relationship there. There were a dozen articles about it, calling them a highlight of the Paris shows, if not the highlight of the season. They were real, in a world of artifice. So went the think pieces.

Reporters had dug up everything they possibly could on Lou: her high school track races, an essay contest she'd won in middle school on what made a good citizen, and her volunteer hours with the Audubon Society. She learned more about Thayer from one listicle than she had in the hours they'd spent together in real life.

The waiter brought their coffees. She texted Thayer, *Can I see you before I leave?*

The world wills it, Thayer responded. *Might as well get on board.*

Lou smiled down into her phone.

"What?" Harrison said.

Lou shook her head.

"Shut up. Thayer de Silva? I knew it."

"You don't know anything."

"I know how she was looking at you in New York. I know how she looked at you when you ate shit off the Chanel catwalk. You like her?"

"I don't know her that well."

"Sometimes, that's the best way."

"Oh yeah? What about Tuck?"

"Who says I know Tuck? And who says we're even talking anymore?"

"Are you?"

Harrison shook his head.

"Why not?"

"Because I'm a fuckup," Harrison said. He got quiet, sipping on his coffee. A woman in a platter of a hat walked by. It was still Fashion Week out here. The looks abounded, even on pedestrians. The air felt heavy again.

"When are you going back to New York?" Lou said.

"That's actually why I wanted to talk to you. I'm moving home."

"What? When?"

"After the shows."

"But you love modeling."

"I like it," Harrison said. "But it's still a job. It made sense before. For a long time. It doesn't anymore. My brothers need me, back in Portland. My dad does. Nobody lasts more than five years anyway. I'm at four."

She thought about Harrison's apartment, how it had felt like a home where she could land, when the craziness of fashion month was over. She must have looked upset, because Harrison grabbed her hand and held it on top of the table.

"You're going to be so busy," he said. "We wouldn't have seen each other anyway. But we will now. Whenever you come home, I'll get to see you."

She felt like she might burst into tears. Her eyes stung, and she tried to swallow her disappointment down into a dry throat. She wanted him to do what was right for him, but he was also her final connection to home, the last 1 percent of battery before she was stranded somewhere, alone, with no directions and no one coming for her.

"Besides," Harrison said. "I'm the one who taught you how to walk. Now I have to retire in shame." He nudged her, and she rested her head on the table. He stroked her hair. "You're my finest work, Lou. While also my most disappointing."

5

She had a few days before her flight to Tokyo, and Thayer asked if she wanted to go on a day trip with her to the sea, near Normandy. What Lou knew about Thayer from the articles about them online: Thayer was twenty. It was her third fashion season, but she was just now gaining traction in the industry, booking bigger shows. She and her ex had a well-documented relationship on social media, but the Internet had deduced what Thayer had told her last night: they had broken up a few months before, after a two-year open relationship, mostly long-distance. She was single.

What Lou knew not from the Internet: Thayer had a wide grin and a hiccupping laugh. She wanted to write plays and act in them. She'd grown up surfing in the Pacific, outside of Vancouver, and she and Mari went together sometimes. She wasn't over her ex, but then, neither was Lou, so they talked about it. It was easy to talk to Thayer. It was easy for the Internet to believe they had fallen in love at first nightmare-fall. In fact, it was very good. Lou kept feeling like every time she picked up her phone, there would be a text from Ivy. She had to have seen it. Everyone had. People from every corner of her old life were texting and DMing her. Her old track coach. Her parents' friends. People she hadn't talked to since elementary school, asking what she was up to, as if it was a coincidence of timing.

No word from Catherine either. Lou hadn't heard from her since they'd FaceTimed, when Catherine was drunk in her dorm room. She wondered what Tuck had said to her parents, if anything. Maybe she should have called them herself. Maybe Catherine had actually just been faking sleep, and after Lou hung up the phone she had gotten back in the car and drove it into a tree and no one had called her because no one had thought to call her, or had any way to get in touch with her, because she was in Paris, tripping in the Louvre.

By the time Thayer picked her up midmorning, Lou felt like she was going to explode from the expectations placed upon them, which were suddenly real, not just an illusion in a browser. She had gotten used to her body being inspected and commented on in person and online, but not her personality, not her love life. People on social media could say all they wanted about her waist and the way her eyes were set and her forehead and her ears, but it felt disorienting to read about who they thought she theoretically was, without a clear grip on who she actually was.

Thayer didn't seem nervous at all. She pulled up to the corner of Lou's model apartment in a tiny rental car with a surfboard on top. She wore a red shirt. Her long brown curls were pulled back in a bun.

"You want to learn?" Thayer said. "I brought an extra wetsuit."

"I want to watch you." She didn't want to explain about her eardrum, how even if she wanted to get in cold water in the fall, which she definitely didn't, she couldn't without doing lasting damage.

It was the first time she'd seen the ocean, or something that looked like the ocean, in months. It was technically the English Channel, but it fed into the Atlantic, somewhere. It was dark and stormy out, but little birds were zipping around. She used to go to the coast with her family almost every weekend in the summer, and often for the holidays. The Oregon coast was cliff-filled and empty. This stretch of beach was made of pebbles, not sand, and there were lots of people walking up and down it. It was almost too cold to sit, but Thayer said the conditions were best in October, with the water breaking off the reefs.

Lou watched her zip up her wet suit and walk toward the water. There were a few other surfers out, black-suited shadows bobbing in the waves. Lou wished she had worn a hat. Her ears hurt from the cold. She watched the people walking by, and it was surreal to be surrounded by families again, little kids. Everyone seemed very short, compared to all the models she'd been around for the last couple of months. A toddler stomped around on the pebbles, with a hovering dad holding out his arms in case the baby teetered too far.

Thayer attached the anklet cord to herself and walked out into the surf without any hesitation, until she was deep enough in to paddle out on her board. So she wasn't the kind of person who imagined her own death.

But when Thayer dived under a wave, Lou's heart started to

race. She suddenly had a very bad feeling, like a storm cloud had appeared, though the day had already been overcast. They were in Normandy, where one of her great-grandfathers had fought for the Americans on D-Day. She'd heard her mother tell the story before. How he'd been in one of the last waves of soldiers, which meant that he wasn't killed, could return to his family's ranch in eastern Oregon and have a bunch of kids. But Lou's mind wasn't on him returning, procreating, raising cattle and children in the mountains. It was on men with guns storming a beach. It was on dodging bullets. It was on the way they might have looked in the water, drowning.

Thayer popped back up and waved at Lou. Lou's throat felt like it was locking up and she couldn't stand it anymore. She stood up, ran to the edge of the water, and waved her arms. Thayer waved back. She was really far out now, in open water where even Lou knew people couldn't surf. None of the other surfers were anywhere near her. Lou tried to keep her eye on all of them, but it was impossible. One would catch a wave, and there would still be four or five out there, plus Thayer, drifting farther and farther away.

Lou was screaming then. She stopped caring. She didn't want to see her go under again. She didn't want to see the sea swallow her. Finally Thayer started paddling back in, and as she got closer, Lou didn't get any calmer. She just felt more and more certain the gentle waves were going to be the ones that sucked her down. It felt like a thousand people were going to come storming just over the horizon. She knew that she was screaming still, but her throat could only make a sound like a whistle.

Thayer was rushing in and asking her something, and Lou didn't know anymore what she was saying. She became aware of just how sore her knees were, and when she looked down, they were black and blue and she couldn't remember how they'd gotten that way, and it felt like they might stay like that forever, like she was dyed bruised, like it was something a stylist had done to her when she wasn't looking. She wiped at them and they hurt more. She became aware that Thayer was saying her name, louder now. But she was saying it like her mother did, *Louisa*, and she had no idea how Thayer knew that was her real name. Maybe Lou had told her. Maybe the Internet had. Maybe it was a lucky guess. Thayer was holding her very tightly and Lou smelled the same detergent from the other night, and that was something solid to hold on to even though it wasn't solid, it was in the fabric, in the air, Lou burrowing her face into Thayer's wet shoulder, the sun suddenly out, warm on them, as if it had been summer all along.

Back in Paris, they had black coffee and sandwiches at a café near Thayer's hotel, and neither of them mentioned what had happened at the beach. They ate quickly, as if they both wanted the day to be over with. Afterward, Thayer offered to drop Lou back at her apartment, but Lou waved her off, kissing her goodbye on both cheeks like she had learned to do, but slowly, like they might never see each other again. Which was entirely possible. Fashion month was over. The shows were over.

Thayer held her by the shoulders and looked at her for a long moment. "Are you sure?" But it felt like she was asking something else.

"It'll be good to walk," Lou said.

"Just don't fall," Thayer said, and the awkwardness of the day finally broke.

Lou really did think she'd feel better if she was alone, with time to process, like she'd had for that single day in Italy. But being alone in the rainy dark in that moment didn't feel at all like the brightness of her afternoon wandering around Rome, people watching and sketching in her journal. It just felt like home.

She missed her parents, and she already missed Harrison, who hadn't even left yet, and she missed Ivy. Lou's shirt smelled like coffee from the café and it brought to mind all the afternoons she and Ivy had spent together in the dark booth in Portland the previous winter, rain battering the windows.

As Lou rounded the street corner toward the tall tan apartment building, she noticed a group of people huddled beneath the awning, near the entrance. As she approached, the group aimed themselves at her, and she realized they were there for her. They were mostly middle-aged men in raincoats and white sneakers, but all of them were holding up cameras, yelling, waving their arms at her, as if there was a roadside emergency she could help with.

"Lou!" they were shouting. "Louuuu!" Her name held that long sounded like a booing crowd.

Their cameras were clicking like a giant machine. She blocked the flashbulbs with her elbow; despite all her training not to blink, she couldn't stop against the barrage of light. She'd never heard that many going at once, a fluttering pack, weaponized against her.

Paparazzi, Lou realized. It felt so bizarre that of everyone on the planet they'd want to ambush, she could be anywhere on the list. She hadn't starred in anything. Hadn't won anything. She'd tripped in the wrong place.

The crowd started to grow as strangers coming off the street held up their phones with screens facing her. As she tried to make her way to the door, she realized they were trying to take selfies with her, craning their necks to capture their own faces beside her in the frame. Most of them probably didn't even know who she was, what she could possibly be famous for, if she was famous at all, or why anyone was taking her picture. They just wanted in on whatever was happening.

"Oh, don't be so shy, Lou," a man said, an American. He leered at her behind his camera. A woman put another phone in her face and Lou saw her own startled expression, her wet bangs with eyes blinking rapidly underneath. She didn't have the word for *stop* in French so she kept asking in English, "Please stop. Stop. Stop."

But no one was reacting to her; it was as if her voice didn't exist, as if her body was moving on without her. As she tried to get closer to the building's entrance, pushing through the humid tunnel of hands and phone screens and camera lights flashing, she lost her sense of direction entirely. On another day, she would have felt panic. But she was already drained of it. The last of it had come out in a whistle scream on the pebbled beach. She didn't know which way to go, so she stood still and let them take what they wanted.

She might have stood there forever, the people rotating around her, if a familiar face hadn't fought her way to the center of the crowd, shouting in French, spitting it, until the people began to back away. Keeley Dot, Alabaman ambassador and vibrator connoisseur and now the officially loudest person Lou had ever met, scaring the shit out of a whole block of Paris.

Keeley Dot grabbed Lou's hand and guided her into the building, elbowing the last few men with cameras out of the way, and locking the door behind them with one last scream over her shoulder in French.

They were both drenched and breathing hard. Keeley Dot broke into a laugh as they climbed the stairs up to their floor. "Well, those folks are a bag of dicks," she said.

"Thank you," Lou said, after she'd caught her breath. The air in the hallway was stale. "I didn't know you speak French."

"Oh, I don't," Keeley Dot said. "But I took two years in high school." She paused at the top of the landing, considering. "Pretty sure I told them to go eat a bicycle. But I sure was commanding, *oui?*"

Dark spots pulsed in her vision, the afterimages of all those needy bulbs. Lou remembered something she'd learned in biology class, about how surgeons wore blue gowns and masks to help with eye fatigue, because blue was complementary to orange. She wondered if that meant organs were more orange than red. She didn't want to know.

Keeley Dot was messing with the key in the lock and chronicling a time when she'd failed a French test because she'd spent the night before stealing a car and driving to New Orleans with her friends instead of studying the conditional tense, but Lou had lost the thread of the story, staring down at the stairs, as if she expected her own body to be at the bottom of them.

Keeley Dot paused, taking in Lou's hand white-knuckling the banister, her wet face. "Oh, honey, who do you want me to call?"

It took Thayer only a few minutes to get there, and Lou was glad to have Keeley Dot to tell the story of what had happened, so that Lou didn't have to explain why she'd frozen like that, or how she was feeling now. The three of them hung out in the apartment for the rest of the night, watching movies with a crowd of other models that Keeley Dot gathered from their bedrooms. People drifted in from after-parties and joined them; some left with luggage in the middle, off to catch flights elsewhere. Jia and Eline came after their shows, even though they were staying in an apartment in another arrondissement. It began to feel like the night of her high school graduation, when she and her track friends had stayed up all night in Catherine's basement, unwilling to give in until dawn, until high school was officially over—giddy with relief and so tired they couldn't sleep. Keeley Dot had told everyone what had happened to Lou, and everyone agreed that while it would certainly be good for her career—all the exposure (and it was, Lou agreed, exposure)—it was still shitty.

"It happened to me after the Milan shows," Keeley Dot said. "I didn't fall off a catwalk or anything, but they're apparently just that interested in what I'm wearing on my way to breakfast. And it would have been fine if I was alone—it was only like three or four of them, nothing like what you just had to deal with, Lou—but my *mom* was with me. And y'all know how much Connie loves modeling, loves fashion, loves the drama of it, but honest to goodness afterward, she told me that she wasn't sure she wanted me to do it anymore, if it was going to be like this."

"Didn't she bodycheck one of them?" Thayer said.

"Sure did," Keeley Dot said. "One of them even tried to sue, but Connie eviscerated him on Twitter, and he dropped the lawsuit."

Some of the other models broke in with their own stories, most of them unrelated to any fame from modeling—one of them had nannied for a famous actor who was going through a divorce and got ambushed with him at the Los Angeles Zoo, in front of the hedgehog habitat, with all four of his children; another happened to be at baggage claim when a K-pop band got mobbed by fans, and described it as the most terrifying experience of their life. Jia had a friend back in Singapore who'd secretly dated a member of the Malaysian royal family when they were in high school, and they'd all been chased onto a mall escalator, trapped at the top and bottom by photographers.

"It felt like we were in a video game," Jia said. "But the photos never surfaced. Someone probably paid a lot of money to bury it."

Eline had once been photographed by the Norwegian paparazzi, when she was dating a fellow member of their national soccer team, but said they were oddly polite. "They kept asking if it was okay, and we were like, no? No, thank you?"

In all the thoughts she'd ever had about photography and why it was too uncertain a career path, Lou hadn't given much thought to the sinister side of it—how images were their own currency, their own power. At least if she went to school for ecology she could just be alone with binoculars at a pond, and worry less about exploiting people.

After a while, Lou got sleepy and zoned out, looking out the window at the rain. Thayer kept her arm around Lou all night, but never tried to make her join the larger conversation. Lou liked how it felt to be close to her: warm, quiet, and safe, surrounded by people who understood exactly where she had gotten herself, but didn't want to look at her.

When Lou woke up in the morning, for a moment all she could see was Thayer in the waves: a dark body, floating, and herself on the shore. Cameras were still clicking in her brain. She felt like she was falling forward. All of it seemed to mean something, but she didn't know what.

Thayer was already awake, looking at her phone. Lou felt calmer, watching her, and for once, she didn't want to second-guess what that meant.

"I don't know where I'm going to live," Lou said. She said it more to herself than to Thayer, after remembering the conversation with Harrison. She needed to make it register.

"Are you going to move home?"

"My plan was to go back to New York. But then my housing situation fell through."

"My roommate Eito and I have a place in Greenpoint. He's with Superb too. It's like a thirty-minute subway ride to the agency."

Lou nodded. "That sounds ideal."

"Come live with us."

"Are you serious? You wouldn't mind?"

Thayer looked at her like she'd never minded anything in her life.

The model on the top bunk lowered a single middle finger to them. "Shut the fuck up," whoever it was said, in a British accent. "Please."

"I wouldn't mind," Thayer whispered.

PART FIVE

I

By Halloween, Lou was smoking a joint through a moose mask, settled on a fire escape with Thayer and their roommate and a couple of drag queens in LED bikinis. It often seemed like people in the industry were wearing costumes around her when they weren't, but Halloween was proving to be a whole other level. Someone inside was dressed as a Metro-Card. Another was a working traffic light, with a green left arrow. Everyone at the party knew professional makeup artists or they were professional makeup artists, and they knew how to sew or their best friend or brother or roommate sewed costumes for Broadway or drag shows or the opera. So far, Lou had had to google three of the four costumes of people she'd talked to. One guy dressed in white and off-white cloth acted offended when Thayer had asked if he was a blank canvas, which Lou thought was a pretty generous guess. He told them he was a Kazimir Malevich painting, and Thayer looked like she was going to punch him in the face, even though Lou had no idea who that was. Thayer said her goal for Halloween was never to be anything so self-referential that she had to explain herself over and over, but for most people at the party, that seemed to be the objective. Lou got it; it felt cool to find the one person who really got and appreciated a deep-cut costume. Then again, one year in elementary school she'd gone as an amoeba, and her teacher was the only one who got it, and that had been embarrassing. Well, also her dad, who was delighted.

When Lou had woken up in Thayer's bed that morning, which was technically now *her* bed, the apartment had been quiet, with no one rushing off to work for once, and she'd walked barefoot to the kitchen and made them coffee, thinking how peaceful it was, how nice to finally be alone after the chaos of the shows—only to have the same rooms turn to bright sexy spectacle by 11:00 p.m., when the partygoers arrived, elaborate as any runway.

Their roommate, Eito, had only decided he was throwing the party that morning. Thayer insisted they dress up in something handmade, and so she returned to the apartment with two grocery bags full of materials and demanded to know what kind of animal Lou would be, if she could be any kind of animal, which felt weighty, like she was asking for her birth chart. They'd spent the rest of the day working on their masks, spread out across the kitchen table with paste and tubes of acrylic and old editions of *The New York Times*. It had been the most normal fun Lou had had since moving to New York, her fingernails sticky with glue and paint, eating spring rolls while the masks dried on the balcony.

Thayer's mask was a toucan. She'd crumpled the long papier-mâché beak by accident when she opened the fridge into it. Now she was wearing it like a hat. Lou's moose was sleepy-looking, with Popsicle-stick antlers. The only moose she'd ever seen had been on a road trip with her family to Yellowstone: she saw one in a meadow, screamed for them to pull over, and her mom almost crashed the car into a herd of bison. That whole trip, she'd wanted to see a grizzly bear—from inside the car, with all the windows rolled up, obviously—but she didn't realize until she was staring at the moose that this was way better. It was enormous. Alien, but cartoonish. Like something out of a Bill Peet picture book. Lou's moose looked a little like a poodle.

On the fire escape, Eito told them the word for *moose* in Japanese translated to *spatula deer*. Lou drew a spatula deer on a napkin, with a long face and antlers that could scoop cake batter.

Thayer was looking at her phone, her head resting on Lou's shoulder. Lou glanced down and saw Diego's name at the top of the screen.

"Someone just set the couch on fire," Eito said nonchalantly. He was looking back through the window behind them. Eito had what their shared agent Yukon called *egregious cheekbones*. His long black hair was tied in a knot at the base of his neck, and he wore a pair of sequined child-size butterfly wings over a motorcycle jacket.

"Should we . . . stop them?" Lou said.

Eito squinted through the glass. "Now it's out."

The MetroCard ducked through the window, pulled Eito to standing, and they started to dance, hands gripping the railing.

Thayer still didn't look up from her phone.

"How's Diego?" Lou asked her. She didn't mean it in a suspicious way. She was just curious. Thayer didn't seem to mind questions like this. She was more confident in what she liked than anyone Lou had ever met. Even when there had been a half dozen paparazzi outside their door when Lou had first moved in—she'd felt grateful not to own any sex benches, with the way their cameras were going off at her piled belongings—Thayer didn't seem to care. She kissed Lou in front of all of them and helped carry her bags to the fifth-floor walkup. It felt so different from being ambushed in Paris. Fun, even.

"Needy."

Lou took a long sip of her drink. It was hard to reconcile needy with the guy she'd met in Paris, with his confident reporter energy. "Why did you leave Paris?"

"He proposed," Thayer said, lowering her bird mask.

Lou didn't know anyone who was old enough to be proposed to. "And you said no?"

"I said not now. Like, try me in ten years, bud. But Diego is big into gestures. He always does things just for the story. His story." Thayer took the joint from Lou and relit it, smiling. "But I like my story better. We still hang out. Sometimes we hook up. Anyway, he'll always be one of my people."

Lou knew Thayer hooked up with other people. They'd talked about it the week she moved in. Lou didn't have any interest or any time to do the same, but it felt lower pressure to have it on the table. "Talking to him now doesn't make you sad?"

"What does being sad feel like to you?"

Thayer was always saying things like this, trying to get to the bottom of things, trying to excavate what was automatic to other people. Last week when Lou said that she was trying to pay attention more, Thayer had asked her what she meant by that, what paying attention actually was, and Lou had no idea how to respond. She wasn't used to having to investigate her immediate feelings, let alone the psychological roots of them, let alone their etymology. But she didn't mind it.

"Like this, kind of," Lou said. "Like not knowing anyone on Halloween." She hadn't known that was the feeling until she spoke it. Earlier that morning, Thayer had read her a scene from her play in bed, in a T-shirt and underwear, the filmy white curtains waving in the open window, and Lou had felt like she was living someone else's life, an adult she'd know someday who'd be incredible company. But as the party wore on, that feeling of wonder had transitioned into something heavier. This was her life, not someone else's—the adult, if she stayed here, would be her.

"You know me," Thayer said.

The way Thayer looked at her, head tilted to the left, Lou felt like she was meant to be overcome by something, that Thayer was used to getting a reaction out of this expression, out of all her tenderness and openness and confidence. Instead, it reminded her of seeing someone over FaceTime, like Thayer was looking at herself in the little window in the corner, not at the camera, not at Lou. Maybe that wasn't how it was intended. Maybe she'd only ever looked this way at Lou. But Lou didn't have her own look to return. She had no practice at this. It wasn't easy for her. The more she thought about it, the more she was surely making faces like she thought the balcony might give way.

"Sorry, I have to pee," Lou said, and stood up. She climbed back through the window before Thayer got another word out. The couch was too covered in a group of people dressed as Ninja

Turtles, with full shells, to see any singe marks, but she didn't feel any calmer.

Lou ran into Sienna on the way to Thayer's bedroom. Lou had invited her, not expecting she'd really come. Sienna wasn't wearing a costume, which made Lou feel too high suddenly. Her hands felt heavy.

"Taking a breather, *cara*?" Sienna said.

"Yeah," Lou said, but sound barely came out. She swallowed. Her throat was dry.

"You need anything?"

Lou didn't know what she needed.

"Wait here." Sienna retreated back through the costumed people toward the kitchen. She returned a minute later with a full glass of water and led Lou into Thayer's bedroom. She sat her down on the bed and handed her the water.

"Thanks," Lou said.

Sienna closed the door behind them and sunk down with her back against it, like she was barricading them in, and let out a long breath. Her black hair was in a long braid over her shoulder. She wore wire-framed glasses over her dark eyebrows and a satin jacket that Lou recognized as Mari's. Or maybe it had been Sienna's all along.

Thayer's mattress was on the floor, covered in a honey-colored afghan her grandmother had knit her, and Lou thought she might be able to sleep right now, even with all the noise outside the room. Her body was so confused by the ongoing jet lag that it never quite knew when to wake up or go to sleep. Sunset was constantly surprising her.

"That yours?" Sienna said, nodding at Lou's Nikon on the desk, one of the only objects in the room that belonged to her.

Lou had barely brought anything from home. Thayer had lived in this apartment for a year, and it was neat but lived-in, with two full bookshelves, mostly stacked with plays and thin books of poetry.

Lou took the camera off the desk and held it in her hands, like that was the real reason she'd left Thayer on the balcony. She liked the weight of it.

"Mind if I take a look?" Sienna said.

She didn't know if she wanted Sienna to see it, but she handed it over anyway. It felt too awkward to say no, too much like she was hiding something. Her SIM card was full, and she hadn't uploaded anything except Harrison in the Boboli Gardens. It felt like if she erased it, the emptiness of it, the blank screen, would kill her.

Sienna's expression was neutral as she clicked through, going backward in time, and Lou felt self-conscious that a professional was seeing her snapshots of friends and teammates and her parents in the backyard. It made her feel like a kid, acting at something.

"I like this one," Sienna said, holding out the camera to Lou. Lou's heart stopped for a second, remembering the shot of Morgan at the top of the falls. But it was only Ivy running, a streak of light, the red towers extending overhead. The fence and grass were in perfect focus. She didn't realize how long she'd been looking at it, zooming in, zooming out, before Sienna nudged her.

"What do you think?" Sienna said.

"Is it good?"

"Does it matter what I think?"

"Yes."

"Why?"

"Because you know what you're talking about."

"And you don't?"

"I know what I like, but I don't know what's good."

"What's the difference?"

Lou took the camera back, looked at the image for longer. Ivy was in the very far corner of the frame, as if she might burst through it. It made Lou feel the thing she felt that night. A longing without end. "It's a good photograph. And I like it."

"Agreed," Sienna said.

"Do you ever need any help?" Lou asked.

"All the time," Sienna said. She took off her glasses and ran a finger over the bridge of her nose.

"With shoots, I mean," Lou said.

"Oh." Sienna smiled. "Sure."

Lou assisted Sienna for the first time at the beginning of December. The yellow gingko leaves had fallen in Central Park. Lou's dad once told her gingkoes were two hundred million years old, which technically made them fossils. That scale of time sometimes terrified Lou, in the way she didn't always like looking at the stars at night, especially when she was alone. In this case, it only made her feel connected to something. These trees and Lou had ended up in the same small field, against all odds.

For the last couple of months, she'd been modeling for a shoot a week, at least. She'd flown to California for a whole week of commercial work. An Adidas photo team picked her up for the shoot in an unmarked gray van at the Arrivals curb at

LAX. Clearly she'd gotten very trusting. Yukon had sent her the license plate number in a text, with accompanying details: *Gray Ford Transit, license htb 236. Photog has worked with our girls lots, but he was rude to me at a Givenchy party so give him some trouble.* Beyond that, she had no way to know these people were who they said they were. The van was full of a crew of goofy German guys who kept making comments about how short she was, the first time in her life that had ever happened.

"You are so tiny," one of them said, "you are practically not even here."

After that, she went back to Paris, where she did an editorial shoot on the banks of the Seine, wearing a feathered gold jumpsuit that kept shedding, and had to kiss a male model in vibrant blue eye makeup. They both kept laughing, and the photographer got frustrated and made them do another pose, in which Lou was a kind of mechanic Icarus and the male model was a sea nymph, maybe, and they were very into each other. Some photographers were so directive that it was like being a mannequin, the photographer grabbing an arm and placing it exactly where they wanted, adjusting it a few centimeters only to move it back. Others wanted improvisation, acting, choice. They wanted Lou to jump and move and then settle back. Others wanted static, like a long slow yoga session, or how she imagined yoga to be—she'd never actually tried it, just watched Thayer in the living room. She knew she should have joined her, would have been able to do weirder and better poses if she was more flexible, but instead she went on long runs around whatever city she was in, too exhausted to stretch properly when she got back. In the week she was in Tokyo, Lou did six shoots, three commercials for cosmetics, and three editorials for Japanese fashion magazines. The cosmetics shoots were easier than anything else, because she didn't have to pose. Just hold her face very still. They paid so well that Lou would have stayed in Japan for a lot longer, saving money, eating conveyer-belt sushi, doing Technicolor shoots, if Yukon hadn't already booked her a ticket back to New York, where her career had more forward momentum, more potential. *Get thee back to the city*, Yukon's email read, with the attached ticket. *We have work to do.*

Lou started to like looking at her face and hair and body changing every day in a different mirror. The runway shows had been so quick, there was hardly time to inspect oneself. But photoshoots meant she was a different character, maybe, or a mood, a feeling, an embodiment of an aesthetic come to life, for only a day or two. When she was just herself, on the stretches of time off, when she slept in and wandered around a city, she didn't always recognize her own reflection.

In the park, Sienna directed her and the model to a spot between the gingko trees and asked Lou to hold the white light reflector on the left side of his body. She felt relaxed and happy, knowing she wouldn't have her own turn in front of the camera but got to enjoy it from this angle.

The model was a sweet-faced man named Wyatt, who'd grown up in Idaho. Lou's dad had once taken her fly-fishing near Wyatt's hometown, when she was in middle school. She remembered the buttery light and the beautiful clear pools and the green shoulders of streams where she and her dad would wait for trout that never seemed wholly convinced by their downy flies. Wyatt told them that he'd moved to New York with his boyfriend ten years prior, after they were both outed in high school. His boyfriend taught high school history in the

Bronx. Wyatt was getting a master's degree in engineering at
City College. He loved it. He loved the city. He was going to
propose to his boyfriend soon. He hoped modeling on the side
would help pay for the wedding.

Sienna talked to him about all of this so naturally, it was
like it was more a part of the job than composing the shot.
As she asked him questions, he loosened up before them, his
movements more emphatic and expressive, his eyes focused in
a different way. When he talked about his boyfriend, his gestures were fluid and light. When he talked about his parents,
about Idaho, everything grew hesitant, staccato. Lou wondered
if Sienna had done the same thing to her that day on the roof,
and how much she knew about Lou from how her body moved.

Wyatt had been scouted at a Mets game. *Was that how it
worked?* Lou wanted to know. Women scouted at malls and
men at professional sports events. What did that say about her
and the landscaping truck?

The shots they were getting that day were just to build Wyatt's
portfolio, so they were low pressure, the same kind of thing
she'd done with Anne in Portland. But this time, instead of
deciding how to pose, Lou was deciding where to hold the light
reflectors to highlight Wyatt's impressive jawline, switching out
lenses for Sienna as she requested them, guarding the bag of
the nicest photo equipment she'd ever been allowed to touch.
Certainly she'd seen nicer at recent shoots, her mouth watering
as she watched the photographers handle it so cavalierly. She'd
never talked to anyone about that feeling. Ivy used to talk to her
about guitars all the time without self-consciousness that she
was boring Lou, as if she knew that lighting up that way only
made Lou like her more, but Lou never really let herself feel

the need of her own obsessions long enough to be able to nerd out about them with anyone. She never assumed anyone would want to listen. But Sienna talked to her the entire time about what she was doing with her camera and the lighting and her angles, as if she was giving Lou a casual master class. She told Lou she'd introduce her to other photographers who'd give her work. But Lou only wanted to work for Sienna. She didn't want to work for a Pete Webbs, or someone worse.

"Any holiday plans?" Sienna asked them. Sienna was going home to visit her parents in Italy, she told them, but she didn't seem very excited about it.

Wyatt had started the shoot awkward and nervous but now he was singing a song for them from a show he and his boyfriend had just been to, very off-key but with utter joy. Lou was doubled over as she realized she didn't want to leave New York to go home. Didn't want to see Catherine, no longer sober, or her parents, who would have all kinds of questions about her future she didn't have the answers to, or even Harrison, who was living the life in Portland that might have been there for her too—going to school and maybe, a hard maybe, dating a member of Fortunato—if she'd stayed. She didn't think too much about it, because sometimes if she looked at it too closely, she wanted it so badly she couldn't stand it. But she wanted this too.

"I don't know," Lou said. "I might stay here."

Thayer had said they could spend the holidays together, if she wanted. Her family were Buddhists. She wasn't planning to go home to Vancouver until her birthday in the spring.

Lou didn't even know if her parents would be spending Christmas together, if they would want to. Before she left, she'd overheard them arguing about selling the house. Her mom had wanted to move somewhere on the east side, where they could walk to more places, be more central. Her dad wanted to stay where they were in the woods, on the edge of things. She didn't actually know what they'd decided on. Her parents didn't mention it on their phone calls. She didn't ask. Her brother hadn't come home the last few years for either holiday. She knew he was staying away on purpose, but they weren't close enough for her to ask why.

Wyatt was quiet for a minute, looking down with an entirely new expression on his face, like he was alone. "My boyfriend and I see his family, back in Twin Falls. My family's just . . . not open to it."

"You miss them," Sienna said, to both of them. Or maybe there was a question to it.

Wyatt bent down to tie his shoe in the fallen gingko leaves. Lou was thinking of her dad, standing on the bed of that creek in Idaho, pointing out different species of tree.

"Every day," Wyatt said.

2

After that, Lou finally promised her parents she'd come home for Christmas. Her parents were renting a house at the coast over the holidays. Her brother wasn't coming, but some of her parents' friends were. The addition of friends to this family tradition was an unnerving sign that either things were better enough between her parents that they could be around other people, or worse, that they needed more buffers than just Lou. But her mom had told Lou that if she didn't come home for Christmas, they'd come to her in New York, and she didn't want that.

"Invite anyone you want," her mom said. They'd be there a week. Everyone was welcome to come and go. Lou invited Harrison and Catherine for a few nights, without thinking at all about whether they would get along. Harrison seemed to get along with everyone. Catherine with no one. But it turned out they could only come on different days. Catherine had said yes immediately; she was on winter break from college. Harrison texted to ask whether he could bring Tuck, for the night he was able to get away. She didn't know they were in touch. But she told him yes, of course, without asking for more details. He hadn't mentioned Tuck once since he moved back.

Her parents had already been at the beach house a couple of nights with their friends by the time Lou's plane touched down at PDX, where they'd left a car for her in long-term parking. She approached the car expecting her parents to jump out from behind it, surprised by how badly she wanted them to be there to greet her, even if she'd been the one insisting it was fine, she preferred just to meet them at the beach. But no one jumped out. It was just an echoing parking garage, with other families' luggage clicking over the speed bumps.

Lou hadn't driven a car since the summer. Her foot felt a little shaky accelerating on the freeway, and she kept breathing on her hands and placing them at different positions on the wheel, as if it could slip out of her grip at any moment, no matter how tightly she held it. She didn't know if she was more nervous to be boxed in by semis driving ten over the speed limit or to be seeing her parents. What if they tried to talk her into moving back? What if there was a part of her that wanted them to? Or at least wanted them to try?

It was a relief not to take the exit for Aldenlight, if only to preserve the version of it that lived in her head. She descended the slick curves of the Coast Range, and pulled over as soon as the ocean was visible, just to be alone for a little longer. New York wasn't made for being alone, at least not in the world she was living in. She and Thayer shared a room in their six-hundred-square-foot apartment. Their roommate Eito's partner practically lived with them. Every room was almost always occupied. A closed door could be walked through at any time. Noises came from every angle. A wall drilled through. The ceiling line-danced upon. A broken snare drum hit in the alley. Sometimes she went to the library just to have her own carrel, her vision blocked out by the wood paneling. Even there, people still walked by, lingering at the shelves just behind her.

From the shoulder of the road, she spotted a wooden staircase leading down to the sand. Being back on the beach felt like the scale of her vision had changed; everything grew larger, wider, brighter, expanded. It was so quiet, her footsteps squeaked on the dry sand. There was no one behind or in front of her.

Lou watched the sunset by herself on a dune, beach grass snapping at her ankles, hair in her eyes, the last blip of gold slipping into the ocean before she remembered that she was there to see people, people who loved her, and she should probably go see them now.

The rental house had cedar shake siding and a yard full of buoys and oars and red madrone trees. It rested on a cliff covered in seagrass, overlooking the ocean. She climbed the steep steps in the dark, a single duffel bag over her shoulder, and the motion detector lights came on. By the way her parents opened the door for her, before she even knocked, they had clearly been watching out the windows for her arrival, which made her feel guilty and low to the ground, like she was a snake trying to slither past them on a trail. Her dad was wet-eyed, and her mom was smiling as they pulled her into separate hugs. Their gripping of her, like she would try to escape at any moment, wasn't like if she had gone away to college, though it should have been—it had been exactly the same amount of time her brother used to disappear from home, when he was away at school. Instead, it was like she'd returned from a one-woman sailing voyage.

The house had a high slanted ceiling, and it was bright and open, with all the lamps turned on and a woodstove roaring in the middle of the living room. It was much larger than any rental house her parents had ever gotten for Christmas before. Usually it was just the four of them in a shabby condo with nautical lamps. This felt more like a lodge than a house. She wondered why this was the year they splurged: if it was for her, their friends, or themselves. She wondered if they were lonely.

Catherine wouldn't arrive until the next day, so for now it was just Lou and a bunch of real adults. All their clothes looked very plain. She didn't know the last time she'd seen a person wear a microfleece pullover. Her whole childhood had been one long backstroke through a pool of microfleece. She loved their fleece, and she loved their terrible jeans and then judged herself for knowing they were terrible.

Her parents let her have some wine, because they knew she'd been in Europe—or so they said, maybe they just wanted her to relax—and she sat out with everyone on the deck. Her dad's two laid-back farmer friends from Wisconsin and her mother's best friend, David, and his beautiful new girlfriend, Sonya, were there; both of them worked with her at the paper. Over the last decade, most of their friends had taken buyouts or been laid off, but her mom and David had hung on. Her mom had mildly shit-talked his girlfriend over the phone, but seemed to be pretending to enjoy her now.

Sonya, eager, asked Lou how college was, and she realized her parents hadn't told anyone about what she was really doing.

"I'm working in New York actually," Lou said.

"I've always wanted to live in New York," Sonya said. It was a thing people said to her a lot now, when she was anywhere but New York. There was always a "But . . ." that followed like, "But it's too expensive" or "But it's too crowded" or "But then I visited." Lou had never wanted to live in New York. Ever since the moose in Yellowstone, Lou had wanted to live in Alaska, where there were both orcas and moose, but if she ever went to Alaska, she would never tell the people who lived there that it was a dream to live there but there was something wrong with it.

"She's living in New York and *modeling*," her mom offered to everyone, like it was still as startling to her now as it had been the past summer.

Then her parents' friends were all extremely curious about what modeling was like, and Lou didn't know how to explain to them. It was like trying to explain a long trip to someone: how she felt changed by it, but the details kept coming out boring or out of context. She ended up telling them about the Pete Webbs shoot but left out all the fucked-up parts. Instead, she told it as if she had been living the life her mom expected when she told Lou to take notes. Like it was all a good story.

But her dad cornered her later that night, when she was about to go to bed, and he walked her over to the overstuffed chairs by the woodstove and asked her to sit with him a minute. For a second, she thought he was going to tell her that he and her mom were splitting up for real, and the next time she came back to Portland, there wouldn't even be a reason to take the exit for home at all. Her throat clenched up, and she had the feeling that the ocean was going to suddenly rise with no warning and consume them up on this cliffside.

"I feel pretty jet-lagged," Lou said. "Can I just go to bed? We can talk in the morning?"

"Just sit a minute," he said. He went into the kitchen and got her a mug of tea and a beer for himself. "Please."

She sipped the tea. It was chamomile, with tiny bits of yellow flowers floating at the top. As a kid, Lou made him dandelion tea from the backyard all the time, and he always drank the whole thing, even though it occurred to her now just how muddy and disgusting it must have been.

Her dad tapped his beer on her mug. His graying beard was shorter, his hair longer, like it always was in winter, and he wore the same green flannel he'd had since she was a little kid, worn thin at the elbows, with his reading glasses tucked in the front pocket. He set his beer down, then watched her with his chin rested on his fist, like he expected her to speak first.

The fire in the woodstove was dying. She wanted to tell him about Wyatt, from Idaho, who reminded her of their fly-fishing trip, and how his family didn't talk to him anymore, and how she didn't realize until she was on the plane home just how sad it made her feel. Maybe her emotions were getting closer and closer to her, with less lag time, or maybe they were just stronger than they used to be, now that there was no one around who knew her very well to ask about them. But she didn't know if she could get all that out right now without crying. Seeing her dad in his old shirt and his sandy jeans, rubbing the back of his neck like he didn't know who she was or what to say to her, made her experience such tenderness for him that she felt like she couldn't ever live up to it, couldn't ever live up to who he believed her to be.

"I went to the library for you," Lou said. "I forgot to tell you."

"Did you see Patience and Fortitude?"

"What?"

"The lions. At the entrance."

Lou's eyes welled up, and she covered her face with the mug. She didn't know why her dad knowing the names of two lion statues made her cry, but it did. She wasn't even sure he'd ever been to New York.

"Lou, are you okay?"

She finished the tea in a few hot gulps. "What do you mean?" she said. Maybe she was stalling, pulling a Thayer, expanding the question out until it was more philosophical than emotional.

"What do I mean?" he repeated, sounding the words out like he was learning to read them. He seemed on the verge of something. Frustration, or fear, maybe, or something closer to the surface, a physical weariness, like she was a trench he was digging into. "I mean are people being good to you? Are you being good to them?"

She'd missed how her dad thought about things, like those were the categories. Like everything was so clear. Maybe the categories became clearer the further into adulthood one got, and the details got fuzzier. She wanted to tell him the real story of the Pete Webbs shoot. She wanted to, like it had been living right under her lungs this whole time and all she had to do was take in some air.

"In Italy, I broke this guitar."

She told him the rest of the story in the present tense, like it was happening to them both together, right then, Pete Webbs standing right over there, telling them to put their mouth on the mic. She didn't even realize that she was still thinking about that moment until just that moment, how it had felt to be on the other side of a stage from him, how no one had said anything, and how she knew it was nowhere near as bad as things that happened to other people in the industry, let alone the world, but what felt the worst to her was that he was a photographer: that he could act like that and still get to be what she wanted.

Her dad leaned over, looking straight at her. "Lou, I'm sorry that happened. It shouldn't have."

"Do you want me to stop modeling?" she said.

"I want you to call me more."

"Do you think I'm good to people?"

"Yes," he said, as if he spoke for everyone, not just her mom in the other room and her brother in another state and her friends all over the world, but everyone who had any love in them, as if answering the real question she had asked. The ocean roared out the window. "You have both fortitude and patience."

"I don't know if that's true," Lou said.

"It's true," her dad said. "And you'll know it."

3

There was a part of her that expected Catherine to look like she had on FaceTime. Small and curled up and drunk, about to put herself in danger. But instead, when she arrived at the house the next afternoon, she looked strong, like she'd gained ten pounds of muscle. Her head was shaved to a quarter inch of white blond fuzz. She wore a Ducks hoodie and track pants, and she hugged Lou so tightly that Lou almost started crying. Her body tensed, trying to prevent it.

"Don't be a pussy," Catherine whispered in her ear.

"Don't say pussy when you mean weak."

"Don't be a dick."

They walked down to the beach together, while her parents made dinner with their friends. The seagulls hovered in place overhead. Her body hummed with the residual fear of being around Catherine, as if she was going to call Lou out for something. Trying not to say the wrong thing slowed all her questions and answers.

"How did the rest of preseason go?" Lou said.

"You mean you haven't been stalking my race times? Because I have been very up on the situation with your model girlfriend and your beautiful love."

Lou blushed. "Tell me about the running."

"Still on the team. Did not get together with the sprinter. Did stop drinking." She said it in one string, as if it all belonged together, objects of similar size and shape. The ocean opened up in front of them, gray and stormy, whitecaps thrashing.

Catherine climbed some rocks on the edge of the surf and Lou felt hyperaware of watching her walk around on them, aware of choosing not to follow her up there, as if everything had suddenly gone HD and Catherine was a too-real person on a screen. A wave rushed in around her, filling in the tide pools, and Lou backed up, but for a second Catherine was marooned there, surrounded on a tiny island, before the tide went back out.

"Can you come back?" Lou called out to her, as it occurred to her that she had invited her two best friends to a giant body of water. "Dinner's probably ready."

Catherine stood for a second, looking out at the receding waves, as if she thought they were going to swarm her again if she moved too quickly.

"Cath?"

Finally, she hopped down from the rocks and put her arm around Lou, like she was about to give an overdue pep talk. Her body was shaking.

"I didn't use to be so nervous," Catherine said. "I'm like you now."

———

Later that night, she and Catherine fielded questions from the adults, who were wine drunk and happy. They all loved each other, and Lou's parents seemed to love each other too, at least right at that moment. Her dad's hand was curled around the back of her mom's chair, touching the gray at her temple absently, and at one point, he kissed her on the top of her head as he cleared the table. Her mom kept glancing over at him, whenever she said something that she thought was amusing. They seemed a unit again, in a way that was confusing; the last time Lou had been home, they'd only ever seemed to talk to each other about the logistics of fixing the house, as if they were going to put it on the market the second she left for college.

Her mom was interviewing Catherine about track. All the adults were impressed that she ran for Oregon. There was a lore to the program that even her dad's friends, who lived in Madison, seemed in awe of. It was how industry people reacted to Lou when she told them she was represented by Superb in New York. Like it held influence that she had nothing to do with but got to claim as her own making. Her parents didn't know to react that way to Superb. She could have been with any agency, walking for any designers; it would have all been the same to them. They'd have thought her equally lost.

"Do you feel like you can juggle academics and running?" her mom said to Catherine.

"Sure," Catherine said. "School's fine."

"See, Lou?" Lou's mom said. "You could do both. Why don't you enroll in New York?"

"It's not the same," Lou said.

"It's an elite level of something," her mom said. "I don't see why it couldn't be the same. Why can't you do some classes at a community college? Get some credits, for when you go to Oregon next year."

"Because I'm traveling all the time." And because she didn't know if she did want to go to Oregon next year.

Catherine saved her, though in doing so, pushed her into a different kind of danger.

"Did you see your daughter's famous now? And that she's dating an international supermodel?"

"You're dating someone?" her dad said to Lou.

"She's famous too," Catherine said. "Thayer de Silva."

"Jesus, Cath," Lou said. "Can you not?"

"What? She's extremely hot, everyone."

Her parents had seen about the Louvre, but they hadn't seen about Thayer, or heard of her, which made sense, given they didn't follow gossip or fashion sites, and apparently Catherine did, or she did expressly to troll Lou. Catherine passed her phone around so the adults could read the articles about her and Thayer, while Lou slunk all the way down her chair and under the table, like she used to do when she was a kid, to get some alone time while the adults crowed overhead. But she was happy to have the information out there, happy not to provide her own explanations just yet, when everyone was staring at her. Catherine said it better anyway.

Later that night, Sonya had started talking about her young daughters, telling an overlong story about their flute recital, when she looked at Catherine and Lou and said, "You two could be sisters, with your hair like that."

Which made Lou's whole body stiffen and screech. The layers of weird were impossible to unearth, would take a full team of gay archeologists. Or psychologists.

"My sister's dead, actually," Catherine said to Sonya, who looked horrified and said she was so sorry, sorry. "And we're just queers, ma'am."

Catherine laced her fingers through Lou's on top of the table, to accent it, and Lou choked on her drink. No one else said anything while Lou coughed ice water all over the empty plates. Catherine just smacked her on the back.

Her parents were washing wineglasses later, after everyone else had gone to bed, and Lou watched them from the doorway, the easy passing back and forth, her dad washing and her mom drying. They were laughing about something. Suddenly, she felt completely outside of them in a way that felt nice and unexpected. Like they could just be two people and here she was, a third person who loved them. She'd unhooked from the space shuttle. She had her own oxygen. Them breathing theirs didn't mean she couldn't breathe hers.

Before Catherine left for Portland in the morning, to go back to her own family, she and Lou went on a run together just after dawn, through the old-growth rain forest behind the house. Everything smelled so fresh, like snapped-off wood, like a freshness that had existed before cities, before the invention of concrete or rubber. Lou had been going on runs but not at this breakneck pace, so Catherine did all the talking while Lou tried to identify ferns in her head to keep from puking.

Catherine's coach had said if she trained really hard, she might have a shot at the NCAA championships in the spring, but then Catherine's tone changed, grew exasperated like she was running uphill, but they weren't. They were finally on a downslope, maneuvering a little ravine. "Just so you know, Lou, I'm sober for running. Not because anyone else thinks I should be. Not my coach. Not my parents. Nobody but me."

"Okay," Lou said, and she was worried that maybe Catherine was going to call her out again, that maybe confiding in Tuck was a bad idea. "Got it."

But then Catherine looked at the creek bed like it was a never-ending track and smiled. "But it's not so bad," she said.

Lou tried to catch her breath. Her muscles burned in a good way. The sun was breaking through the woods, right in their eyes.

Maidenhair fern.

Lady fern.

Sword fern.

After Catherine left, Tuck and Harrison's arrival loomed over the rest of her time there, projecting some knowledge of Ivy that flickered at her from the corners as she and her parents and their friends built fires on the beach and ate warm and elaborate meals. Even on Christmas itself, after presents, when her parents asked if she was actually dating Thayer, the woman from the articles, and Lou said, actually, yes, and they were living together, and they wanted to know all about her, she was still thinking of Ivy. Why was it so easy to tell them about Thayer, when for years whenever the topic of Ivy came up, her body felt like it was going to erupt into flames and spread through the house?

The aggression of how badly she'd once wanted Ivy seemed out of scale in relationship to Thayer, who'd been texting her cute pictures all week from Berlin, where she was doing a shoot. It turned out you could just like a person, and they could just like you. It didn't have to be a volcano you were studying for years. It could just be a hill, and you could walk to the top and look around and tell everyone later how nice the view was.

The boys arrived after dark. Lou heard them coming up the long gravel driveway before she saw the car pull in, and watched from the window as Harrison and Tuck got out. But then a rear door opened and Ivy emerged, wearing a T-shirt and black jeans and no coat, even though it was forty degrees out. Lou wanted to run down the steps to her full speed, tackling her like she would have at Aldenlight Park before they started being careful around each other's bodies. Instead, Lou waited like a normal person for them to come to the door, but her hands were trembling as she unlocked it. She was nervous and happy, and nervous at how happy she was.

The boys hugged her hello and there was no way not to hug Ivy too without a full-on sidestep. Ivy hugged her back, but barely, her bare arms freezing, her energy so quiet that Lou knew immediately that something was wrong. She was definitely stoned. Her glances kept avoiding any surface for long, as if there was a glare coming off them.

Harrison pulled Lou into a downstairs bedroom as soon as they were inside and let out a long quiet apology for bringing Ivy, followed by a lot of information that made Lou feel like she was feeling around in a dark room for a light switch.

"I would have given you more of a heads-up—or you know, asked if she could join us. But her dad and stepmom are visiting her stepmom's family in Wyoming, and Ivy was just going to be alone, like *alone* alone, because she didn't want to go with them, and Tuck was really fucked-up about it, and I wanted to spend it with him, because—well, there's a lot that's happened I need to catch you up on, like, maybe he's my boyfriend now? Maybe. Anyway, I'm sorry. I hope it's okay. We can leave, if it's not."

"It is," Lou said. "It's okay." She felt calm suddenly, knowing Ivy was in the other room, that she wouldn't leave, or couldn't, and maybe she felt safer knowing that she had Thayer somewhere else as a shield between them, as easy proof of how well she was doing now without her, that she could move on. See? She had moved on. It. Was. Fine.

Really fine.

"What happened with Tuck?" she said.

"They were on break from tour, for the holidays," Harrison said. He seemed calmer now too. "And he texted me."

"That's it?"

Harrison shrugged. "I'm not as sad when I'm with him."

Lou tried to decide if that was a low bar or the only bar. "Is the sex good?"

Harrison laughed. "That's an important part of erasing the sadness, my petite librarian." He asked where she was staying now that the shows were over, and when she told him, he said, "Sorry, you're *living* with Thayer?"

"I'm subletting from her."

"Is that like a lesbian sex term?"

Lou's dad was feeding Tuck and Ivy enthusiastically in the kitchen when she and Harrison emerged from the bedroom, and he gave Lou a curious look, like maybe Lou had just gone into a bedroom to make out with a flagrantly beautiful boy while her parents and her ex-crush and the beautiful boy's maybe-boyfriend were all eating dinner without them. There were way too many dynamics to manage, and so Lou didn't plunge into any of them. She watched everyone without really talking. Ivy still hadn't spoken to her.

Lou's mom and her friend David were standing in the sea-grass together, looking out at the ocean, and her dad kept glancing through the window at them. Lou didn't know where the others were.

Harrison, Tuck, and Ivy left to go walk on the beach, and Lou stayed to take a shower and clear her head. When she came back out into the hallway, hair wet, head no less full, just warmer, her parents were talking in the bedroom next to the bathroom. She could hear them through the door.

"You need to let it go," her mom said. She was almost pleading with him.

"Let what go?" her dad snapped. He rarely raised his voice, but Lou could hear something harsh in it that was never there, like a residue built up from something else. She stood there frozen, listening.

"He didn't mean anything by it," her mom said.

"Oh, sure he did. He absolutely did."

Lou didn't know who they were talking about, but it was a tone of voice they'd used to talk about David in the past. Lou's heart started racing in a familiar way, like it had back home when she knew that eavesdropping on them would feel terrible, but she had to anyway.

"Then what do you want me to do about it?" her mom said. "Seriously. I'm asking."

They went quiet, and her mom swung the door open, blinking at her in the dark hallway.

"Sorry," Lou said.

"Are you guys all set? Dad and I are going to bed."

Lou held her gaze, and her mom didn't look away. "All set."

Lou met Harrison, Tuck, and Ivy down on the beach with an armful of newspaper and dry logs from the house to start a bonfire. Lou worked at it for a while before it got going. Ivy was silent. Harrison and Tuck held every thread of the conversation in their hands. They were sitting cuddled up on a log. Tuck was wearing a puffy blue jacket and a beanie; Harrison wore a coat that looked like sheep's wool. Ivy was sitting by Tuck, bare-armed, hugging her knees, and Lou was on the opposite side of the fire, huddled in two quilts, watching the three of them, their faces orange in the firelight, like they were in a different movie than she was.

Tuck started talking about a band, a pretty famous one, who had asked Fortunato to open for them, for one show, but then maybe a whole leg of a tour, if it went well. He seemed to be unabashedly trying to engage Ivy, asking her questions about what it might be like being on tour with them, whether it was the break they had been waiting for or just a distraction, but she wasn't responsive.

Tuck was getting frustrated, his right knee rattling up and down, like he was playing a bass drum really fast. "Ive. You said you'd think about it."

"I have thought about it," Ivy said. Her voice was hoarse, like maybe it had been days since she'd spoken, not just the last few hours. "I don't want to do it."

"But you're not even listening to what I'm saying."

Ivy didn't answer.

"It's a huge opportunity," he said. "They're not that douchey."

"They are," Ivy snapped. "They're like a fake band in a movie. Their songs don't mean anything. Maybe they used to. But the writing is bad. The musicianship is lazy. You don't like them either."

"Their last album sucked," Harrison offered. Tuck shoved him playfully, and Harrison laughed.

"I thought it was subtle," Tuck said, but he gave up after that.

They watched the fire for a while. Lou started telling them about the shoot she'd done in Tokyo, to try to lighten the mood. "I was wearing a dress made out of pool noodles, basically. They made me swim around in one of those gymnastics pits, with all the foam cubes, you know? It wasn't a ball pit, but it was kind of the same idea." She directed the last bit to Ivy, who didn't smile.

"Is it depressing that that makes me miss it?" Harrison said. "My life is like, get up, make my brothers breakfast, go to class, read all night, sleep, repeat. I miss how absurd fashion is. Eito told me about your orgy Halloween party. His boyfriend hooked up in your bathroom with that guy from the Valentino campaign I've always had a crush on."

The fire crackled. A bit of ash spit out and landed on Lou's sleeve. She fingered the tiny singed hole in the fabric.

"You miss the orgies?" Tuck said to him.

"That's not what I meant," Harrison said. "I mean, for sure, yes, who wouldn't? But I just wanted to know if Lou and Thayer are having the wild time that I—"

"We went to bed before that happened," Lou interjected. She tried to eye-contact Harrison off the Thayer topic, but Ivy stood up abruptly and slapped the sand off the back of her jeans.

At first, it looked like she was heading toward the dunes, back to the house, but then she veered in the direction of the surf.

"Sorry," Harrison said to Lou. "I didn't think she'd—"

"No, it's fine." She stood up.

Ivy had left her jacket at Tuck's feet, and Lou grabbed it and took off after her, her eyes adjusting to the dark. Ivy wasn't walking very fast, but she seemed to know where she was going. Lou caught up and stayed alongside her, stumbling on the uneven sand. She held the jacket out, and Ivy didn't take it, so she threw it over her shoulders.

Ivy stopped abruptly, slipped off her boots and socks, and left them on the dry sand. Lou did the same, even though she hadn't entered a body of water, even a full bathtub, since Morgan drowned.

The lights of boats on the water were so distant. She followed Ivy to the damp, packed sand, then to the edge of the surf. As they entered the water, the cold shocked her, then turned to pain. They were ankle-deep in water, the wind picking up, before Lou realized Ivy wasn't going to stop.

"What are you doing?" Lou shouted, grabbing Ivy by the elbow. She felt a sudden rage that she'd only ever directed at her parents. A frustration that no one was solving their own problems, just circling them or being circled by them.

Ivy turned suddenly, as if she had just noticed Lou was there with her. Her hair was whipping all over her face, and she pushed it back with one hand, like she was trying to wipe something away.

"I don't know," she said, almost inaudible. Lou's feet were totally numb, but she could feel the waves pulling gently at her legs.

Lou steered them back to the dry sand and Ivy let herself be led. They sat on the edge of the dunes for a long time without speaking, as Ivy's breathing changed to something more like crying, or heaving. Lou couldn't feel her hands or feet or face, but she put her arm around Ivy and waited until it passed and Ivy finally asked if they could go back.

All the lights were out in the house. Lou had texted Harrison that they were fine, and the boys weren't around when they got inside. She had a million questions about him and Tuck, but she was too worried about Ivy to ask any right now.

Lou led her to the main floor bathroom, turned the shower on as hot as it went, and left Ivy in there, closing the door behind her. Twenty minutes passed. The ocean roared behind the glass. Lou stripped off her wet clothes and changed into sweatpants and a T-shirt, then wrapped herself in a blanket on the futon, which hadn't been made into a bed yet. Ivy reemerged into the living room, hair wet, face flushed, steam pouring out behind her. The ceiling came to a peak above them.

Ivy turned out the light and sat beside her on the futon, so they were facing the window.

"I'm really tired," Ivy said, her voice cracking. "Today is my mom's birthday, and I don't want to talk, okay?"

Lou opened up the blanket, and without another word, Ivy nestled in beside her, like they used to do in her bedroom. Her arms were still cold, but her back was warm from the shower, and she smelled like soap. They fell asleep like that, from muscle memory alone. Lou didn't dream or surface from sleep until late morning, and when she awoke, everyone was gone.

Lou's mom had left a note saying that the adults had gone into town for breakfast. Harrison had texted around eight to say they'd taken off early for Portland, he had to take one of his younger brothers to a swim meet. It felt like the whole previous night hadn't happened. There was no proof of it anywhere. The coffee maker was going. The kitchen was spotless.

She walked down to the beach, right to the spot where she and Ivy had been the night before, their footprints wiped clean, replaced by shards of sand dollars and long ropes of kelp. A line of pelicans, usually long gone by winter, swooped toward the waves in a long, organized line. Lou squatted down, sinking her hands into the wet sand until they were numb.

4

The night Lou returned to New York, climate activists were gathering in the park near the apartment, preparing to march, speakers taking turns at a megaphone. After watching them gather and pass by her window for an hour, listening to her roommate Eito play bass through the wall, she finally went out on the street just after dusk, got caught up in the throng of people holding Sharpied cardboard signs and painted banners, and followed their slow movement for miles along the East River. It was the kind of movement among strangers that she liked, where she could be part of a tide, the observer, not the focal point. There was no performance. There was only showing up.

Thayer wasn't due back from Berlin for a few more days. Lou went out alone every night with her camera, documenting the marches and posting the edited images on her Instagram. She loved to be around people who cared about what she cared about, without having to meet anyone new. She felt like a guilty wad of a hypocrite, taking planes everywhere on a moment's notice, then taking part in collective action for climate justice, but when she voiced this to her dad over the phone, he gave Lou a long talk about how oil companies invented the concept of the personal carbon footprint and how the world was going to have to legislate their way out of this no matter how many "good" personal choices individuals made. Lou had called him wanting to ask about what was going on with him and her mom—what had happened at the beach house and whether he was all right—but she didn't know how to phrase it without admitting that she'd been eavesdropping.

After the infamous show in Paris, work hadn't slowed down, but now it was slow. Yukon said that was how winter always was, right up until shows started again in February. She wasn't ready to return to the fever of the shows, but she missed seeing her friends. Mari was in Rome, trying to patch things up with her girlfriend, who'd just gotten a job in an orchestra. Jia was doing commercial work in London and still texted Lou curated playlists. Eline had quit after the past season and returned to Norway to study physical therapy. Keeley Dot was the face of Dior, living in Paris.

New York was less lonely when Thayer got back. Some nights, Thayer would be reading a book in bed and Lou would be editing photos on her laptop at the desk, and their life together felt nice. Calm. Easy. They didn't see each other often during the week because their work schedules were so variable, but on Sundays they'd layer up to get coffees and bagels at a place near the park and eat them on a bench, watching people walk by, or go out for steaming dim sum with Thayer's friends, a discord of actors clamoring for dumplings, or go to the Met for the afternoon, just the two of them, making their way and making out systematically from wing to wing, in an order that Thayer had devised when she first moved to New York. For Lou's nineteenth birthday, they went back to the American Museum of Natural History, just so she could see the meteorite in the Hall of the Universe again. These pockets of time were almost what she had imagined she'd have in New York with Ivy. It didn't feel like the fantasy of it had, but she was starting to learn that nothing ever did. Sometimes you got close to the thing you wanted, and that was enough. That was adulthood. It was a relief to have this confirmed, how it made everything she thought she might have lost easier to lose, like someone smudging out the edges of a drawing until it was hardly there; until it was the background, ready for something new and sharp and simple to be sketched on top of it.

"I want to meet your friends," Thayer said, one of those Sundays, on their way back to the apartment from a matinee that they'd gone to with two of Thayer's friends. Outside was even brighter and colder, after the dark warmth of the theater.

"You've met my friends," Lou said. She listed off models they both knew. "*You're* my friend."

"I mean from the before times."

"Are these the end times?"

"You're the American. You tell me."

Lou spent a lot of her time around citizens of other countries who pitied America and its bleakness and its inability to save itself. But what was Lou doing about it? Working on ad campaigns? Promoting capitalism? Living with her head in a cloud of hair spray?

"Will you chain-immigrate me to Canada?" Lou said.

Thayer laughed and cupped her hands around Lou's, like Lou was a child she was humoring. "Someday. If you're very good."

Thayer let the thing about her friends drop, but Lou knew she was keeping a reliable distance between them, and Thayer could sense it. She never talked about her friends back home, or her parents. Thayer talked so vividly about her life in Vancouver and Paris that Lou could have told anyone all the names of her cousins and their spouses, her workshop classmates from university, the name of her family dog two dogs ago, even the other people she slept with: a poet she dated sometimes who she'd seen in Berlin and was always half in love with; a university student in Paris she and Diego had both been involved with. She felt like Thayer was building a bridge toward Lou from one side of the shore, and Lou had built nothing, so Thayer's was just hanging in space, perpetually unfinished.

Thayer had been dropping hints around Lou coming back with her to Vancouver for her birthday, and Lou didn't know why she still felt reluctant, even as she was flattered that of the people Thayer was dating, she most wanted Lou with her for an occasion like that, with all her family. They'd been having a really good winter together, but Lou was surprised by how relieved she felt when the shows started back up in New York and they had less time together.

This season, Lou went to castings herself, then assisted Sienna as she photographed models at other castings. Her schedule was even more maddening than the fall. She had gotten better at being late, but now she didn't know which to favor: working for Sienna or modeling. The shows paid ten times more, some-times twenty, but she preferred to be at Sienna's side, watching, loading and unloading camera equipment, listening to Sienna handle the clients. Now, when the casting directors made com-ments about how her ears were oddly placed, or her hips were too large, or her eyebrows were too flat, she felt annoyance, not dread. She felt more sure of how her body was, and if they didn't want her body how it was, fine. No one ever stopped threaten-ing her and the other models that a million other girls were waiting to take their places, but instead of feeling intimidated, she tempted it more and more, as if it would make the choice easier. Whenever she was at a casting as a model, she felt a yearning to be at one with Sienna, as an assistant, and whenever she was with Sienna, she'd see the pictures her friends posted on Instagram of castings she was missing, which meant she was always rushing through the city in a haze of FOMO no matter her destination.

Even with all the rushing around, the bailing last minute, the lying to Yukon about going to castings she didn't end up mak-ing, she booked twice as many New York shows than she had in September. Many of them she'd walked for the past season. This time, it was like a reunion. The stylists hugged her hello instead of directing her immediately to hair and makeup with-out really seeing her. The newer girls often had earlier call times, and now when Lou arrived early she was told she could wait, have a snack, hang out.

One of her favorite makeup artists, Xavier, joined her and Thayer for pizza outside the Michael Kors show. Xavier loomed large in her memory for being the only makeup artist to ever ask whether she minded if he applied fake eyelashes, and when she said yes, respected her preference. There was no avoiding thongs, but the opportunity to evade cold glue on her eyelids was something she'd always be grateful for.

They sat in the winter sun just outside the warehouse door, on some folding chairs set up for smoke breaks, wearing only bras and jeans. It was the one show Thayer and Lou had booked together, and there had been press about it that Yukon had sent her, speculations about where their relationship was at, how things were progressing now that they were living together. They'd been photographed on a few of their outings, and each time Lou felt both violated and exposed in a way that was proof of something.

"What's new, X?" Thayer said.

Xavier folded his slice over, grease caught by the paper plate. "Usually people ask me that, and I'm like, 'Oh, you know, things are good, I'm doing well, big things always on the horizon,' even if I'm depressed as shit, because I am that Capricorn middle child who hates making waves, but honestly? My husband just told me he wants a divorce. So that's been fun. That's new."

Lou was trying really hard to eat without messing up the lipstick that Xavier had applied a few minutes before, but clearly Xavier didn't care. He also wore a full face, and was digging in anyway.

"You're joking. Ollie did?" Thayer said.

"No fucking joke. Last weekend, he comes home. He says he isn't in love with me," Xavier said. "He said it *exactly* like that. Like, 'I'm moving out. And, oh, I'm not in love with you, maybe I've never been in love with you.' Like it was a fucking order of fries. Not even the entrée."

"He should have lied," Lou said.

"He should have lied!" Xavier exclaimed. He took another slice of pizza, folded it in half, and ate it in four bites. "What about you guys? You fucked-up over anyone?"

Thayer and Lou glanced at each other, and Xavier snorted. "No, I know. I'm just playing. I know. Everyone knows. And it's real cute. At least until someone comes home and blows up the life you've built together. Because of what? Boredom?"

This was what Lou had always imagined her mom was going to do. Walk in the front door after work and announce her departure. Sometimes it felt like she was looking over all their shoulders at some other future or past that didn't include them. Lou had never wanted to be like that in her own life, but lately, living with Thayer, she felt guilty of it.

A stylist popped his head out the door of the warehouse. Emmett. He was from Tennessee and Lou wanted to bottle up how he spoke. She had just spent thirty minutes with him inside while he debated teal socks or slightly less teal socks for her look. He said one of the pairs of socks reminded him of the sky back home at dusk and the other reminded him of the sky back home before dawn.

"What in gay hell are y'all doing out here?" Emmett yelled. "If call time wasn't in ten, I'd fire all y'all. Get dressed. Honestly, Thayer, you should know better." Emmett gasped, and Lou thought for a second that he had seen a truly famous person in the alley and was going to faint. But he was looking down at Lou's feet. "Lou, baby, I changed my mind on the socks. The dawn ones, we're going with, not the dusk. Dawn all the way. Say it back to me."

"Dawn," Lou said. "Got it."

Emmett held her gaze until she realized he was asking for

it verbatim, and maybe he'd stand there all day until she gave it to him.

"Dawn all the way," Lou repeated.

"That's right, baby. All the way. It's always darkest before the dawn." He sang the last part, holding the note so long and with such vibrato that the others started to cheer.

Later that week, she had an editorial shoot with clothes from one of the shows with a Finnish guy in his thirties named Mikko who'd said at the casting that he liked Lou because she wasn't too friendly, like some of the other Americans. She hadn't known whether to take that as a compliment, because it was something she'd been criticized for before, that she wasn't smiley enough in the castings, even though she was expected to be dour for the shoots or shows themselves. But Mikko had seemed to mean it sincerely.

The shoot itself was fine. Mikko was respectful and had interesting ideas for poses. He wasn't bossy or overly friendly. But when it was over, after everyone had packed up, he asked her to get something to eat with him. She'd mentioned that she was into photography, and she thought he was going to offer her advice, or be a good connection. She'd been thinking more about what Sienna said, about finding more people to work with, expanding her circle to get more of the kind of work she wanted. Broadening her choices.

She and Mikko walked to get sandwiches together and sat by a fountain on the Upper West Side. They talked about his cameras, and a recent trip he'd taken to Portland, where his sister and nephews lived. He'd gotten a new tattoo there, one of a tiger shark that Lou really did think had beautiful linework. It was only when they were parting ways, Mikko to get into a cab to go back to his hotel, and Lou for her apartment, that he kissed her. She was so startled, she didn't pull back right away, and he took her by the waist and kissed her more deeply, his beard scratching, his fingers gripping her side, until she stopped him, pushing his chest away with her hand, blushing, and made an excuse about catching her train.

"Can I see you again?" he said, as if he had no idea that he'd done something she hadn't wanted him to do.

She let him add his own contact to her phone, because she didn't know what else to tell him when he was standing right there, then blocked his number as soon as he was out of sight, her palms sweating. It reminded her of when a crew had bleached her hair without asking, a few months prior, on the last day of an editorial shoot. They told her they were just going to add a little dye, a touch-up, as if her natural hair color needed to be touched up, and instead bleached the whole thing before Lou realized what was happening. It took several hours, her scalp burning so badly that it might have been numbed. When she got home, Thayer helped her dye it back to brown in the bathroom sink, but the texture of her hair was all wrong now. Fried out and wispy when it had been naturally wavy before.

Back at the apartment, she told Thayer what had happened with Mikko, and they ordered takeout and binged lesbian movies where no one ended up with a man or died at the end. It wasn't a long list. Halfway through the second movie, Thayer told her that during a fitting a few weeks before, a designer had slipped his hand up her skirt without asking, and she'd kneed him in the jaw. The designer had threatened charges.

"You want to know what my booker said to me, when I told him?" Thayer said. "'If no one hit on models, we wouldn't make any money.'"

When Lou woke up nauseous in the middle of the night, remembering Mikko's breath as he leaned in, she wrapped all of her limbs around Thayer, pressed her cheek against the center of her bare back, and focused on the whir of the window fan until she fell asleep.

5

That spring, Lou saw herself in an ad campaign for the first time. It happened a week after she got back to New York from her second season of European shows. She and Thayer were walking down Fifth Avenue on their way to an editorial casting when suddenly Thayer swerved toward the window display of the Reebok store, posing as if she was going to kiss the model in the poster on the cheek. It took Lou a few moments to register that it was *her*, wearing blazing-white sneakers, mid–high kick. She expected to feel proud or at least pleased, but instead she wanted to run into the store and rip it down.

"Do you want me to take your picture with it?" Thayer said.

"That's okay," Lou said. "I'm good."

Which Thayer didn't understand. "You should be proud!" she kept saying at the casting later. "You looked awesome in it."

But it wasn't a matter of that. Up until then, it had been easy to forget modeling was inherently linked to advertising, to business. The runway shows felt so much like art that the commerce on the other end of it hadn't always seemed as obvious.

All the shoots that had piled up that fall and winter were being published and posted. Some of the magazines or ads were out in different countries or cities, and Yukon would send them to her later. Some, she never saw. Her face was just out there in the world without her, like a lost pet and all its posters.

The next day, her mom texted her a photo of Lou in an H&M campaign in a magazine she was reading in a waiting room. In the ad, Lou was wearing menswear, with her hair slicked back and her mouth open. She looked like she was about to go unsuccessfully hit on someone at a wedding.

Is this my daughter? her mom wrote.

One of them, Lou wrote back.

Lou agreed to go to Vancouver for Thayer's birthday. Her family was throwing her a big party on Saturday, and she wanted Lou to meet her friends, her parents and sisters. It was weird to sit beside her on the plane as the snacks and drinks were distributed, like they were really together, Thayer napping on her shoulder. She was excited, she realized, by the weight of Thayer's body against hers. Maybe this was what she needed: to be immersed in someone else's life, to know that she could be a full part of it too.

Thayer's parents were warm and effusive, both political science professors at the University of British Columbia, and her sisters and their husbands all hugged Lou hello. The house was in a neighborhood with a canopy of old trees running down the center parkway. The birthday party was full of people who knew Thayer, who loved her, who wanted to know all about her adventures, and they asked Lou all about hers too. That was how everyone phrased it: *your adventures!* It was so surreal to be thrust into this whole life, Thayer's family enveloping her in love, enveloping Lou too. Here was a warm mess of people feeding her and taking her in without doubting that she was someone they would want to know, without doubting that she would be here for the long haul.

For the first time since the protests, Lou posted something on her Instagram that wasn't one of her modeling shots. It was of Thayer, surrounded by her family, blowing out twenty-one candles on her cake. Her eyes were closed, but she was smiling. Lou captioned the photo with a heart and a crown and tagged Thayer. Because Lou had a public profile, at Yukon's insistence, the comments started pouring in, the heart eyes and the stans and the trolls. Lou was getting better at ignoring it all. She wanted to document this. She wanted it somewhere she could look at, whenever she needed to.

Later, they went on a walk around the neighborhood, after dark but before everyone had gone home. Thayer had slipped her hand into Lou's and led her out the back door, away from the crowd and heat. It was cool out, and misty, and it smelled like Portland, like pine and wet soil and something colder, more northernly, the edge of frost.

"Are you having a good birthday?" Lou said.

"Are *you* having a good my birthday?"

Lou grinned. "I'm having a lovely your birthday."

"This feels like real life, doesn't it?" Thayer said, as if she was asking for confirmation.

––––––––––

Lou's phone started buzzing early the next morning. The sky was bluing out the window of Thayer's room, as dawn approached. When she finally dug the phone out of her jacket pocket, the screen glared 5:00 a.m. Tuck was calling. Her first thought was something had happened to Harrison.

"Lou, hey."

"Um, hi."

There was wind on the line, and repeated honking.

"Have you heard from Ivy?" Tuck's voice was gravelly.

"What do you mean?" Lou said. She walked out into the hallway, closing the door to Thayer's bedroom behind her. She tried to keep her voice low. Thayer's whole family was sleeping.

"She— I don't know, I don't know where she went."

Lou's chest started pounding, and her vision started blinking, like she was staring into headlights. He sounded scared, like he had the day at the falls, and she heard his voice echoing out from the boulders toward the water: *Where did she go? Where the fuck did she go?*

"What happened?"

"We got into a fight last night and she took off. In downtown Seattle, in the middle of the night. Her phone's going straight to voice mail. I thought maybe you could—I thought maybe you'd heard from her."

"No," Lou said. "We haven't been talking."

Tuck was quiet on the other end. "Okay, well. Let me know if you hear anything."

"I will. Sorry, Tuck."

Back in the bedroom, Thayer was asleep, peaceful and warm. Lou lay back down, trying to calm her heart. She stared at the wooden shades, moving in the breeze through the open window like a chime, but all she could think about was Ivy on the dune back home.

Her phone started buzzing again, and she slipped out of bed and walked into the bathroom. She turned on the light and the fan, her own bright face startled in the mirror.

"I heard from her," Tuck said. "She's safe. She went to her uncle's, a couple of hours from here. We have another show here on Wednesday, but I don't know if she's going to come back for it, let alone the rest of tour."

"Thanks for telling me," Lou said.

"I don't want to say anything that Ivy— I just know she really cares about you. And she could use a friend. A friend who isn't also one half of the band."

When Lou came back to the bedroom, Thayer opened her eyes and lazily touched her fingers to Lou's cheek.

"Everything okay?" Thayer whispered.

"Yes," Lou said. She turned the brightness down on her phone and texted Ivy, *Hey. Are you okay? Tuck called me.*

A few seconds later, there was a reply. *Yeah.*

I'm on the West Coast, Lou texted.

I know, Ivy answered.

Later that morning, Thayer made them breakfast and asked who called her earlier. It was her real birthday, but no one else was up yet. It had the feeling of a Sunday that might go on forever.

"A friend from home, Tuck," Lou said. She paused, then decided to forge ahead. There was no use lying. "He was worried about Ivy."

"Is she okay?"

"I don't know. I think I want to go see her."

Thayer just nodded. Lou had told her about that night on the coast, after they both got back to New York, how she'd been worried about Ivy ever since, but didn't feel like she had any right to ask what was going on. "That sounds like the right thing to do."

"Are you sure?"

"My family will be glad to have time alone with me," Thayer said.

But Lou couldn't tell if there was an edge to it, like, it would be better if Lou wasn't there after all, if she was going to be fielding calls in the middle of the night regarding other women. Which would be a very fair point to make, and yet, Thayer looked decidedly neutral as she drank her coffee and flipped a crepe, and there was no going back on it now.

6

Lou took the train. She hadn't been on Amtrak since she was a kid. It was so different to get to sit just above the ground, looking out, watching the green countryside going by, the sun shimmering on the tops of the wheat fields, giving in to the joy and fear and sense of escape cascading over her, instead of the attentiveness of driving. Maybe that was why she forgot that she was actually going somewhere, that the journey ended at Ivy, until the brakes hissed and the train slowed to a stop in Silverhorse, a small Washington town on Puget Sound that Lou had never heard of. Her only luggage was her JanSport, which Yukon teasingly called her rucksack, as in *It is overdue for you to ditch your rucksack for something more elegant—something leather at least. Throw me a bone here.*

Ivy was waiting on the platform, her hair long and messy under a beanie, wearing an oversize coat, jeans, and work boots. Lou didn't know how she expected her to look, if she wanted her to look as upset and frayed as she had at the beach, to warrant the middle-of-the-night panic, or the journey itself, but she looked okay. Herself.

Lou could see Ivy's breath emerging in little bursts, even though it was almost spring. The sky was darkening with a coming storm. Everything felt like it was happening in slow motion. Ivy hugging her, the full weight of her in the stiff canvas jacket, her soft cheek, the train pulling away, a man with his hand out the window, waving to his family on the platform.

Lou followed her to a silver pickup in the parking lot. Ivy reached into the driver's-side window and unlocked it manually, like she'd done it a million times.

"How was Vancouver?" Ivy said, as she got into the driver's seat. Lou took the passenger seat and tried to look straight ahead, not at Ivy's face in profile.

"I went for a shoot." It wasn't technically untrue. She had booked something for a few days after Thayer's party, a commercial shoot for Herschel.

"And your girlfriend's birthday."

So she'd definitely seen the post. "She's not my girlfriend, exactly."

"Oh."

They didn't say anything for the rest of the ride, as Ivy drove them on a long quiet route out into the country, on a wooded road that hugged the vast edge of Puget Sound, which could have been the ocean, could have been the edge of the world, with the trees clinging to its cliffs.

They arrived at a small shingle-sided house with a view of the water out the back. It sat in a field of tall grass at the base of the thick forest.

"My uncle left on a backpacking trip this morning," Ivy said. "He'll be back Sunday. So it's just us."

There was a steep path to get to the water, and Ivy took off down it. She stepped confidently with her boots, and Lou followed in a half slide, gripping roots to keep from tumbling all the way down, mucking up the soles of the brown loafers Yukon had given her.

A weathered dock extended into the water, and Ivy settled cross-legged at the end of it. Lou stayed standing. Lou knew orcas lived in Puget Sound, some of them year-round, and she kept her camera up, scanning the water. She wished she had binoculars. Or a longer-range zoom lens.

"You look like you're scouting for *Planet Earth*," Ivy said.

Lou had made Ivy watch a lot of *Planet Earth*. "I'm scouting for the perfect whale model. She'll be enormous, and no one will care."

"Do people give you shit about your weight?" Ivy said.

"No," she lied. In addition to Yukon's comments about her losing an inch or two off her waist size, as if that didn't mean shaving down her actual bones, several stylists had remarked on how it would be helpful if she were skinnier. That was the word: *helpful*. Nonaggressive, yet suggestive. The Paris shows had banned size zero and pubescent models, but no one else had. "Not really anyway. It's part of the job."

"But it shouldn't be."

"I know, Ivy. I agree." She kept staring into her viewfinder. All she saw was dark water. "Aren't there parts of music you wish weren't part of the job?"

"All of it."

Lou looked down at her, and snapped her picture. She was

gripping the soles of her muddy boots. "Is that why you're out here?"

"A few nights ago, we were sleeping at this guy's house, some guy Tuck met at another show, and the floors were slate, and there was no furniture in the whole place, and it was literally freezing. I was like this tiny ice worm in my sleeping bag, and I thought, like, am I going to freeze to death here? On this stranger's floor? But what was I going to do? By the time everyone else woke up, we still had to wait for the other band to wake up too, so we could all get breakfast, which is how it always is. Then it goes: group-consensus our way to some diner with grody food, then drive seven hours. Get to the venue, at long last, then sound check. Then wait around the venue, because there's nothing to do and we don't know anyone in town. Then play. Repeat. The music is like one *tiny* part of it. I haven't been able to write a single song since we've been on the road. I'm never alone long enough to hear myself think."

Lou put down her camera and sat beside her. The water was wide and blue. It wasn't the ocean, but it smelled like it.

"Maybe I'm not cut out for it." Ivy's voice was as slight as Lou had ever heard it.

"What do you mean?"

"I don't know if I even want the responsibility of leading us. Tuck has just been so depressed, first because of Morgan, and then because of how confused he was about everything with Harrison, and things are getting better now, since he figured out that maybe it's better to risk being happy than to cancel it before it's begun, but this whole year, I haven't known how to help him, which made me feel ineffectual at everything, even the stuff I always thought I was good at, like guitar, or taking care of myself, or whatever; it all feels like it's gone out the window. We fought last night over nothing, like literally nothing, he just looked at me one way, and it was like I couldn't stand it, how he needed me, needed me to make choices, needed me to drive the van, find us dinner, book the venues, write new songs, keep us moving. And I've just felt like I *need* that, to keep moving, and if I can do that, everything else will get fixed, because I can get a handle on it, but maybe that's the worst thing I could be doing. Mostly the people we've met are so good and they love my songs and I love playing for them. But I keep feeling like maybe I did this wrong. I should have just gone to school in New York. I should have come with you. I should have just chosen a place and stayed there. I keep making the wrong choices."

Lou shook her head. "For real? Name one bad choice you've made."

"Dude, I don't know, diving off the rocks that day?"

Lou's head was fuzzy, and her heart started racing. She'd always blamed herself for suggesting the trail, for being the only reason they were there in the first place. She had no idea Ivy might have been doing the same.

"Why did you?" She regretted it as soon as she said it. There were a thousand reasonable answers. *Because it was hot out. Because it was beautiful. Because it's the kind of thing people do every day without dying.*

"I was showing off. It was so fucking stupid. Because you hadn't said anything, after I played the song, and I was pissed, and I didn't really care what happened to me, if you didn't feel the same way."

Lou's head was buzzing. She pressed her palms into her eyes and saw bright red shapes.

"I used to have these terrible thoughts," Lou said, without

looking up, her camera heavy around her neck. "Like I was so grateful it wasn't you. As if it could only be one person, swapped out. As if it had to be anyone. You're the last person on the planet I would have wanted it to be. You still are."

Ivy's body was so warm next to hers. She smelled like soap and something else, something that was always there, cedar sawed off to make a perfect edge. Lou touched her hair, looping a long piece around her finger. It was soft, and she wanted to put it in her mouth. Their eyes met, but then Ivy glanced away, out at the water. She inhaled sharply, then took Lou's head with both hands and swiveled it, positioning it to the left, just off the shore, where there was a wide swath of sun, and for a second, Lou didn't know what she was meant to be looking at, except the yellow light.

But there they were, spouts erupting in the water. They were so far away, they looked like tiny wisps of white. Little geysers. One, two, three orcas. She watched them, mouth open, and then held up her camera, hands shaking, and zoomed in, her shutter going. It felt like a fleeting something that she had caught with her bare hands, something so fragile it would disintegrate as soon as she moved her eyes away.

The inside of Ivy's uncle's house was small but neat. Ivy made them coffee, and they curled up together on the sofa. Her stuff was piled at the base of it, two guitar cases and an amp, a duffel bag and jackets.

"He lives here alone?" Lou said.

Ivy nodded. "He moved here after my mom died. She left me the house, but he needed somewhere to live after his divorce. So we kept it."

"You grew up here?"

"Where did you think we were?"

Ivy stood up and headed down the dark hallway. She paused, gesturing for Lou to follow her. When she flipped on the light, it took Lou a second to register that she was looking at a child's bedroom. Or someone on the border of childhood to adolescence. Fender decals on the bedposts, and the same stapled collage of singers from Ivy's room in Portland, an almost exact replica, and a dresser painted with starfish. There was a stuffed dolphin on the bed. Dolphins swimming on the trim of the wallpaper. Dolphins. Everywhere.

Oh my god, Lou mouthed to herself. She almost started to laugh, but the air between them was still too tense to let it out. After all of Ivy's teasing about dolphin girls, it had never occurred to Lou it was coming from a place of recognition, not judgment.

Ivy reached for her acoustic, which was resting on the bed, like she needed something to do with her hands. She gripped her guitar for a second like they were unacquainted, then sat down on the window seat. When she started fingerpicking, Lou sat down beside her, watching the clouds over the water as they disappeared in the dark. The song was either new, or too old for Lou to know it.

"You can sing," Lou said. "Please."

Ivy leaned back against the glass, and finally looked at her. When she started to play the next one, it sounded just like the record. She took the same breaths between verses. Lou had them memorized. The verses and the breaths.

See it in your eyes
When you're dialing in a view

You tell me please hold still,
I'm trying to get a good shot of you

And then you run through the brush
flashing fear like a caribou

Should I follow or am I
just coming unglued,
Lou Lou Lou

Is there more to know
Or am I left in the unknowing
Scared of following through
Scared of what I might be showing

With the mountain at your back
I know you see it too

It's bigger than we both knew
Please come on come on
Lou Lou Lou

She sang it through twice, singing Lou's name so softly it buzzed against the glass but barely made a sound.

"How did you know?" Lou said, when she was finished. "Know . . . how you felt."

Ivy didn't say anything for a long time. So long that Lou didn't think she was going to give her a real answer. But then she said, "Remember when we watched that meteor shower?"

It had been the very last week of their senior year. Lou had showed her the spot on her roof where she used to hide out as a kid, just outside her bedroom window, where they'd be invisible from inside and outside the house. They'd taken a blanket out there and some pillows and watched for hours.

"That was the anniversary of my mom's death."

There were a couple of sailboats floating. Lou could see a small figure on one of the decks moving around.

"And it was the first time in four years I didn't want to spend that day alone," Ivy said. "I wanted to spend it with you."

"Will you tell me what happened? You don't have to, I just—I want to know, if you want me to."

"You've never looked it up?"

It had never occurred to her that she could. She didn't know Ivy's mother's name.

"She drowned."

Somehow, this knowledge was already planted in her, but now it unfurled in a plain way, like it had been there all along. After Morgan died, Ivy had shaken off everything Lou had said about how horrific it was, how unbelievable. Because it was the worst thing that had ever happened to Lou. But it wasn't the worst thing that had ever happened to Ivy.

Ivy's parents had divorced when she was seven, and after that, she'd lived with her mom in this house during the school year and with her dad during the summer. Her mom was a research scientist, who'd moved to Washington from Montana, where she'd grown up, in order to study marine life and coastal biology. She'd gone to Western Washington, in Bellingham, where she met Ivy's dad, and then got a job here, at a field station a few miles away. That was when Ivy's parents divorced. Most of her dad's family lived on the Warm Springs Reservation, near Mount Hood, and he wanted to be closer to his parents, his family, a bigger city. He got a job at the research hospital in Portland and remarried. Ivy had wanted to stay with her mom. Her mom always told Ivy stories about her lab or fieldwork that weren't sad, even if what she was studying was how much humans had messed things up. Instead, her stories were about the things she'd seen that had surprised or delighted her. The caretaker of a summer camp who lived alone on an island in Puget Sound all winter, building guitars and canoes by hand. The sea lions that sounded like her grandmother's honking laugh. But Ivy was alone a lot of the time, with their dog and sometimes a sitter. Her aunt and uncle lived with them for a while, taking care of her, filling the house up, until Ivy was in middle school. Then they moved back to Montana, when Ivy's grandparents got too old to live alone.

"That's one reason I expected to like being on tour more," Ivy said. "I thought I liked being around people all the time. I thought it would be more like shows, where you're in a room together, but you don't have to interact if you don't want to. No one's relying on you for anything except music."

Her mom took a kayak out every morning. One Sunday, her mom left for her normal route. Ivy went to her piano lesson, down the road at the neighbor's house. When she came back, her mom still hadn't returned. The dog wouldn't stop barking.

"It felt like if I just went to school the next day and pretended everything was fine, it would be. She'd come back. But then my dad came into town to drop something off, and he wanted to talk to my mom about something, and I told him that I didn't know where she was, and that was when I realized something was really wrong. And because I wasn't there for it—

With Morgan, it felt like, we saw it, you know? We *saw* it. It was so real that there was no question. It made sense. But there was no storm when my mom went out. Nothing. They never even found the kayak. She was only forty, but she had a will. Her instructions were so specific for me. My uncle's still the only one who can admit that maybe it was on purpose."

Lou looked out at the water, imagining an empty kayak, floating. It felt terrible to receive Ivy's pain like this. It felt terrible not to be able to do anything about it. The world felt very wide and very difficult. She wished they had longer than a day or two before Lou needed to get back to New York. It felt like she'd never be alone with Ivy for a long enough amount of time, even if they were alone every day for the rest of their lives. On the nightstand beside them, there was a photograph of a woman in her thirties, maybe, and a tiny Ivy standing beside her, with her dark eyes and hair and an object in her hand that Lou had to lean in and squint to figure out what it was. The stuffed dolphin. They were on the dock, the same one Lou could see out the window, but the wood looked fresh, and there was an old Labrador at their feet.

"Can I show you something?" Lou said. She flipped back in her camera photos until she came to it, and this time, she didn't skip past it. She knew it from the light that day alone. But then she second-guessed herself. Who shows someone the photo of someone about to drown right after they tell you about their mom's drowning? What was wrong with her? Why was this the only thing she had to give?

"It's okay," Ivy said. "You can show me."

So she handed her the camera, and Ivy seemed okay. Not mad, anyway. Like how she understood it was the best Lou could do.

"She looks so determined," Ivy said.

"I was too scared to warn her."

"She wouldn't have heard you. She didn't hear me, and I was right there. We couldn't have stopped it, Lou."

She knew Ivy meant they couldn't stop it now. Not Morgan, or her mom, or anything else that was coming for them that they couldn't foresee. And for a minute, it felt like something she could live with, or learn to.

"Do you think I should go back to school?" Lou asked.

"Do you want to?"

"Sometimes I want to study ecology like I'd planned and feel like I'm doing something to help instead of just fucking things up more."

"You're contributing something."

"How?"

"Fashion's about beauty, right? Whatever beauty is. And I don't think that's inherently bad. I think helping people see beauty means they want to save things that they otherwise wouldn't even see. I'm just saying you don't have to be a scientist or a full-time activist to do good."

"Will you think I'm a coward if I don't go back?" Lou said.

Ivy shook her head. Her eyes were so dark and so open. She put down the camera between them. "Will you, if I don't finish the tour?"

Lou kissed her, and this time, there was no stopping it, no interrupting it, no second-guessing. Ivy's mouth was so soft and warm, and her hand slipped up to Lou's neck, pulling her closer, and it felt just like it had in New York, that feeling of running downhill, picking up speed. They were so alone, the birds were the only echo out the window. There was no stopping the feel of

Ivy's skin under her fingers, or the smallest sound Lou had ever heard from her mouth, when Lou slid her hands down her soft stomach to the band of her black cotton underwear. The quiet she contained was stunning compared to the onstage noise she could make.

"Is this okay?" Lou asked.

"Yes."

"Is this?"

"Yes."

They moved to the bed, and then Lou was underneath her, slipping a finger inside of her, then two. Ivy ground against her, eyes closed, and Lou couldn't stop kissing her skin, how soft, how impossibly soft, pressing her body as close as she could to her friend, stomach to stomach with this girl, this bare girl.

Ivy slipped her hand between their bodies, kissing Lou's neck, licking her ear, whispering something, and Lou shuddered and pushed back, wrapping her legs around Ivy, touching the curve of her neck, tugging her hair. Lou flipped her over so she was on top and pressed her mouth between Ivy's legs.

"Oh fuck," Ivy said.

Lou kept going.

"Oh fuck."

They spent the whole night in the dark, waking up, starting and stopping, sleeping, making the slow move to fucking, that push and pull, and back to lying there, someone's arm holding someone's body. Ivy's fingertips on Lou's neck, her stomach, her legs. Lou's mouth on her ear, her hair, her mouth.

Every time Lou opened her eyes or pulled back far enough to see where she was, she was surprised, again and again, like holding the roving beam of a flashlight, or more like the dark around the hand that grips it. Something you can't capture when it's still. Ivy the light, Lou the dark around, on top of, beside, in her. How if you stare long enough at a face in the dark it disappears, but in this case, becomes more itself. Showing, *Here you are, here you are, here I am, here.*

PART SIX

I

The next morning, Lou could make out the very tops of the evergreens and the negative space between their limbs, familiar and gray. She hadn't slept at all, even in the last few hours when they'd finally slowed—it wasn't actually physically possible to sleep when her body hummed like this, fatigued to the point of giddiness, reluctant to miss any of it. She finally let herself look at her phone, hoping she'd missed her train back to Vancouver. But it left in two hours. There was plenty of time not to miss it.

Lou rolled off the bed, untangling her jeans, then her bra and flannel from the sheets, but she couldn't look away from Ivy on the mattress. Ivy naked made Lou's head feel light and gauzy, and Lou climbed back into bed and buried her face in Ivy's soft, soft neck. If she was going to pass out from desire, she already would have sometime in the last twelve hours. She licked the shadow of Ivy's collarbone without moving her head, something she hadn't ever realized she'd wanted to do, but it turned out she did. Badly. She did it again.

"Don't go," Ivy said into her hair, and that was when Lou's anxiety kicked in, reliable and fluttery. She did have to go.

"I don't want to." Lou stood up and started pulling her clothes back on again, and one of her shirt buttons got caught on her hair, and she winced, trying to untangle it, but as she worked at it, it just got worse and worse. "Did you know people in the industry say *stable* of models? Like a gaggle of geese? Or a pod of dolphins?"

She'd heard it for the first time during the New York shows, when a casting director told Lou that because her agency wasn't with their usual stable of models, she was a long shot for the show, but they liked her look. It had been meant as a compliment, but Lou was so hung up on how casually he used the phrase, like they were racehorses and no one was trying to pretend otherwise, that she'd never forgotten it.

"How many can you do?" Ivy said. "Really?"

"A cackle of hyenas. A raft of otters. A wake of vultures."

"What, did you memorize these for school or something? Was it like the fifty states song?"

"A siege of herons. A parliament of owls. A bale of turtles."

"I feel like you're making these up now."

She wasn't. She was just getting going. She was still stuck in her shirt. She could stay like this all day and then she wouldn't have to leave. Her favorite nouns of multitude were for animals that never actually got together in groups. Who ever saw a bunch of owls together?

"A charm of hummingbirds."

Ivy stood up, held her still, undid the whole shirt, unwound the hair from the top two buttons carefully. Then she pulled the shirt down, rebuttoned it, fixed her collar and her hair, and looked her in the eye. Kissed her. "You get one more."

"A walk of snails."

The train ride went by quickly. Ivy held her hand, looking out the window. Lou didn't want it to end—she wanted to already be a forty-year-old nature photography hobbyist that her hot musician wife kept fed and insured in a cabin on the water, because if it was a fantasy why not let it be the all-the-way fantasy.

"Stay with me," Ivy said in her ear, as they called the stop for Seattle, the brakes screeching. Tuck was already waiting for her at the station. "Take a break from modeling. Come be my tour baby."

"You're asking me to do what you stopped talking to me for."

Ivy laughed. "Maybe I'm selfish."

"You can't just take a break. They forget about you."

"Come to the show tonight, at least. One last hooray for Fortunato. Maybe forever."

Lou couldn't say no to that.

In the minivan, Lou texted Thayer that she wasn't coming back to Vancouver, then emailed Yukon that there'd been an emergency, she needed to cancel the Herschel job, and that she'd be back in New York in a couple of days for her next shoot. She recognized as she made both decisions that there would be consequences later. But for once, she didn't care.

Thayer texted back right away: *Okay, I'll see you when I'm back from Paris then. How is Ivy doing?*

Lou watched the back of Ivy's head in the front seat. *She's fine,* she wrote, but couldn't quite bring herself to add the rest—*by the way, I slept with Ivy on your birthday and I think I've been in love with her this whole time.* Instead, she wrote, *Just figuring out her life. See you next week!*

That night, the show was at a real venue, a big one, on Capitol Hill. Harrison hadn't driven up for it since he had class, and so it was just her, alone in the crowd. When Fortunato came on, Lou was right up close to the stage with her camera. Just being near a stage made her relieved she didn't have to perform; she could finally relax into the night, take pictures, not be stared at by anyone. She had forgotten how much she loved the dirt of shows, the sweating bodies and sticky floor and people around her who had all chosen their own clothes for themselves. Everything on photo shoots and at runway shows always had to look too perfect, too designed, too clean and exact and in place, and all she wanted was to watch a room of people jump around and sweat on each other and what she *really* wanted was a girl singing so hard into a microphone that her spit shone in the spotlights and the crowd spit back, and nobody was beautiful and nobody cared. Ivy onstage was the old Ivy, the one who held power and command of the room with just the way she looked up to the rafters and looked back down to the crowd, like she knew every single one of them, wrote this song for them.

There was something about the way that Ivy jerked the neck of her guitar up on certain notes, as if she were trying to pull something out of it that was deeper than a sound, that killed her. It just straight-out killed her.

Ivy addressed the audience. "I wrote this next song for a girl."

She looked down at her guitar, tuned one more string, then looked back out at the audience, right at Lou. "I'm kind of in love with her."

The crowd screamed, strangers rejoicing in what Lou had never been able to, and it was the first time she wished in her whole life that someone could take her picture without her knowing it, so she could have remembered what she looked like, right then, when she flat out lost herself to the night, to the moment in front of her, to what was finally swallowing her whole.

Thayer had flown straight to Paris from Vancouver, so when Lou got back to New York she was in the apartment without her. It felt like Lou was suddenly encroaching on a space that had never belonged to her. None of the things hung on the walls were hers, none of the clothes in the closet, none of the miscellanea. Lou's objects were contained to a few shelves and her bags. It hadn't struck her before how compartmentalized she'd kept her life there, how separate. She might as well have been living in a space station model apartment.

But there was nowhere else for her to go, so she stayed. At the end of the week, Thayer was supposed to get back from her birthday part deux in Paris. Lou was walking back from a casting the night Thayer was due to arrive back in New York and called Catherine on an impulse, hoping to talk it out with someone, but when Catherine picked up, she was suddenly shy asking for advice. She never asked Catherine for advice. It had always been Catherine confiding in her. Or both of them avoiding a topic altogether.

"How's training?" Lou said.

Catherine paused for so long, Lou thought maybe her head-phones weren't working. "I'm actually out right now. Landed weird on my knee the other day at practice. I'm in PT now for it. But who knows."

"That really sucks." Lou wanted to ask if she was drinking, but she didn't want Catherine to think she was policing her. "You doing okay?"

"I joined a fraternity," Catherine said dryly. "Pledged Sig Chi. They're keeping me sane. Keeping me pilled up. We're doing a lot of keg stands."

"Just don't fall in love with any of them," Lou joked back.

"First of all, ew. But speaking of," Catherine said. A long pause. "I know you used to have feelings for me, and it's been an awkward subject between us ever since"—Catherine's tone was dry and a little teasing, back to her old self, and Lou grinned— "but I just wanted to let you know that I have a girlfriend."

Lou felt the sharpest flash of jealousy, something so dormant she didn't even know what it was at first. She was walking by a pair of boys sitting on a stoop, chest passing a basketball back and forth. One of them fumbled a pass and it bounced off a step toward Lou. She grabbed it before it rolled into the street and threw it back to them. Maybe she was just jealous at how clear it sounded, coming out of Catherine's mouth. *Oh, I have a girlfriend.* Lou wanted things to be that straightforward for her. She had half of two things. She had Ivy. She had Thayer. But no names for what they were to her.

"Are you actually mad?" Catherine said.

"What? No." She shifted into overenthusiasm, and as the questions came out of her mouth, she knew that Catherine could sense how weird it felt too but thankfully didn't comment on her hesitation, just told her that she was dating a pole-vaulter from her team named Raquel. Raquel was a junior philosophy major, and Catherine was getting her ass handed to her.

"She's very intense about track," Catherine said. "And school. Actually, she's very intense about everything. So we are imperfectly matched. But she knew Morgan. They lived in the same dorm their freshman year and had an intro English class together. Apparently Morgan once said really smart things about a poem that Raquel remembers the professor was impressed by. Who knew?"

"I could see it."

"What's going on with you and the supermodel?"

"Well," Lou said. Suddenly things felt very awkward. She fumbled with her key in the door. There was a man lurking on the corner, and she kept glancing back over her shoulder at him, aware that no one else was on the street. She was cornered at the top of the stairs, but she guessed she could jump over the railing and into the bushes if she needed to, and then slink along the side of the house, screaming at the open windows.

"Lou, focus. Are you texting?"

The key finally worked, and she got the heavy door open and locked behind her. She sat down on the living room carpet. Her roommate Eito's bedroom door was open, which meant he wasn't home, and she was relieved. She could actually say what she wanted to. "Actually Ivy and I—"

"*Oh, Jesus Christ,*" Catherine shouted. "You finally figured your shit out?"

Catherine started laughing. A genuinely pleased laugh. Something Lou'd maybe never heard out of Catherine, so unabashed and open. A sound Lou wanted to take a long bath in.

"I really need your advice," Lou said.

Catherine was a good listener, but she didn't tell Lou what

she should do. She told her that she needed to decide what she wanted.

"What *you* want, I mean," Catherine said. "Not what you think other people want for you."

When Thayer got back that night, she kissed Lou on both cheeks, like they were meeting at a party, then went straight into the bathroom and turned on the shower. They'd texted a little while she'd been in Paris, but nothing else about Ivy. Lou wanted to say something the second Thayer walked in the door, because the longer she waited, the more it felt like she was going to back out of saying anything at all. But the shower ran for a half hour, and then the hair-dryer for a long time after that—so long that Eito, back from a shoot and coated in glitter, banged on the door, demanding Thayer get the hell out, because he had to pee and he didn't want to do it in the alley, because the last time he did that, the neighbor woman had sprayed her kitchen hose at him and threatened worse, and he didn't want to have to register as a sex offender just because his roommates couldn't respect a bathroom schedule.

When Thayer finally opened the door, Eito stalked past her. Lou was starving; she'd given in and started trying to lose an inch for the shows, which meant going on longer runs and eating less and it still didn't seem to be working. Her hips stayed a stubborn thirty-five inches. Every time Yukon measured her in the agency, they asked if she was sneaking macarons, and she knew it was a joke but it didn't feel like a joke. Her uneasiness felt heightened by her hunger, which meant that she was hovering like a weirdo in the kitchen while Thayer fixed herself a snack, and she didn't ask if she could have any because it didn't feel fair to ask for anything from Thayer right before she broke up with her. If she ever got there.

"How was it?" Lou said.

"I'm always sad when I leave. I'd like to move back someday."

"When?"

"Oh, I don't know. Five years? Whenever I finish this play and no one will work with me anymore? Don't worry, I like being here now with you."

Lou stared at her. "I actually need to talk to you. About that."

Thayer glanced at the window, like she was afraid Lou was going to crawl out of it. "Okay . . ."

"When I saw Ivy, things became clear—clearer, anyway. Things I've been trying to figure out for a long time."

"Did you guys hook up?"

Lou paused. That wasn't what she wanted to start out with, but it was effective. And true. "Yes."

Thayer shrugged. "I hooked up with Diego in Paris. Like, the whole time I was there. And someone new, actually."

Lou's face burned. She was jealous, in spite of herself and her intentions for this conversation. "All right."

"I'm not saying that to fuck with you, I'm just saying that I don't care. You're allowed to hook up with other people. I know that you haven't. But I don't want you to think this is some kind of double standard."

"But I've been too slow. With us."

"I like that though. You're thoughtful. Intentional. I mean, sometimes it's annoying as shit. Sometimes I feel like you're here, and other times it's like you slip into a hole in the wall and you're in some other place that I'll never be able to access.

It's incredibly frustrating, to have you present for a day or two at a time, maybe even a week, and then you go off in your head again, check out, wall up. Like, it's okay. But it's also aggravating. But I figured it was just anxiety-driven. I used to get like that, when I was a kid."

Lou nodded. She bit at her knuckle. "You've been really patient with me."

Thayer sat down across the table from her. Lou wanted to look away but she didn't.

"I'm in love with her," Lou said.

Thayer looked frustrated. She was squeezing her hands together, the same way she did when she was trying to solve a scene in her play. "So? I've been half in love with Diego since we met. I feel like I've been pretty open about that. But I can also be in love with you."

When Lou was little, her parents had seemed like they had a big version of something—of love, or something bigger—and then as she got older, and they did, it was just smaller and smaller until it didn't even seem like it was there anymore, like it wouldn't even fill a room. Whenever Lou was in a room with Ivy, it was so full, she couldn't see around it. She didn't want a smaller version or a lesser version. She wanted it to be enormous, endless, or at least endless as far as anyone could predict. She wanted it to be a volcano she studied her whole life.

"I can't," Lou said.

Suddenly, Thayer laughed, and it started to build and build, until she was half crying, like something was coming out of her she couldn't stop, like she'd just tripped off a runway at the Louvre, like she was the kind of person who reacted to pain with joy. "Then what are you doing here, Lou?"

2

A barrage of online articles about their breakup arrived the next day. Lou turned off her news alerts. She didn't know how the media found out, but all the same sites that had posted about their cute Fashion Week love now bemoaned its end. Maybe Eito leaked it. Maybe someone just caught Lou moving her bags out of Thayer's and back into the model apartment with the faulty lock and the greyhound woman. She was on a bottom bunk again, surrounded by all the new girls. A blank stable.

Sienna called Lou about an assisting job, and it turned out to be her agency's new-faces shoot, an annual event. This year, it was at the Superb office in Midtown, not an apartment. She and Sienna set up in the conference room that doubled as a studio. Lou unrolled the backdrop and set up the lights. She had grown to love the mechanical parts of photography, the assembling and disassembling, always with an armful of extension cords. It felt like mental prep work that she didn't get when she was thrust into other situations in fashion. It felt like good planning.

The makeup artist was her friend Xavier, who told her all about his new boyfriend, the first after his impending divorce, a Gemini with a moon in Taurus (Lou nodded enthusiastically, even though she didn't know what this meant) who worked on criminal justice reform and had introduced Xavier to his entire Long Island family on the fourth date.

The girls showed up one by one. There were seven of them. Sienna wanted to shoot them clean, with minimal makeup, near the window, in front of a light backdrop. Lou's main job was to hold the light reflectors where Sienna wanted them, which she was getting better at predicting.

While Sienna shot, Lou watched the other models laugh and talk with one another. She could tell immediately which one was the Mari and which was the Lou. The Mari led the conversation, and when she got in front of a camera, she was so magnetic that the shots Sienna was taking came out so beautifully it only took a few minutes. The Lou was a girl who seemed flustered to the point that every time Sienna asked her to do a new pose, the girl could only unclench her fingers.

A few days later, Lou was sitting directly in front of the air conditioner in the living room of the model apartment, having her morning coffee and looking at a picture Ivy had sent of Puget Sound, when Mari and Thayer burst through the front door, wearing matching peach jumpsuits.

"We're going on an adventure," Mari announced to Lou.

"Where?"

"It is finally time. You will learn to surf today."

"I have a job today," Lou said. It was a Tuesday at 7:00 a.m. She was doing a beauty shoot, which was her least favorite kind of job. They required a lot of up-close face shots and mascara wand jabs in the eye.

"Call in sick," Mari said. Thayer was hovering half behind her, as if Lou was a small animal she feared startling.

"It's a lot of money." She'd forgotten how exorbitant the model apartment was. It was like staying in a hotel in New York, but without any privacy and with strangers poaching your shampoo and bodywash, one drop at a time. But she hadn't been able to find another lease with such short notice, and so she was staying there for now.

"Don't care."

"Yukon would kill me."

"It is a *perfect* day." Mari kissed her head. "Sienna has generously agreed to drive us to New Jersey in her ex-wife's very cool Japanese van. We are going. You are coming. We have already rented you a board and a wet suit over the phone. Prepare yourself."

"Guys," Lou said, her anxiety nosediving into the ground. "I really can't."

"You really can," Mari said, grabbing her hands and yanking her up off the sofa.

Lou didn't want seeing Thayer to make her feel sad anymore, if they were going to exist in the same world. She didn't want Thayer to feel like she had to hide, and she didn't want to feel like she needed to hide either. "I'll go for the beach and the company. But I'm not going to surf."

Thayer gave her a sympathetic look, but Mari just laughed. It was only when she was in the last row of seats in the cream-colored adventure van with a roof rack, feeling mildly carsick from Sienna's lurching driving, that she fully realized it was almost exactly a year since Morgan had drowned. The montage of Morgan's dive had finally boxed itself away sometime that winter, but now the heat dragged it out from her memory, so swiftly, like clothes she hadn't thought she'd ever wear again. Morgan on the rim of the waterfall. The slippery moss under her feet, the way the water glistened off it. Details Lou wouldn't have even been able to see from where she was sitting but asserted themselves in her memory of the events anyway.

"How's it been going?" Lou said to Thayer, who was buckled in beside her.

"Eito misses you," Thayer said. "He thinks he finally has me pegged as the one running up the water bill, since you've been gone for most of the month."

"Isn't it a fixed charge?"

Thayer smiled. "Sure is."

They drove past the exit for Asbury Park, which she knew from her mom playing almost exclusively Bruce Springsteen records on repeat throughout her childhood, and she got very excited, and nobody else knew what she was talking about. She took a picture for her mom, who sent her a series of GIFs of Bruce Springsteen gyrating, and she was happy she'd decided to come along, if only to get out of the city. At the board shop, a guy talked down to Mari and Thayer in the way that Lou had often been talked down to at bike shops, but they clearly knew exactly what they were talking about and managed to get a discount just for him being a douchebag.

Out on the beach, it was already humid and it was only
11:00 a.m. Thayer and Sienna went out immediately, and Mari
and Lou stayed on the shore, watching them. Mari had packed
them an enormous lunch, but Lou was too nervous to eat. She
drank from her sticker-covered Nalgene and tried to watch
the surfers who weren't Thayer and Sienna, though at a certain point she couldn't tell anymore, as they mixed together and
drifted out.

Mari wedged a bag of potato chips between Lou's legs.

"You look skinny," Mari said.

"I'm trying to lose an inch before the shows."

Mari dumped a handful of chips on her head. "Eat with me.
I ended things with Rosana."

"No!" Lou said. She felt surprisingly let down by this, even
though she hadn't really known Rosana. She had grown to love
the saga of their relationship anyway. What Rosana wanted
from Mari was the same thing Lou had once wanted from Ivy,
or maybe it was what Ivy had wanted from her, in always asking Lou about the art she wasn't making: for them to want to
live the same kind of life, together. "But I thought you always
wanted her in your orbit."

Lou had hung on to this, in all her longing for Ivy. The idea
that someone could always be there for you, even if your lives
looked incredibly different.

"Orbits change," Mari said.

"Isn't that against the physics of the universe?"

"Actually, no. It's one of the laws of the universe. Ellipticals
shift. Massively."

"I thought you studied music. Not physics."

Mari stood up. "Get on the fucking board."

She placed the board right side up on the sand and gestured for Lou to stand on top of it. Lou pretended she was on a wave, and it was fine until she actually looked at the water and then she felt like she had at the beach in France with Thayer, like someone was storming the ground she was on, forces coming at her she couldn't understand.

Mari showed her how to go from lying down to standing up on the board. Lou let her zip up the back of her wet suit, so she at least looked the part.

"We're not even going to try this today," Mari said to her. "I'm just going to hold on to the board while you cling to it, like a tiny lizard."

"I don't know if I can do that."

"We are here now. You have learned to walk in heels. You endured the humiliation of ruining the Chanel show and came out the other side a star. Dammit, you are a strong person and a fierce model. You can float on a surfboard while I guide you around like a child at a swim lesson."

It was a good pep talk. Lou followed Mari into the water. She knew the water was cold, but the wet suit prevented her from feeling it all the way. It felt good and salty on her face. Mari waded out with her, holding her hand and the board.

"I know how to swim," Lou said. "You can let go of my hand."

"Then get on the board."

Lou let the waves break against her body, walking out until they were chest-deep, then she slid onto the board, gripping both sides with her hands. Mari guided the board over the waves, jumping with the surf. Out farther, Thayer and Sienna were cheering for her. She knew that she could get swept away at any moment, that a riptide could come for her, that Mari herself could be swept away, but she started paddling. She swallowed some water and coughed it back out, as it burned the back of her throat.

The sun was hot on her back and cheeks, as she crested the tops of the waves that weren't quite waves, waiting for the right one. But the right one never seemed to come. They were too weak or too strong, and she kept floating. Finally, Mari shouted at her to choose, to commit, and she did, positioning herself toward the shore, paddling her arms through the water until a wave caught her and lifted the back of the board, pushing her forward, the force underneath her out of her control. She gripped the sides of the board, but kept her head above water and her eyes open, all the way into shore.

Lou lay there for a while, looking up at the specks of sand in front of her, sifting through it with her fingers like she used to as a kid, her hand an hourglass.

Mari walked over, dripping salt water and sand onto her. "Like a baby sea turtle," she announced, "going the wrong way."

They ate the extensive picnic out of the cooler, separated into tiny colored Tupperware containers of different kinds of fruit salads and one labeled cucumbers that held only a handful of Cheetos, while Mari and Thayer talked about the new season, when castings would start, which labels they'd book again, which they badly wanted to walk for the first time. Sienna was looking out toward the waves. Her hair was messy and sticky. She was wearing a mismatched bikini, Birkenstocks, and men's sunglasses that slid down her nose. It was the least put together Lou had ever seen her. She was smiling absently at a little boy playing in the sand with the plastic mold of a starfish.

"Are you going to do the spring shows?" she asked Lou.

"I don't know." It was the first time anyone had asked her. It was assumed she would. She was on the train. The train was moving. Why would she not do them? It wasn't about money anymore; finally, she could pick and choose, not just take everything that was thrown at her for the sake of making a living. It would be easy to let go of the thread of her old life and commit fully to this one, even though everyone said it didn't last. Their meaning wasn't as obvious as *your body or youth couldn't last*, but instead, that the industry would take you down. You couldn't endure. Or you wouldn't want to.

Lou watched the little boy hurl the plastic starfish. He fetched it for himself. Then hurled it again, empty of sand.

"Can I ask you something, *cara*?" Sienna said, looking at her closely.

"Definitely."

"Fashion doesn't speak to you. I can tell. The models can tell. Photography, sure, that I can tell you love. But if not that, what speaks to you? What would you take pictures of, if you could take pictures of anything in the world?"

Lou paused and looked out at the shore. She thought of Ivy on the dock in Washington, the spray in the sound. "Whales?"

Sienna laughed, harder and longer than Lou thought it really warranted. Sometimes she forgot to tell people who she was, and when they found out, they thought she was kidding.

Sienna dropped her off last. Since passing Asbury Park on the way home, "It's Hard to Be a Saint in the City" had been playing on a loop in Lou's head. When they pulled up to the curb, a neighbor boy was practicing pirouettes under the streetlamp, saintlike in the soft light. Sienna idled at the curb, and Lou didn't get out right away.

"Do you want to go get a coffee?" Sienna said. "I have to return this van, and there's someone I think you'd enjoy meeting, given our earlier conversation."

"Yes," Lou said.

The van belonged to Sienna's ex, Alice. Alice was a middle-aged woman with messy braids and a kind face. She looked like one of Lou's many aunts. Her mom was the youngest of four, and her aunts all talked with their hands and had varying shades of reddish-gray hair, wild around their shoulders, and they were always talking to Lou about her potential, as if there was a reservoir of it she needed to use before it dried up.

Alice told her she lived in Portland, Maine, but she was driving down to get to an assignment in the Florida Keys. She was a nature photographer who did contract work for the U.S. Geological Survey, protecting natural resources. As soon as Lou started asking her about the birds that she was going to photograph in the Keys, what equipment she was bringing, how long her trips in the field were, she realized Alice was one of her people. It was like how Harrison talked to stylists, or her mom talked to other journalists: like they were finally speaking the same language.

"Lou has a good eye," Sienna said to Alice, like that was the highest compliment she could give. No one had ever said that about her before. Once, her beloved art teacher in high school had described her as *timid with the brush, but greedy for meaning*, and she'd never worked out whether it was a compliment or not.

Alice asked how old she was and Lou told her she was nine-teen. Alice remarked that was quite young, and Sienna defended her. Lou wondered if Alice thought they were sleeping together. She didn't know if Sienna had a reputation for that, given the situation with Mari. She didn't want Alice to think that, but if she did, she probably wouldn't have given Lou her phone number and told her to call when she got back from Florida the following week, if she wanted to talk more, if she was interested in working as an assistant on some shoots in the States or Canada.

Sienna walked Lou back the few blocks to the model apartment and hugged her goodbye.

"Call Alice, *cara*," she said.

When Catherine qualified for the NCAA national championship at the end of that week, she called Lou to tell her but didn't extend any invitation to come watch her run. At first Lou was just relieved to hear that Catherine had recovered from her injury, that it hadn't caused her to spiral. But then it struck her that she could go. That she had to. She'd fly to wherever the championship was just to see Catherine run for fifteen minutes.

That was before she saw the location.

Hayward Field. Eugene, Oregon.

Her first impulse was to go back on the plan. No one knew she'd cleared her schedule to go, so no one would miss her if she didn't show up. Ivy had finished out the tour, then gone back to Washington, staying with her uncle and trying to work on writing some songs, and Lou didn't want to interrupt that just to have someone coach her through her anxiety. She tried to coach herself—yes, the idea of going back to the University of Oregon campus alone made Lou queasy, but Catherine *lived* there. Lou could do it for a day.

She flew to Portland on a Friday night and slept in her child-hood bed. She brought all her things back with her, her two suitcases and her JanSport. That was still all she had.

The next morning, she helped her mom weed the vegetable garden out behind her parents' house. The garden had always been her dad's project, but her mom seemed invested now, in a way she'd never been when Lou lived at home. Lou's hands were sweating in the gloves, but she was barefoot and in jeans, and she'd forgotten what it was like to sit on the ground like this, surrounded by soft brown pine needles, with her hands in the dirt. They were on the edge of the shade from the ever-greens, in the only patch of sun the yard really got.

"Do you think I should keep doing it?" Lou said. "Modeling?"

Her mom paused and wiped some soil off her brow. She seemed to be carefully considering her response. "To me, it seems like the kind of thing that could go and go if you want it to. Lots of things could, that aren't exactly right. Relationships. Jobs. Places you're living. You can tolerate things that aren't right for you for a long time. Some people do it forever.

"It doesn't have to be dramatic," her mom added. "The leaving."

"What do you mean?" Lou said.

"You can just decide to stop a little bit at a time."

Lou sat up, looking at her mom. She dug into the dirt, beneath the tomato plant, to extract a weed with thick roots. The tomatoes weighed on their vines. They were ripe. The arti-chokes had bolted, flowering up above their heads.

"Are you and Dad getting a divorce?" Lou said. She'd been avoiding asking it all year, not wanting to know the answer. Maybe the last few years with her mom had been some version of that morning in New York with her mom, the girl with the camera circling, trying to get at the truth of them. For whatever reason, with the sun inching higher over the evergreens, she finally felt like she could get at the truth herself, that she was ready for it.

But her mom didn't seem offended, like Lou was expecting, or defensive. She didn't ask why Lou would think that, as if they both knew the details her answer would contain, the dead air in the mornings at the house when Lou was in high school, or even the look between them in the hallway at the coast. Instead she asked, "Do you think we should?"

"I don't know anything about love," Lou said.

"Sure you do," her mom said. "As much as anyone."

3

That evening, Lou called Alice, asking if she had any assisting gigs coming up that she could apply for. Alice told her to send her portfolio, and for a second, Lou thought she meant her modeling portfolio, which she still hadn't unpacked from the plane ride. But of course Alice meant her own photographs, which she didn't have. She spent the whole night sorting through her hard drive, her heart pounding with excitement, until she found the right files to edit and compile, and maybe there were too many people, and not enough landscapes, but at least they were all her people. Ivy at the radio towers. Catherine midair on the trampoline, with the two neighbor girls. Her mom weeding in the garden. Her dad hopping down a dune. Thayer sitting on a mossy curb in Vancouver. Harrison looking over his shoulder at the Boboli Gardens. Mari at the show in Rome. Fortunato onstage. Morgan on the U of O campus, beneath the maples.

The NCAA championship track meet was Saturday at Hayward Field, not far from those maples. It was an overcast day, raining on and off. She was so worried about being late that she arrived on campus two hours before Catherine's event time. She sat in a parking spot for a few minutes before pulling back out and driving her mom's car to the trailhead for the waterfall. It was so automatic, she didn't realize where she was taking herself until she was on the right stretch of road.

Walking the trail took way less time than she expected. It was only three-quarters of a mile. It was damp, from spring rain, and foggy. There were a few older hikers, gripping walking sticks, looking for other trails that forked off from the main one. It felt like she was trespassing, returning there, as if spoiling the worst memory she had was against the rules, would take something larger from her that she had to sit in the shadow of.

The waterfall was heavier than she remembered. The mist coming off it didn't look any different than the mist coming out of the sky. There was a path leading around the pool that she hadn't seen before, carved into the side of the eroded rock, and she walked out onto it, gripping the side of the wall with her fingers, like she was rock climbing. The pool was clear but covered in little droplets echoing down. When she reached the platform under the falls, she aimed her camera up. She wanted to walk under this moment, as if she could slip backward in time, to open her eyes and be back there. To hear Ivy and Morgan laughing overhead, to see herself and Catherine and Tuck on the shore, in the moment just before something changed. It wasn't that Lou wanted to reverse anything; she understood that she couldn't. She just wanted to stay present there, to look around without any dread.

At first, she didn't feel anything. But then came the frustration at feeling nothing. She thought she'd moved past that blankness. She wanted it to be over. Lou threw a rock out into the water and it landed with a heavy splash. She threw another, and almost lost her balance.

Someone was yelling at her from across the shore. She thought, for the quickest moment, that it was her past self. But it was a woman in a red raincoat, a large dog beside her. She was waving her arms at Lou, and Lou walked the edge back carefully, suddenly relieved that someone was watching her, making sure she made it back safely, as she let herself look down at the black depths of the pool.

"A girl died there last year," the woman said, as Lou stepped back onto the trail. "Please be careful."

"I'm going back now," Lou said. "I promise."

The woman watched her leave, then stayed on her tail almost the whole way back to the car, her dog panting, close to her side. Every time Lou looked over her shoulder, the woman was there, watching her. She wondered how many people the woman had trailed in this same way, vigilant, untrusting that they would make it out without her.

Lou had run at Hayward Field in high school, her last two years, both times drenched at the finish line from spring rain, finishing somewhere in the middle of the pack. Their senior year, Catherine had drawn on a Steve Prefontaine–inspired mustache in brown eyeliner for her race. Everyone had joked about the mustache, but it hadn't seemed like a joke to Catherine. Catherine had lost that race, badly, because she spent the whole previous night doing shots with the boys, whose races were over. At the end of the season, their track coach had given them all T-shirts, in honor of making it to state. It read: *Stop Pre.*

At the bleachers at Hayward Field, she spotted Catherine's parents almost immediately. They sat a couple of rows down, in matching Ducks sweatshirts, looking older, grayer, than they had at the memorial. They were next to the dark-haired girl Lou recognized from Instagram as Raquel, Catherine's girl-friend, not that Catherine was the kind of person who posted any declarations of a new relationship. Raquel didn't either, but Lou had gone deep enough into their tagged photos to fig-ure out who she was. Raquel was talking to Catherine's par-ents, pointing out different things on the track. Catherine's dad laughed at something she said, and Lou's body was filled with a humming delight, which built even more when she spotted Catherine down on the track.

Catherine wore a green tank jersey and shorts. She was stretching, with her muscular arms and white-blond head. She looked sharp as she leaned into her stretches, jumping up and down. Lou thought about going to go sit with her parents and Raquel, but she preferred to be alone, to take in the moment apart from them. She didn't want to distract from Catherine.

The other runners headed to their marks, and Catherine looked up into the stands before making her way over, waving to her parents. She noticed Lou right after, making eye contact, and that was when Lou stood up, blew her a kiss, and pointed to the shirt she was wearing.

Stop Pre.

She thought she saw Catherine smile as she turned to take her mark at the track.

Lou knew Catherine's 3,000-meter time almost exactly, from the years of trying to come within spitting range of it, but she'd never watched her run a 5,000-meter race. The race was twelve and a half laps, and halfway through the second, Catherine was toward the front of the pack, neck and neck with two other runners.

Lou's jaw was clenched, her eyes so focused on Catherine's moving body that they started to water. At the end of the seventh lap, Catherine started to lag. She looked tired. When another girl took a clear lead, that was when something shifted, like Catherine realized that whatever she was doing wasn't working, not if she wanted to win, and her posture changed, her strides were longer, cleaner, faster, as if she'd turned a corner inside herself. She gained on the lead runner, until she was near the front of the pack again.

The last lap was when she took the lead. Her body was faster than Lou had ever seen it; so this was what it looked like when Catherine tried. Everyone stood up, dead quiet, but as she rounded the final corner, pushing forward, Catherine's parents started screaming her name and so did Raquel and Lou did too and then the whole crowd was behind them, like the raw force of their voices might thrust her to the finish line.

When it was over, Catherine was crying and she had finished first. She collapsed on the track, her teammates swarming her, throwing towels and spraying her with water. When she looked up at the crowd, still cheering her name, she blew a kiss back to Lou.

Lou walked down the steps to the aisle where Catherine's parents were and they hugged her, gripping her so tightly she could hardly breathe.

"Can I ask you something?" she said to them.

4

Lou met Catherine back at her parents' house in Portland a few days later. They sat on the deck together. The trampoline was gone, replaced by a grid of rosebushes, all in bloom. Catherine had just gotten back from a run, and she was sprawled in an Adirondack chair in sunglasses and her dirty socks.

"Don't you get to take a break from running?" Lou said. The boards of the deck were warm from the sun, but it was still breezy out. She was wearing brown corduroys and a red T-shirt and sneakers. And boxer briefs. This was the longest she'd gone without wearing a string thong in nine months, and she was so happy.

"It's better not to stop," Catherine said. "Or else maybe I'd never want to start again. I'd probably get really into crocheting or something instead."

That was how Lou felt about modeling. Like all momentum had been lost, but infused somewhere else, in the heart-pounding process of curating her portfolio for Alice. She hadn't booked a ticket back to New York, and she hadn't heard from Yukon, who must have been focusing on the new faces. Since Lou wasn't going to castings, she wasn't booking any shoots. Maybe her mom was right, and she could just turn down the volume until she couldn't hear it anymore, or until they couldn't hear her.

"Crocheting?" Lou said.

"Raquel does it," Catherine said seriously. "It helps her focus before meets."

Crocheting was the kind of thing Catherine would have mocked to death when they were in high school. There was a girl who used to knit in their algebra class who Catherine used to tease by unraveling her yarn, but now it occurred to Lou that maybe she'd just had a thing for her.

Catherine's dad walked one U-Haul box out at a time and placed them in front of Lou. "Take good care," he said, squinting at the boxes, then back at Lou. There were four total, all labeled in neat handwriting. Maybe it was Morgan's. Maybe someone else's.

"I'll have them back soon," Lou said.

"Will you send us the photos?" Catherine said. Her dad rubbed his palm over the crown of her head, looking out over the backyard toward the mountain, which was out.

"If they're good," Lou said.

"They will be," Catherine said.

Silverhorse, Washington, was four hours away, and Lou borrowed her mom's car and drove north the next morning. She'd unpacked the U-Haul boxes the night before, which were lighter than she expected, and steamed everything in her old bathroom upstairs. She'd seen enough stylists do it to do a passable job. Then she hung everything up and draped it over the back seats of her mom's car, like she was going to a wedding. The freeway was fast. It was green everywhere, even greener than the spring, and the clouds were speeding along.

Lou drove on the outskirts of town until she found the right spot. She knew it as soon as she saw it, off a forest road: the way the teals of the moss and the groundcover matched the buttons on some of the blouses, and the rich bark of the cedars pulled out the burnt reds of the fabrics. The colors were right. But the light.

The light was what made her pull the car over.

She walked through the brush, out into a clearing in the forest, and looked around. Part of the forest had been clear-cut, and new trees had been planted, only a year old, based on the sign off the side of the road. The sun shone through the new growth, soft-needled lime. Her dad had once named these to her as secondary forests. He thought it was very beautiful that even though human disturbance, logging, any of it, could take down a forest, they could still regrow completely. They needed help, but they usually came back.

Putting on the dress again was surreal. She changed in the front seat of the car, the seat pushed all the way back. No one was around. She felt less exposed than she did when she was changing with a hundred people around her. The postcard from the artist in Italy, the artist in precipice, was still in its brown paper sleeve in the zipper pocket of her backpack in the passenger seat, and Lou pulled it out, looked at it for a while, wanting to occupy the opposite feeling: the feeling of feet on the ground, the gravity pulling downward, someone exactly where they were. Not in motion. Just still.

When she took a test shot of herself in the clearing on a timer, she didn't feel inside out wearing the dress. She didn't feel like herself, exactly, standing in a ball gown in the woods, but she felt powerful. It wasn't the dress itself but deciding who saw her in it and how. The photos were for Catherine and her parents. But they were also for her.

It felt in some ways like the last year had been practice for this, and in another way like she was doing something for the first time. She knew how she wanted to look, knew what looked good, but she'd never taken photographs of herself like this. They weren't self-portraits, really, because at first she just wanted them to show off the collection, like she was doing a catalog shoot. But somewhere halfway through, it became an editorial of Lou herself. She shot the whole thing using the timer, which meant she had to guess at how they'd turn out and whether they were even in focus. She put herself in the center of the frame. She walked back to the camera and took another shot. It was slow going. Morgan had a lot of work. Over forty pieces, which Lou styled into different looks, trying out different combinations of tops and slacks and skirts. Every piece fit like it was made for her, which was the beauty of sample sizes. It would probably be the last time samples fit her like this, if she didn't go back to New York. She was too hungry.

When she was finally finished, she called Ivy. She felt like she'd been walking all year, and now she could finally sit down and look around. She didn't want to talk, didn't want to decide any-thing; she just wanted to see her, to be with her for a little while.

They met on the shore of the sound, on a rocky beach. The light was foggy and dim, everything suffused with shallow gray, as if they'd spent all night on a red-eye and exited into a new day in a novel and faraway place. They sat on an overturned tree, its roots extending out sideways.

"How was it?" Ivy said.

Lou felt overcome, but not like things were slipping out of her fingers: like her pockets were filling with objects she wanted close to her always. "Good," she said. "How's the writing?"

Ivy looked at her out of the corner of her eye, and smiled, her mouth higher on one side. "Slow."

"But it's coming?"

"I think so, yeah. Better than before."

There was hardly any tide, and only a few other people, dark figures down the beach, kayakers out on the water, paddling smoothly along. Lou kept an eye out on the horizon for whales, her camera still around her neck, but mostly she was think-ing about the shoot, how the photographs had turned out. She wouldn't post them anywhere, just send them to Catherine and her parents and that would be that. She wasn't even sure she would look at them herself, whether she could at this point. Maybe someday.

"I used to come here with my mom," Ivy said, and Lou took her hand.

There was a woman walking by them, with two big unleashed dogs who zoomed around her like they couldn't believe their luck, mouths open to the clouds. They galloped out into the water, and the woman started to laugh as they disappeared up to their necks. She looked at Lou and Ivy, her other witnesses, and gave a little wave.

"Excuse me," Lou said, standing up. "Would you take our picture?"

The woman smiled and accepted the camera. She took a few steps back and looked through the viewfinder at them and started counting down as Lou returned to her place at Ivy's side.

The dogs swam farther out, heads bobbing. The fog was burning off.

Lou pulled Ivy close on the overturned tree, and it was like all of her emotional jet lag caught up with her all at once, or maybe the delay just meant she felt more, now that everything she wanted was so clear to her, now that she could look straight at it, as bright as it was, and not blink. How badly she wanted to stop time and wanted to speed through it, wanted to be better, to be good, to stay exactly as she was, to be with the person next to her, with her and *with* her, to love her like this, even if only for an afternoon.

As the light started breaking through the clouds over the water, the feeling in her was enormous and physical, as wide as the water, as full, spreading through the best parts of her; and Lou wanted to remember this always, every second of how she felt, here, right here, finally here, as she waited for the shutter to close.

ACKNOWLEDGMENTS

Deepest thanks to my agent, Dan Conaway, for absolutely everything. There aren't words, you know? Thank you to Taylor Templeton for making this story better, one phone call at a time, and for believing in me and Lou from the beginning. Thank you to everyone at Writers House, particularly Genevieve Gagne-Hawes for edits and zeal at a pivotal time, Lauren Carsley, Andrea Vedder, and Chaim Lipskar. To Peter Carlin for putting it in motion.

Thank you to my editor, Anna Kaufman, for seeing this novel as it could be, for getting all my deep-cut jokes, and for being a dream come true. My gratitude to you is eternal. Enormous thanks to the incredible team at Vintage, especially Zuleima Ugalde, Edward Allen, Erica Ferguson, Maggie Carr, Sarah Bowen, Nicholas Alguire, Julie Ertl, Annie Locke, and Perry De La Vega. Thank you to Jami Attenberg, Deirdre McNamer, Kimberly King Parsons, Rufi Thorpe, and Jess Walter for your brilliance and generosity.

I am profoundly grateful to all my friends and family who read and reread drafts for me with love and attention, and all who gave me advice or help along the way, especially Alyssa Kennamer, Sarah Dozor, Michelle Seibert, Evelyn Langley, Emily Oliver, Jeff Whitney, Eric Ohman, Brett Puryear, Alicia Mountain, Emma Quaytman, Hali Engelman, Chris Benz, Lisbet Portman, Sarah Kahn, Bryan Di Salvatore, Cathy Cain, Jan Kurtz, Robert Stubblefield, Debra Magpie Earling, Monica Berlin, Chad Simpson, Nick Regiacorte, Sherwood Kiraly, Caitlin Delohery, Elisabeth Geier, Laura Lampton Scott, Emilly Prado, Andrew Simon, Hilary Shirk, and David Gates. Thank you to my Montana MFA family for the inspiration, community, and every Flip & Dip. Thank you to Roland Jackson, Kate Barrett, KJ Kern, Courtney Bird, Sierra Bellows, Brendan Fitzgerald, and Hannah Withers for your work and uplift. Thank you to Dee for showing me how to be a writer, a teacher, and a person.

Thank you to the Knox College Creative Writing and Green Oaks faculty. In memory of Robin Metz, who told me I was a novelist and helped make it true.

To my friends for the beauty you bring to the world. To KB for every poem, for every call, and for creating the queer joy we want to see in the world. To Tijana for answering every injury-scenario text, and for your belief and love. To Shawn for taking me seriously as a kid who only wanted to talk about books. To Jesse, Joan, and Marc for your enduring support and every beautiful hike. To Isaak for the rainy drives on Skyline. To Nack and Claire for the last two decades of true friendship. To Allister for steadfast friendship and poetic ribbing. Cathy, thank you for always seeing me. Michelle, thank you for your genius brain and letting me borrow from it. Sarah, I'm on my way to you now. Thank you to AK for being my most trusted reader for as long as it took, and for always rooting for Lou and Ivy. To Hannah, the Scooter to my Goolz, a double rainbow, classic-car-parade kind of friend and person; thanks for being in this with me.

To my family for your unwavering love. To the Joneses for welcoming me into yours with such warmth. To my brothers and my parents, most of all. Jack and Mandy Ohman, for your constant belief. Jan Dunham and Doug Waugh, for all you've given. To my dad, for your creativity and faith in mine. To my mom, for being my guide and heart in all things.

To my wife, Jess Jones. Guitar nerd, Fortunato lyricist, whale watcher, first reader, the most of anyone.

This novel is dedicated to my grandmother Susan, who saw the best in people and helped me see it too. Her love made everything possible.